Open Links

Dominic Holland

Dom Holland Books

Copyright

Proceeds

*All authorial proceeds from this novel are passed on to **The Anthony Nolan Trust**, the charity that saves the lives of people with blood cancer.*

Blood cancer is an indiscriminate disease. A random occurrence irrespective of lifestyle or genes. It can afflict anyone and survival might hinge on receiving a bone marrow transplant.

Anthony Nolan funds and curates the largest register of potential donors in the world and every year, their work saves literally hundreds of lives. Every twenty minutes, a person in the UK is diagnosed with blood cancer. Imagine the numbers worldwide and the simple equation this presents; the larger the donor register, the more likely patients can be matched and have a chance of life.

You can find out more at www.anthonynolan.org - how you can join their register and possibly save a stranger's life.

By buying Open Links, you have already contributed to this life saving work.

Please share it with your friends and leave a review online so that other readers might discover it and contribute to this worthy cause.

Glossary of Terms

For readers not familiar with golf and/or Mr Holland's purported humour and writing style, here follows a Glossary of terms used throughout *Open Links* which some readers might find helpful.

Tee

Not to be confused with the drink so loved by the British and why it has a different spelling.

A tee is a delineated patch of ground from where a golf hole begins and where the golfer hits the first shot of any hole. A second shot hit from the same tee box is affectionately known as 'knob out'. This is funny, but rude and likely to offend in these sensitised times.

Tee Off/Tee Shot

The first shot of an individual golf hole.

Driver or 1 wood

The golf club that hits the golf ball the furthest distance

(supposedly). Also known as the Big Dog, the Daddy and depending on ability, a 'useless piece of...'

Par

The number of shots permitted to complete a hole in golf.

This can be 3, 4 or 5 shots. Completing a hole in par (the regulation number of shots) is the aim of the game.

The par of a golf course is the aggregate of 18 holes and their individual pars. Most golf courses have a par between 67 and 72.

Par Golf

Also known as 'scratch' golf - playing the course (18 holes) in par; playing each hole in par. Par golf is the benchmark of the pro golfer.

Birdie

Completing a hole in one less shot than par. 1 under par.

So, playing a par 3 hole in 2 shots. A par 4 hole in 3 shots or a par 5 hole in 4 shots.

This is where the playing professionals live.

Eagle

Completing a hole in two shots less than par.

This is where the golf Gods live. The author of *Open Links* has never achieved an eagle. His sons have and like to remind him of this frequently.

Hole-in-One

Known also as an ace. Completing a golf hole in a single shot. Mostly, but not always on a par 3. The author of Open Links... (see, Eagle)

Bogey

One shot more than par. So, taking four shots on a par 3 hole...

Double Bogey

Two shots more than par. So, taking five shots on a par 3 hole...

Bunker

A large hole dug into the course (or forming naturally) and filled with sand from which the golfer must play the ball without grounding the club.

A links

A coastal golf course, bordering the sea (UK) or the Ocean (US). The Open Championship is always held on a links golf course.

Caddie

The person who carries the golfers bag and can be blamed by the golfer for any poor shots. Caddies are usually very good golfers, although not always. Caddies provide precise yardages for their player, and they offer advice on club selection, plus encouragement and commiserations.

The Green

The piece of ground with the most manicured grass and where the hole is positioned. On the green is where the player putts.

Chip Shot

A short shot on to a green (hopefully) and as close to the hole as possible.

Thin Chip
When a golfer hits the ball only and it scoots onto the green and off the other side. A highly painful experience.

Fat Chip
When an anxious golfer takes too much earth, so the ball has insufficient energy to reach the green. Like the food variety, fat chips eventually lead to cardiac arrest.

Fairway
Prepared turf where the tee shot is supposed to land. Easy to play from. Difficult to hit.

Rough
The unkempt (unmown) ground bordering the fairway. Difficult to play from. Easy to hit.

Putt
The shortest shot in golf, played on the green and with a putter. Each hole allocates two putts for par. So, on a par 4, the golfer has 2 shots to hit the green and then 2 putts to make par.

Two-Putt
Regulation putting because each green is designed to be completed with 2 putts.

Three-Putt
Taking three putts instead of two. A painful experience.

Pin

The flag and the pin that marks the hole and what professional golfers aim at. Ordinary golfers pay no heed to pin location and concentrate on just hitting the bloody green.

Hole positions are moved each day over the four rounds of a championship with the most difficult hole positions used over the weekend, the last two rounds of a Championship.

The Cut

A Championship is staged over four rounds, from Thursday to Sunday. Only the top half of the field (the players with the lowest scores) qualify to play the last two rounds (the weekend). The players in the bottom half are CUT from the competition. This is brutal and why golf is the hardest and cruellest sport.

Prologue

I t was no good. He gave up pretending to sleep and opened his eyes for good. He sighed, heavily.

Everything felt wrong; or nothing felt right. He couldn't decide. It felt like he hadn't slept at all. Not a single wink - and this added to the acute sense of anxiety that had started yesterday afternoon. And not any ordinary anxiety or nerves; that much he was used to. This was something else. Something he hadn't experienced before. It felt untoward and unsettling.

The fear of the unknown; don't they say that's the worst fear of all? And if so, then why should he feel normal, on a day like today?

It was just after 4.30am, half an hour before his alarm was scheduled to wake him. His tiredness aside, nothing felt normal or safe. Unique circumstances, he reminded himself again; quite possibly the most important day of his life. And in all likelihood, today was a one-off, never to be repeated... so shouldn't he just relax and try to enjoy it?

That made him laugh.

Gently, he pressed his thumbs onto his sore and swollen eyes. Flat on his back, he opened his heavy eyelids, focused on the brilliant white ceiling with its cheap artex swirls, and tried to reassure himself that everything was fine – but it was no use. He couldn't explain it, but something had changed. Something had happened, but he didn't know what, and it made him feel vulnerable and afraid.

'Come on, Ricky. What the fuck, man, snap out of it.'

Today was supposed to be a special; the day he'd dreamed of for years and worked so hard to achieve.

He splashed cold water on his face in the plastic en-suite bathroom and tried to reason with himself. Of course his circumstances were extreme. Of course his senses would be heightened. Today was never going to be just another ordinary day at work. Apart from anything else, it was Sunday, the day of our Lord - and how Richard Randal needed a God now. Any God would do.

And if not a deity, then at least his bloody dad.

His hotel room was located in the eaves of the modern ugly building, at the mercy of the brilliant dawn sun; its first rays easily breaching the gap between the flimsy blinds and the edge of the roof-pitched window. Laser beams, he thought, prodding, and poking away at him; ironic that they should be called blinds.

Not that he could sleep, anyway.

Ricky peered at his frightened reflection in the mirror above a sink that was really too small to shave in – a handy excuse not to bother, perhaps?

The horrors of yesterday's experiences at work flooded his mind and made him wince; like a rogue piece of tin foil connecting with a tooth filling. It had been an utter humiliation. Little wonder he hadn't slept.

He checked his phone, hoping for a message that might

explain everything but there was, of course, no such enlighten-ment. Just one voicemail from his wife Maggie, reiterating what they'd already discussed and agreed on; that what happened yesterday was in the past, that it could not be changed and so he needed to just put it behind him, move on, and try to relax.

It was pretty thin stuff and hardly inspiring, but he was glad to have it all the same. He listened to it again.

Hey Rick, it's me, love. Just to say that I love you and I'm really proud of you - and what happened yesterday was not your fault, not really - and I'm still so proud of you, and so are the boys.

Her message was kindly, but it was fatally undermined by *not really* and *still*. He appreciated it anyway, especially given that there was no message from his work colleague, Patrick - no doubt still smarting also from yesterday's unusual events.

Ricky pinched the bridge of his nose as the painful memory stabbed him once again. He'd gone over it in his mind, over and over, trying to understand what had happened but he still couldn't explain it. It just made no sense.

No matter, he told himself – he was a professional and so was Patrick, and today at work they would just have to get on with their jobs.

But then, recalling Patrick's last words to him, he blanched and almost had to sit down. He thought for a second but quickly dismissed his fears. There was no way. What Patrick had said was in the heat of the moment and he hadn't meant it. Absolutely not. And besides, today was a big day for him too. He wouldn't miss it for the world. No question.

Good Lord. He better hadn't.

Ricky looked at his watch; two hours exactly until his shift started. His work wasn't really a shift - but it was certainly a grind. Sitting on the toilet now, he slapped both his thighs hard - over and over.

'Come on, Ricky, you can do this. You can *do* this. It's just another day. It's what I do. It's what I've always done and what I do brilliantly. I don't do anything else as well as I do this. So what's to worry about?' He was shouting now. 'Nothing. Nothing. There's nothing to worry about, Rick. Just get out there. Get it done and enjoy it.'

But his pep talk had a hollow echo. The words were fine, and they made some sense, but he needed to hear them from someone else – and someone he trusted. Ideally from his dad, if only the old bastard had hung around long enough. And this terrible feeling he had, that made him feel so completely impotent? What the hell was happening to him?

Ricky squeezed his eyes shut again and massaged his temples this time, pressing hard into his skull as another wave of anxiousness enveloped him. His breathing was turning shallow and he wondered if he wasn't about to have a full-blown panic attack. He'd heard of such things and how debilitating they could be, but he clenched his fists and raised his knees and thankfully it passed. But everything was cumulative and it all added to this feeling of helplessness.

Even his unsuccessful bowel movement was a concern. He'd managed a couple of hard pebbles which were fooling no one. Acting like a cork and a warning of what was lurking within. A full bowel waiting to be evacuated, and no doubt biding its time – something else to think about, then.

And yesterday was his fault as well. Sure, Patrick bore some responsibility; but ultimately, it was his name on the office door. In his line of work, Ricky owned the glory and the failure. He had lost count of the people he'd met, envious of the way he made his living. But people had no idea.

Living – that was a bloody laugh. His income had been barely sufficient in his twenties and now, two decades on, he was still at it, earning even less but with a family to support. Maggie, two boys and one more on the way.

What the hell were they thinking? Going for the girl, Maggie called it. Heading for a cliff, he preferred.

He left the motel and instinctively scanned the sky to assess the day's weather ahead, sniffing at the air, trying to get a feel. He'd already checked the forecast. A bright day with a swirling and gathering breeze later - little or no chance of rain.

At just after 5am, he had the adjoining motorway service facilities all to himself. Inside was a lone cleaner with a mop in hand and a large expanse of floor - a task with parallels to his own, Ricky thought.

The man was old to be a cleaner and he looked exhausted; hopefully he was ending his shift and not starting it. Dressed in green overalls, he looked up at his visitor and a quiet moment passed between them. The old man smiled kindly, making Ricky feel a little guilty. He smiled back as best as he could.

Now, at least, he was mostly awake and mindful to dwell on only positive thoughts. *Today is going to be a fucking great day,* he assured himself and then he yawned like a lion.

He loathed the self-help guff that his colleagues seemed to use so effectively. Self-help; the new American science. The legitimate performance enhancing drug, the ability to access one's inner goldmine for untold fame and riches. Endless positive bullshit. Ricky grimaced, having reasoned a long time ago that a battery with only positive terminals is entirely useless.

He checked his kit, making sure that everything was present and then slammed his trunk shut. He was growing a little angry now, the more he thought about it. No doubt Patrick would be hurting as well - but what he had done was outrageous. The sooner they cleared the air, the better.

As he slipped into the driver's seat, he ceded some power and placed a call; it went straight to voicemail and his anxiety heightened further. Surely Patrick was up by now – and if so, why hadn't he switched on his bloody phone?

He squeezed at his steering wheel as the ghastly thought recurred.

It was about a ten-mile drive to work but at this early hour, the roads hadn't yet choked up with the inevitable traffic. Of course, there was accommodation much closer to the office, but it wasn't for employees on his pay grade. At a push he could even have stayed at home - which he had considered but decided against. For this line of work, he needed to stick to his routine.

Ricky viewed one of the many cranes a way off in the distance and immediately felt another dollop of adrenaline drip into his bloodstream. There was some movement below now as well; another warning sign of what lay ahead. It was a horrible reality, feeling nervous on your way to work. *Stupid bloody job.*

It wasn't fair to regard himself as being on a different pay grade, either. His 'stupid' job was actually entirely meritocratic. No nepotism or old school networks at work. No famous offspring miraculously prevailing. His was a numbers game. A pure results business, and technically, he earned the same as everyone else. Or, at least, he had the opportunity of doing so - and something to shoot for, then.

Ricky drove in through the gates. A man in an orange high vis stood sentry and another man pointed to where he could park. The first available space was hidden by a muscular black BMW X6, which was lacking only a turret. On the other side was a shimmering grey Aston Martin with a private number plate that was probably as valuable as the car.

He eased his Astra estate between the two, like a piece of dirty grout separating hand-cut marble tiles. He cranked on his handbrake and got out, carefully.

So much for his hope that this feeling of dread would

recede once he got to work. He felt utterly lost and wanted to jump back into his car and drive home; Maggie would understand.

He laughed – no, she bloody well wouldn't. She'd be furious, and rightly so, and quickly he thought of his dad again, and what he would be expecting from his son today.

'Fuck's sake, Ricky, get a grip, man. Get a fucking grip. Just another day. And whatever happens; tomorrow will be Monday. The world will go on. And so will you...'

But who was he kidding? Today was not a normal day at all. Today was the third Sunday of July. The final day of the Open Championship. The world's oldest and most prestigious golf tournament. Ricky's first ever Open. His first major championship and in fact, his first event on the main tour in more than eight years.

He needed to hurry now. He slung his clubs over his shoulder, still no sign of Patrick, his caddie. And Ricky was the first match out this morning, teeing off at 7am.

Thirteen over par and in seventy-second place. Or flat last.

Just an ordinary day, then...

For such a small country, the United Kingdom boasts an impressive and significant coastline. Over eleven thousand miles, in fact; more than Brazil and Argentina combined. And, of course, some stretches of this coast are better known than others. A mull, anyone? On its own, a word which has little use and not much more meaning - until it's combined with Kintyre, and suddenly it makes perfect sense. Brighton is known for its pebbles, an IRA bomb, and now for its gay and green life. Blackpool for its tower and its fat - both chip and human. Hastings for its battle...

Or how about a small stretch of land on the east coast of

Scotland? On the Duncur Road, leaving the town of Gullane for North Berwick in East Lothian? A strip of coastal land better known as Muirfield Golf Club, and home, no less, to the honourable company of Edinburgh golfers.

No one does pride quite like the Scots, and Scotland is a proud nation with good reason considering what it's given to the world: television, telephone, radar, whisky, the bicycle, the steam engine, penicillin, haggis and perhaps the greatest and the most stupid game of them all - golf.

Golf is a preposterous notion; if it was invented today, it'd stand little chance of surviving. Much like alcohol and tobacco, it'd almost certainly be banned. But the sport continues to thrive because it's become engrained in our culture, without which it would be seen off by two formidable modern-day lobbies. Water is a finite resource and so is land, the environmentalists would scream. Sons and daughters of rock stars and other privileged types would fling themselves in front of JCBs to prevent such large swathes of land being dedicated to a single game. And women would surely rally in opposition if their husbands or 'life partners' expressed an interest in this new game which takes four hours to play and often accounts for an entire day if the bacon roll and post-round pint/s are factored in.

But for now at least, golf lives on. It's a game with a rich history and an array of colourful characters and champions, past and present. It has fashion and artistry. There's a purity to the game, pitting player against the land and the elements. And few can argue against the beauty of the golf course. A manicured green carpet, sweeping and undulating away as far as the eye can see - and particularly stunning is the links course, covered in wet dew each morning with the ocean beyond and a single flag poking above the early morning mist.

Trying to establish which sport is the greatest of them all is a folly and a waste of time. Some will argue for archery, others judo or fencing - and who would argue with them? But quite possibly it can be agreed that golf is the hardest game of all. A game measured over vast distances and hundreds of strokes; but ultimately players are separated by mere millimetres and single shots. Often a cruel game, and always a tough one; and Muirfield Golf Club is one of the most formidable courses on earth, nestling confidently within one hundred and eighty acres of Scotland, a country where the national flower is a thistle.

Eighteen holes stretching over seven thousand yards with only seventy-one shots allowed for par: a foreboding challenge for even the very best players in the world - and so a stupid bloody game, then?

These words played large in the thoughts of Ricky Randal as he made his way quickly towards the clubhouse where he expected to finally see his caddie, Patrick, looking sheepish and contrite.

Sorry, Ricky, mate, honestly. About yesterday. Fuck me, what was that? I don't know what came over me. It was like I was possessed, like it wasn't me, d'you know what I'm saying? Anyway, look, can we just forget about it? Here, give us your bag...

But there was no Patrick to be seen, and a new wave of fear gripped Ricky. Just where the hell was he?

He tried ringing him again but got his wretched answerphone again and now he knew that something was awry.

He stared at his watch in horror. It was 6am already. Where had the time gone? He was due to tee off at 7am and he had much to do – but chiefly, to locate his bloody caddie.

Ricky wanted to get into the clubhouse quickly. He needed some space to think and time to compose himself, but just as importantly, he didn't want anyone else to see him lumping his own golf bag around. It was fine on the lesser pro-tours, but it was not okay on the full PGA tour - and certainly not on the final day of the sodding Open.

Just then, Justin Rose emerged from the side of a huge articulated truck emblazoned with the livery of one of the global golf brands. Ricky quickened his step. If he had a golf cap, he would have pulled it down low. He knew Justin from his amateur days, but since then their lives and their careers had diverged wildly.

'Hey, dude,' Justin called out.

'Shit.' Ricky muttered to himself, caught now in a dilemma.

'What are you doing? Where's your caddie?' Justin called and seemingly out of genuine intrigue rather than to make a point.

Justin Rose was a nice guy - a rare breed for such an overachiever in such an individual sport. Ricky was further unsettled by Justin's use of the word 'dude'; he wondered if the superstar couldn't put a name to his face. After all, it'd been a very long time. Way back in 1997, in fact, when they'd played Walker Cup together.

Or even worse, perhaps Justin didn't recognise him at all. The years certainly hadn't been as kind to Ricky as they might have been. He'd thickened around the middle; his thatch of curls had thinned and his golf scores had kept him completely off the sports radar.

But then Justin bounded over and grabbed Ricky's holdall before he could protest; and even as laden-down as he was, Ricky wished that he hadn't.

'Great to see you, Rick,' Justin said. 'How are you doing?'

Ricky smiled, unsure whether he was relieved or not to have been recognised.

'Yeah, you know. Generally shit.'

Justin smiled. 'Yeah, I saw what happened yesterday. That was tough, mate, I'm sorry.'

Ricky shrugged it off as best he could. Maggie had first alerted him to the fact that his incident on the 16th hole had led the sports bulletins. Of course it had. And safe, then, to assume that everyone knew about it and no doubt, had enjoyed a damn good laugh.

'Yeah, you know. But there's always today, right?' Ricky offered, without any confidence. 'And it's not like it matters, eh?'

'Er...' Justin began.

'The Open's every year, right?' he added quickly, to highlight his humour and defuse any awkwardness. Justin chuckled along.

'So, what about you?' Ricky continued. 'You still playing?'

Justin Rose, US Open Champion, Olympic Gold medallist, former World number one, gazillionaire... and generally, star golfer, now laughed out loud. 'Yeah, you know... now and again. When the mood takes me.'

He picked up easily on the train of banter, clearly recalling Ricky's sense of humour - although Ricky would have preferred to be remembered for his golf. Not since pro-celebrity golf on the telly had a golfer made any money from being funny.

'So how come you're here so early?' Ricky asked. 'What are you, one under?'

'Ah, you know. I'm staying in a house here on the course. I woke early - you know what kids are like, and I needed some club adjustments, plus I have some sponsor stuff and press...'

Ricky nodded as if he understood. He was staying at a Travelodge. He didn't have anyone to adjust his clubs, and he didn't have any sponsors either. And as things currently stood, he didn't even have a bloody caddie.

Justin stopped to sign an autograph and have his photograph taken with two Japanese women, who were both wearing fluorescent Marshall bibs and so really should have known better. Loitering to one side, Ricky glanced up at the large leaderboard ahead, to the left of the Muirfield clubhouse.

Rose. 5th place -2

Ricky had him at one under par. *Sorry, mate.* Justin had the game and every chance of winning today and what a popular winner he would be. About time, England's best golfer bagged himself an Open.

Other early birds were now joining the hunt for photographs; Ricky took his chance to get away. He grabbed his bag back and nodded good luck to his old mate. Justin had stuff to do, and so did he.

'Hey, Ricky,' Justin called after him. 'Go well, eh?'

'Yeah...'

'Seriously, I've a got a good feeling about you today.'

Ricky nodded. *Really? I wish I did.*

'Something in the air. I can feel it.'

'Yeah, thanks, mate.' Ricky waved.

It was a kind thing of Justin to say, but he didn't feel much buoyed by it. In fact, he still felt awful; timid and anxious to the point of nausea. And exhausted too, after his night in his oven loft room with his thoughts pounding his mind and keeping him awake.

Never mind the golf; all he wanted to do was to go home to his family.

'*...we'll have live updates throughout the morning from the Scottish links, and then BBC Radio 5 live will be at Muirfield with John Inverdale from 2pm when the leaders go out, including the likes of Woods, Rose, Spieth, Rahm, Fleetwood and McIroy - and we'll stay with the golf until the close of play this evening when the champion golfer of the year is announced. The first pair is due out in just under an hour, including*

England's Ricky Randal who achieved infamy yesterday with his caddie on the sixteenth green. Let's hope the pair fare a little better today in the final round...'

Nowadays in professional sport, nothing is left to chance. Preparation is key - and particularly so in golf, where players each have their own routine, adapted and refined over the course of their careers. But even though their sport centres on the individual player, golfers are not alone; they're accompanied by their agents, managers, therapists, coaches, sponsors and equipment providers, and most importantly of all, their caddie or wingman. Their man within the ropes.

The caddie bears a great responsibility – he's much more than just a guy lumping a golf bag about. Very often scratch golfers themselves, they know the game intimately. They maintain the clubs and they make the correct club available to the golfer, in perfect condition, as and when it's needed. And crucially, they know what to say. They know when to speak and when not to, in order to get their man around the course as economically as possible.

And Patrick was not in the clubhouse. Ricky was growing frantic now. Where the fuck was he?

He tried calling him again. This time the phone rang and Patrick finally picked up. *Oh, thank God.*

But then Ricky's world came crashing down around him. And given what Patrick had to say, he spoke with remarkable poise.

'Are you fucking kidding me?' Ricky spat, grateful that the locker room was empty.

'No, I'm not. And no, I can't explain it and for this, I am sorry...'

'Sorry! You're fucking sorry?' Ricky screamed.

'Yes, I am. I'm sorry. So, best of luck Rick. Play well.'

Ricky stared at his phone. His muddled mind was beginning to break down. Frantically, he played the conversation over in his mind as beads of sweat formed on his brow. Was this an elaborate joke and Patrick was about to walk in through the door?

But the doors remained shut; Ricky was now distraught. He needed to call someone. He hit contacts on his phone, with his vision blurring as he scrolled aimlessly. But what was the point? He was in Scotland and teeing off in less than an hour. Who could he call?

Impulsively, he charged out of the locker room and into the bar area, hoping to see Patrick standing there with a big grin, at which point he would have hugged him and then killed him later - after his round. Or failing that, he hoped to see a young assistant golf professional with nothing to do for the day and happy to caddie for him.

But no such luck. The only people at the bar were a bunch of old duffers in blazers and odd coloured trousers; they glanced over at him knowingly. The incident on the 16th, no doubt?

Quickly, Ricky headed outside, past some reserved parking bays and around the corner to the pro shop. But then he stopped in his tracks.

The place was stiff with people. It was manic. Of course it was. This wasn't a monthly medal. This was the Open. Justin Rose was chatting with Ernie Els and some other players he didn't know. Young Turks who lived in the gym, looking more like middleweight boxers than golfers in their immaculate outfits. Journalists fluttered about like pigeons waiting for scraps, a film crew loitering nearby and self-important officials barking into walkie-talkies.

The prospect of entering the shop and trying to hire a caddie was out of the question.

'*Sleeve of balls, please, bag of tees, er... the long ones, and do you know anyone who could carry my bag?'* The press would have a field day.

Panic welled within. His mouth dried out and his heart thumped - and unfortunately, it wasn't alone.

Ricky froze as something stirred below. His eyes widened. Now, his most urgent worry was not his impending tee time, but the pressure against his sphincter. And this wasn't a casual message from bowel to brain. This was no gentle alert, a suggestion that he might like to consider a visit to a cubicle. This was an emergency. His absent caddie was, for now, forgotten.

Justin Rose looked over at him curiously, as did Ernie Els, the Big Easy.

Ricky turned and lurched like a gazelle that's been spooked and began to hurtle for the clubhouse in great haste. But without a full stride, because it couldn't be trusted.

He kicked the clubhouse door with a force that might have killed a member exiting at just the wrong time, tore through the comfortable lounge, and dived into the locker room – which, mercifully and strangely, was still quiet. He smashed his way through into the toilets.

At this point, if the stalls had been occupied, he'd have been given little choice other than to dangle himself over a urinal or even worse, a sink. An ignominious way to achieve golfing immortality. But thank Christ, there was an open door ahead.

With no time to spare, Ricky dived inside, ripped at his belt buckle, and got himself onto the pan as sheer panic and adrenaline poured out of him.

Oh, thank God.

Golfers are frequently told just to let things flow, and in this particular case the relief was awesome, but sadly short-lived.

His body continued to empty and as he went on fidgeting

with his phone, he remembered his truly awful circumstances. But who could he call? He looked at his watch again. Just why the hell was this happening to him?

'Shit. Fuckety shit, shit, *shit*,' he muttered aloud. They seemed appropriate expletives.

He heard a water tap being run somewhere in the toilets outside and his spirits sank even further. It meant that someone had overheard his terror. Of course they had - and given his day so far, the man was probably a journalist who now had an idea for his column. Even more likely, it'd be Peter Alliss, the voice of the BBC or Ken Brown, the ex-pro and on-course expert.

Ricky took a moment, hoping that he'd finished and that it was now safe to stand up. He did so gingerly, hovering briefly before reaching for the loo paper.

A few moments later, he stepped out of the stall with as much confidence as he could manage.

Better out than in, eh?

In contrast to the clamour outside the clubhouse, the toilets were still deathly quiet - which, again, was unusual and troubling. Had he got the wrong course? Or had the other players simply arrived earlier this morning, fully dressed, bowels voided, and ready to play? Were his fellow professionals sitting on their tailgates pulling on their shoes in the car park, contravening one of the sport's golden rules? The locker room should be a hive of activity already and yet it was desolate. Empty but for Ricky and one other person.

The other occupant of the toilets was an old man wearing a green apron. Ricky had seen him scrubbing and wiping throughout the week and had exchanged vague pleasantries with him more than once. He had a kind face, framed by a shock of white hair and a thin moustache, light eyes and an intelligent expression. Maybe sixty or so, and small, not much over five feet. He carried himself with the wiry alertness of an ex-serviceman and looked significantly over-qualified to be attending toilets. For the second time this morning, Ricky empathised with someone holding a mop.

'Nervous?' the old man asked. Casual as you like. The understatement of the year.

Ricky nodded. Yep, shitting myself, as you just heard. There was little point in denying it.

'It's only a game,' his new friend added kindly. 'Anyway, they all get nervous, even Woods.'

Ricky eyed the clock on the wall. Ten more precious minutes had elapsed. His playing partner would now be rolling in the last of his practice putts, having already spent some quality time hitting balls on the range with each of his clubs in turn. His caddie would have washed his irons and placed them in correct order in his bag and was probably holding a banana at the ready, should his charge need a quick calorie boost.

Ricky's eyes widened as his bowel suddenly twitched again - but then it settled quickly enough, thank God.

The old man smiled. 'Hello. I'm Marshall.'

'Marshall?'

'Yeah, I know - don't ask.' He offered his hand, taking Ricky a little by surprise. He didn't look like a Marshall. The only Marshall that Ricky knew of was an American buddy from university - not an old English duffer like this guy.

More embarrassingly, he realised, he couldn't actually take the man's hand, not before he'd washed his own – and something which Marshall should really have accounted for. He quickly scrubbed his hands clean and flung them dry, ignoring the high-tech dryers which always promise more than they deliver. Finally they shook hands.

'Shouldn't you be out there, son?' Marshall asked. 'You're the first match out, aren't ya?'

Ricky pulled at his face. He wanted to cry. He didn't even

want Patrick to appear now - only Maggie. She'd just hold him and make him feel all right. Or his old man; and he thought of how upset his dad would be if he could see his boy in such a predicament.

Marshall smiled again. He had a knowing air about him. 'It's your caddie, right? After all the hoo-hah yesterday? What is he, a no-show?'

Ricky stared glumly at the little man. Hearing his reality made it even more real and pressing. He had no option. He would have to withdraw from the Open Championship. This would be humiliating, not to mention expensive, forgoing the thirty-three thousand, three hundred and sixty one euros for finishing last - and this was assuming that he didn't manage to improve on his position.

'How about I carry it for you?' Marshall suggested.

'What?'

'Your bag? Carry your clubs for you?'

Ricky was startled. He stared at the odd little man, trying to process his offer; and when he did, all he could do was to laugh. It was a release - it felt good, being able to laugh. An antidote to the bewildering feeling of pain and uncertainty that had laid upon him since yesterday afternoon.

'You want to carry my bag?' Ricky asked, incredulously.

'What? How hard can it be? I used to be in the army. I've carried heavier loads for miles, and not on bloody grass, either.'

Ricky forced himself to focus. It wasn't the physical side of Marshall that was troubling him. It was more the man's circumstances. He was on the advent of the most important round of his life, without a caddie - and his best option was a toilet attendant?

'Unless you have another offer, of course?' Marshall asked mischievously.

Sadly, Ricky didn't.

'You could always carry them yourself, I suppose,' the old man added, with a grin.

Ricky thought about this. Carrying his own bag would be impossible. He'd be a laughing stock. A toilet attendant was way better than nothing.

'Are you sure?'

Marshall chuckled. 'Course I am. Why wouldn't I be? It might even be fun.'

Ricky wasn't convinced.

'And these toilets are clean enough, right?'

'Yeah, I guess...' Ricky said, weakening now - something which Marshall sensed and seized upon.

'Great. Then I'm in. Better to be out in the fresh air, eh?'

'Yeah, I guess,' said Ricky, almost numb.

Marshall grinned in triumph. But then his face fell. Suddenly he darted past Ricky, looped around the back of him and then came full circle to face him again, frowning urgently.

Ricky gave him an enquiring look.

'What?' he asked self-consciously.

Marshall didn't answer. Instead, he shot past Ricky again but this time, he disappeared into a little office just beyond.

'What size pants are you?' the old man called out.

'Pants?'

'I mean trousers. Trousers. What size trousers are you?'

Ricky's eyes widened. 'What? Why'd you want to know that?'

'What, thirty-six? Thirty-eight?' Marshall continued, rummaging around inside his office. 'We haven't got time. Get those things off. What is it with you lot and white trousers?'

Ricky suspected what the issue was now - and once again he felt like he was about to burst into tears. Obediently, he unbuckled his belt and pulled down his trousers. Immediately he let out a little yelp. His trousers were ruined. A rude jagged line of brown ran all the way from the gusset to his belt-loops with a great deal of splashing on either side.

Whatever score he would shoot today, Ricky was already heavily in debt to Marshall - and he hadn't even picked up his bag up yet.

Lee Pah was Ricky's playing partner for the final round. On the practice putting-green, the young Korean star handed his club to his trusted caddie and took the stick of gum that was being held out ready for him.

A gaggle of admiring girls watched him from a respectful distance, clutching pens and programmes for the player to sign. He pulled his sunglasses on, tugged his golf cap down low and began striding purposefully towards the first tee. The girls didn't even get a glance from the star twenty-year-old.

He looked resplendent in all-white clothes that had been personally tailored for him and never worn before; figure-hugging, sharp, and emblazoned with the names of his six sponsors, all of them fighting for attention and hoping for coverage. Back home in Korea, this would've been a certainty; Lee was the newest national sensation, but for how long. The growth of golf in Asia being what it is, there was a steady succession of ever new and younger sensations lining up behind him. There is no time like the present for the Asian golf prodigy.

There was no real crowd to speak of, on the first tee at five minutes before 7am. Present was the match referee who'd drawn the shortest straw - this being the first match out and with no marquee players.

A few stewards and marshals were milling about, but, curiously enough, there wasn't a full complement of professional golfers as yet. Lee preferred to arrive onto the tee after his playing partner; just a habit he had developed. Making himself top of the bill, perhaps? But today he was first onto the tee and with no sign of the English journeyman he was partnering.

As ever, the starter Ivor Robson was in place. An urbane Scot, the man with the easiest job in the world of sport; that is, to read a list of names out loud. Nice work if one can get it.

Nevertheless, Mr Robson took his job very seriously, and right now he was feeling greatly perturbed by the presence of only one player. He had a field of seventy-two to get underway. Television networks across the world and an audience of billions were counting on him.

He glared at his watch. One minute to go and the Open would start with a disqualification. That was a story that nobody wanted to see. But where could Randal be? What could possibly be making him late?

And then, without a second to spare, Richard Randal burst through the tunnel under the surrounding grandstand and onto the tee. He was out of breath, and on his own. It was quite an entrance; everyone present was staring aghast at what stood before them, and this was even without seeing the state of Ricky's caddie.

Marshall, now lagging unseen some considerable way behind him, was already struggling. As soon as he'd got under the bag, his knees had buckled and Ricky had panicked. *The Swiss Army, was it, Marshall?* Ricky envisaged the old boy keeling over and dying on him mid-round, and immediately he'd thought to lighten his load, jettisoning stuff from his bag that he could do without. He'd already lost one caddie and he needed to keep this one alive.

Each match at the Championship has its own on-course referee, and with radio in hand the man in question now marched towards Ricky with a sense of indignant purpose.

'Where's your caddie, and what the fuck are you wearing?'

he barked, dispensing with the customary handshake, good luck and play well.

Ricky just shrugged. He hardly knew where to begin. *Well, you see, I woke up with this morning with this strange feeling...*

'My caddie's on his way.'

'And the clobber?' the referee snapped, pointing angrily at the offending garment.

'It's a kilt...'

'Yeah, no shit, Sherlock. I can *see* it's a kilt. But this is a golf course and this is the fucking Open, so what's it doing on you, a professional golfer?'

A little aggressive, perhaps, but it was a reasonable question – and Ricky didn't know where to begin answering it. He glanced over his shoulder, wondering where the hell Marshall had got to.

'Well?' The man demanded.

'Er...' Ricky dithered. What to say? It was all Marshall had in his cupboard. His choice was a kilt or a pair of plus-fours that he couldn't squeeze into. So it was the kilt or nothing if he was going to make his tee time.

The match referee continued to glare at him. Golf has famously strict rules for what attire can be worn. No jeans, and only tailored shorts with long socks. But did it state anywhere that kilts weren't allowed? But it didn't need to. No exposed knees – and, not-to-mention that Ricky looked preposterous. At worst, it came across that he was cocking two fingers at the venerable game's long and proud traditions.

Ricky didn't have a golf cap either, but this was always going to be a minor infraction against his kilt. He had a cap in his golf bag and would get to it the moment Marshall eventually made it onto the tee. It would complete his attire as a professional golfer and further lighten Marshall's load. A win-win, then?

But matters were not helped at all when Marshall finally crawled onto the tee.

'Here's my caddie now,' Ricky said with some relief as the referee glanced over in the old man's direction. He looked anything but impressed.

He snapped his glare back to Ricky. 'Just what the hell is going on here? Are you taking the piss?'

'What? No. Look, I've had a disastrous morning. You see, I had white trousers...' Ricky began. Quickly he stopped himself. 'It's my knees, isn't it?' His voice faded out into nothing, and he opted instead for his best mournful and pleading look.

'And your caddie?' the referee asked again.

Ricky grimaced. 'He's there.' He pointed at Marshall, who might at least have stood up straight.

'Him, who, where?' the referee barked. Ricky's nerves were shredded already and snapping his fingers, he beckoned Marshall over to him; the old man approached gingerly, probably wondering if the toilets might have been a better option after all.

'This is Marshall. He's my caddie.'

The ref stared at Ricky. '*Marshall?*'

'Hello, sir,' Marshall chirped confidently.

'Yes. This is Marshall,' Ricky repeated urgently and a little angrily. Marshall was as much as he knew. 'He's my new caddie. I can change my caddie, right?'

The referee's eyes narrowed as he considered his options. His finger was twitching over his radio. It was almost 7am and time to get the final round underway. But this was very much an ongoing situation. Fluid. But for now, the final round of the Open needed to begin and so this disaster on the first tee had to be allowed to proceed. He couldn't hold up the Championship. Beyond his pay grade. *OK, people, let's play golf!*

After a cursory handshake with both players, he began to

back away with his radio to his mouth, itching to report in to his boss.

'I'm sorry about the outfit,' Ricky offered vaguely but the referee ignored him. This was all Patrick's fault, Ricky thought to himself, imagining exactly what he would do to his ex-caddie once his round was finished. Take to him with an eight iron, perhaps? Or better still, a wood.

And then it finally dawned on him. In the mania of the last hour, he'd forgotten that he was about to play the final round of the Open Championship. Suddenly his legs felt heavy and his mouth dried as the match referee continued to gabble into his radio.

Ricky shook hands with his playing partner, in a daze now, quickly they exchanged match cards. Lee Pah looked just as agog as everyone else. He said nothing other than hello, but there was a little smirk with his caddie which Ricky caught and decided to ignore. It was fair enough. Ricky would have done the same. After all, it was funny. A golfer turning up as though he was late for the mid-week medal and in fancy dress.

One thing was certain for the day ahead. Ricky was going to make the sports bulletins; the early ones, at least, and possibly even the later reports. And not because of his golf.

Chapter One

Richard Randal, ENG
Open Championship + 13
72nd place
Prize Money €33,361
1st Hole
450 Yards, Par 4

 '... *ithout getting onto his outfit, which is only going to add to the infamy of one Richard Randal. Certainly not a household name by any stretch of the imagination. Forty-five years of age and playing in his first ever Open Championship.*

'*He came through qualifying at Sunningdale, which I think is fair to say was a surprise to most people because after a glittering amateur career - he was the amateur champion twice and a Walker Cup player – but since making the leap into the professional ranks, that good form deserted him. Only one top-ten finish on the European tour. And not known for his flamboyance*

on the course either, until today when his kilt puts John Daly, Ian Poulter and everyone else into the shade.

'Just what he's thinking with such a garment is anyone's guess. But rest assured it will be exercising the golfing authorities as we speak. We are of course, in Scotland, where the kilt is the national dress, so technically, is he breaking any rules? I don't know, and a debate will ensue, I am sure.

But anyway, here he is... playing the 1st with the young Korean sensation, and rather more traditionally dressed, Lee Pah. Randal has teed off. He's found the semi-rough, and as I look at my monitor, it would appear that he's in two minds about which club to take for his second shot... but the Open is underway.'

'Thank you, Russell. More from Russell Fuller throughout the morning from beautiful Muirfield here on BBC 5 Live, when our live coverage begins at...'

Given his circumstances, not to mention the immense pressure that comes with the Open Championship, Ricky was mightily relieved that he'd managed to hit his first tee-shot at all. An air shot wouldn't have surprised him; it was why he had decided not to hit his driver, with his brain racing and his vision blurring after the events of the morning.

Still, it was a genuine release to finally be on the course and away from it all, albeit straight into the rough. It had been a poor tee shot, but at this point, as he marched up the first, he didn't much care. His hopes that once he got his round underway, he might revert to feeling normal and in control were fading rapidly.

His tee shot had been greeted by the silence it deserved, apart from a rather telling 'good shot' from his new caddie, confirming his worries that Marshall would be a bag-carrier and nothing more. Better than heaving his own bag, though. That would have been even more humiliating than wearing a kilt.

Spectators were gawping at him from all sides; he kept his head down and avoided any eye contact. People stared slack-jawed and there were sniggers as well. Was it really that funny? A man wearing a kilt? In Scotland?

What a morning. Ricky gazed down at his knees as he walked; a constant reminder of his awful reality. Just what the hell was happening? He felt utterly bewildered; like a whirlwind had scooped him up and was carrying him along - but to where, he had no idea. Fortunately, the course was still quiet and allowed him the chance to daydream as he marched up the fairway before making a left turn into the rough where the ball marker was waiting for him.

He thought about Maggie and what she would make of it all. Should he text her, since he was likely to feature on television? Not that he would be able to explain himself.

By the time he reached his ball, he still hadn't calmed down. Nothing made sense. Nothing felt normal.

His ball wasn't lying well; the BBC 5Live correspondent had called it exactly right. Ricky was between clubs and in two minds. Time then, to defer to the expertise of your caddie - himself, of course, an expert golfer and someone who knows the game of his player in minute detail through many years of intimate collaboration.

Or not.

'Bloody hell, it's not a race, you know,' Marshall huffed, finally catching up to him.

Ricky shook his head and tried to focus. He *needed* to focus.

'Why didn't you hit driver?' Marshall puffed.

Ricky bristled at the implied criticism.

Because I was shitting myself, that's why.

As a general rule, caddies tend not to criticise their employers - and certainly not after their very first shot.

'Seriously, a driver would have had you over all of this crap.'
Ricky twitched a little, but still managed not to react.
Caddies know when to speak and they know what to say.
Caddies advantage their player. They advise, cajole, placate
and encourage. Not Marshall, though, it seemed.

Looking down, he could barely see his ball, but he couldn't
miss his knees. Just how many rules was he breaking? He'd be a
laughing stock. He could just imagine the flustered conversations in the rules office and the hilarity in the locker-room.
There would be consequences, of course, but he tried to banish
such thoughts from his mind - along with the moaning from
Marshall about his back. The thing he could least afford right
now was a blazing row with his new caddie.

'...because you'll never make the green now...' Marshall
continued.

Ricky fired a quick scowl at the man. A warning shot which
seemed to register; he shrugged in response.

'I'm only saying...'

'Well, don't...' Ricky snapped. 'Don't say anything at all,
OK? Jesus, man, really. Just shut up.'

Marshall took a moment as if absorbing the hit, and then
smiled broadly. It was a warm and welcoming smile and yet, it
was grating in the present circumstances.

'What?' hissed Ricky. 'What's with the smile?'

Marshall said nothing, but continued to smile as though
without a care in the world.

Ricky did not join him. He was acutely aware of the match
referee still glaring at him, and he carefully avoided any eye-
contact. He should have played his shot already.

Quickly, he put his rescue hybrid club back into his golf
bag and selected a five iron instead. An unusual swap, given
that he literally needed to be rescued. He glanced up at
Marshall, hoping for something helpful. A nod of approval over

his club selection, perhaps, or just anything positive. But Marshall tutted and shook his head.

He couldn't believe it. It wasn't even a single tut. But plural. Ricky was seething.

Golf is a game of confidence. All tour professionals are capable of hitting perfect golf shots. They can all shape the ball either way, or make birdie on any single hole, but what separates the household names from the chasing pack is their self-belief and their ability to call upon those shots precisely when needed. Such capability is a mental skill, not a physical one, and that skill is rooted in confidence. And if confidence comes in balloons, then Marshall's tut was like a sharp pin - and this was only his second shot of the day.

His second shot of - hopefully - only seventy-one shots in total and already he wanted to kill his new caddie. Who, sadly, still hadn't finished.

'If you're gonna hit five iron, then you'd better really middle it...'

Ricky squeezed his eyes shut, trying to block out Marshall and everything else bearing down on him.

'Otherwise you'll be short and left. And you'll take three to get down.'

In their manic dash from the locker-room to the first tee, he'd established pretty confidently that Marshall was not a golfer - and now all of a sudden the man was a bloody expert.

'At least three, that is...'

And now Ricky backed off from his ball and looked up at his new colleague.

'Marshall, what the fuck? You're supposed to be helping me.'

'I am helping you.'

'No, really, you're not. You're not helping. If you want to help, then you need to stop talking. Okay?'

Finally, Marshall seemed to get it. He held his hands aloft. *OK, I'm done.*

Ricky shook his head. His eye had been drawn to a young spectator who was watching their rather heated exchange. The young boy, thirteen or so, was staring at them with a curious look. He was alone, and dressed in a golf jacket and mismatching golf cap. Ricky had noticed him on the first tee; he was the only spectator apart from the gaggle of Korean girls who were now on the other side of the fairway where Lee's ball was sitting pretty.

With yesterday's incident in mind and in particular, his loud vernacular, Ricky felt embarrassed enough to gesture an apology in the boy's direction. The boy smiled and returned a thumbs-up sign.

It was the first sign of encouragement Ricky had received all morning and he was grateful for it. Shame the lad wasn't a little older or he could replace Marshall. Anyone can carry a bag, right?

Lee Pah had chosen to hit driver off the tee and had been duly rewarded. He was standing by his ball with his next club already in hand, waiting patiently for Ricky to play first. No selection issues for him or reasons to shout at his caddie. And, just to nudge up the pressure a little more, the television cameraman who'd captured Ricky's hollow tee-shot had followed him down the fairway and still had his lens trained on him. Ricky worried that his exchange with Marshall might have been captured; going by his morning so far, it almost certainly had.

Ricky re-addressed his ball and tried to steady himself, but Marshall's tuts and doubts were still reverberating through his head, making mince out of any positive thoughts he could otherwise have mustered.

He swung his club hard and made a decent connection, but

straight away he knew he was going to be short. The ball's first bounce was particularly absorbing - an upslope, perhaps – and it slowed rapidly before coming up short and left. *Fuck it!*

Ricky handed his club back to Marshall without looking at him. He didn't trust himself and what he might do if he caught another of his caddie's broad and smug grins.

His playing partner's ball landed safely on the putting surface. *Good shot, mate* - although Ricky didn't say anything of the sort as he got on his way again with Marshall hurrying alongside him.

'So, what's your story, then?' Marshall asked.

Ricky turned to give the man an incredulous look. Like he had time for a general get-to-know-each-other? Marshall, though, was undeterred.

'Was it your dad who played, and you followed him? That seems to be the usual route. Westwood, Woods, Rose...'

Ricky shrugged. 'Yeah, and now Randal.'

Marshall shook his head and looked a little lost.

'That's me. I'm Richard Randal.'

'Oh, yes. Sorry.'

Ricky shook his head. His caddie didn't even know his name.

'And is he here today? Your dad?'

No, thank God, Ricky thought. 'Not unless he's looking down.'

'I bet he'd have loved to see you play here, eh? In the Open?'

Ricky felt a little pang - because Marshall was right, of course. His dad would have absolutely loved it. But now wasn't the time to reminisce and reflect. He had other, more pressing things to deal with. Like forty yards to the pin with a tuft of woolly grass to overcome and far too little green to work with. Marshall had been correct. He would need three shots to get down, at least.

He grabbed his wedge and, being a quick learner, this time Marshall remained silent - or maybe he approved? On order now was a deft chip and then two solid putts to make bogey. Ricky gripped his wedge gently and whispered to himself, *soft hands.* He brushed the wet grass a couple of times, visualising the perfect shot. On a normal competition day, he'd have already hit at least fifty such practice chips on the range. Today, though, Ricky had hit none - so no real surprise that he thinned it horribly. His ball screamed across the green; he closed his eyes and hung his head.

When he looked up, his ball was still moving, rolling on further from the target. Finally, it settled; some sixty feet from the pin and barely still on the green. A horror shot.

Marshall didn't react. He seemed calm and unmoved. Ricky scuffed at the grass with his foot as he handed over his offending wedge and grabbed his putter. The boy spectator was still watching, and he apparently knew enough about golf to avert his eyes as a furious Ricky Randal stomped onto the green. Lee had already marked his ball and was leaning on his putter while his caddie had a quiet word with the match referee.

Ricky stared down at the monster putt that faced him. It was more guesswork than calculation, with at least two obvious breaks to negotiate, plus a swale that could go either way. All that was missing was a mini-windmill in his path. What a stupid bloody game; and with only Marshall for company, Ricky felt completely alone.

He looked over at the television cameraman, who was still covering his every move - for novelty purposes, presumably? And a couple of stills press photographers had joined the party as well now.

Marshall shifted a few feet to his left to get a look at the

putt and even bent a little at the waist. Lee Pah sighed. It was
going to be a long day.

Ricky thought of Maggie again. He wanted to whip out his
phone and call her and the kids. They were just over the border,
a little south of Berwick, but a world away from the tinder-keg
of the Muirfield Open. He looked out to sea and wished that he
was on it. Bobbing in a boat with his boys and a fishing-net.

Marshall joined him now behind his ball and seemed to
sense his alarm.

'It's more to the left than you think,' he offered gently.
'Maybe as much as five feet?'

'Left?'

Immediately Ricky panicked. *Left! You have it as left?*

He pulled at his face, pushed his tongue around his dry
mouth, and decided to march the entire length of the putt
again. *Fuck the Korean superstar, and the TV cameraman as
well. They can all wait. This is my Open and my putt.* He felt
like asking the cameraman to move on.

*Oi, mate. No one knows who I am. So why don't you and
your camera just fuck off? No one at home wants to see me play
golf, and you've got your funny shots of the dick in the kilt
already. So, move along, why don't you? Nothing to see here.*

The cameraman stayed exactly where he was and Ricky got
about his putt. He settled over his ball, his mind still scrambled
and his heart still lurching so hard that he began to wonder if
he could even get through the round. Plenty of people had died
on the golf course; Bing Crosby, most famously.

He set up left, with Marshall's advice in mind - a sure sign
that he was desperate - and then he even borrowed a little more,
because why the hell not, before striking his ball firmly.

And off it went. Up and over the first faint swale, before
heading right as it took on the second mound and slowing until

it barely breached the summit; a PhD in physics in just one putt.

Rolling downwards now, the ball picked up some energy and began to track towards the hole. So far, so very good - but now the speed was key. Would it have enough energy to resist the pull from the final borrow? Within ten feet now, and the ball kept nearing the pin that Marshall was patiently tending. Finally it came to rest some four feet short, and crucially, below the hole.

It was a brilliant putt, he realised; a shot of real skill, guile and nerve. Under the circumstances, possibly the best putt he'd ever hit without seeing his ball disappear.

Marshall was grinning broadly but Ricky didn't look at him; instead, his attention was drawn to the young spectator who was clapping wildly. If he'd been wearing a hat, he'd have doffed it for the camera and whoever was watching at home.

Lee slid his birdie putt by the hole but was assured of his par and a good start. What golfers would call solid. Quickly, Ricky settled over his second putt, took a slow breath and struck it. The ball dropped. A brilliant two putt. Bogey.

'...well, that's damage limitation. Right there, that'll feel like a par for Randal because it could've been so much worse after his horror chip.

'So a bogey, then, but his fashion faux pas remains. I can tell you that the referee of this match hasn't been off his radio and he isn't the only one who's exercised in this match because Ricky Randal is taking up from his round yesterday. He's been animated, muttering away and barking to himself and already using his feet in a way more becoming of a footballer than a golfer. But he's nothing if not entertaining, and he's about to step onto the second tee...'

A brilliant putt, sure - but Ricky wasn't feeling very buoyed. It was still a bogey, and it continued his disastrous run of dropped shots that had begun on the ninth hole of yesterday's third round. He was playing bogey golf, the mark that his dad had set his sights on. He looked skyward, thought of his old man, and wondered if he might be watching. He hoped not.

Marshall had been right. His dad had introduced him to the game. He used to joke that he was a two-rounds-a-day man. His milk round in the morning, followed by his round of golf in the afternoon, and at weekends further rounds in the clubhouse; a typical amateur golfer. Absolutely awful, but he played the game with an unfailing enthusiasm. Fat shots, thin shots, shanks and hooks, all interspersed with the occasional 'perfect' shot sent by the golfing gods to tantalise and keep him playing the world's most difficult game.

As a young boy, Ricky had acted as his dad's chief ball spotter - more accurately, a ball finder. It was a task that Ricky had taken very seriously, charging ahead to whichever offending bush had dared to get in the way.

'Found one, Dad.'

'Good lad.'

'What are you playing?' Ricky would call out.

'Er...'

'Was it a Titleist, Dad?'

'Indeed it was.' That'd do, anyway.

And young Ricky would swell with pride. At first, he'd assumed this was the nature of the game and that his dad was finding bushes on purpose - until he realised that his old man just wasn't a very good golfer. And the more he came to understand that, the more his excitement waned.

He'd been eight years old, on their annual holiday down the coast from Newcastle to Bamburgh in Northumberland, when he made the discovery that would change both of their lives.

Bamburgh Golf Club is not a links course, even though it hugs a coastline with magnificent views of the castle on the beach and the ocean beyond. A challenging course, with the inevitable coastal winds to contend with and the fairways lined with heather and gorse. One day, on the sixth hole, seeing his dad's ball disappear into a particularly dense thicket, Ricky grew exasperated and screamed at his father, 'Dad, why don't you hit it straight?'

His dad laughed wildly as he teed up another ball, and then handed Ricky his club.

'Well, come on then, hot-shot. You hit it straight.'

And he did. Straight down the middle. A fluke - or beginner's luck? His dad chuckled and reached for another ball.

Having watched his father play, the young boy knew exactly what not to do, and his second ball followed the first; but this time Ricky stood rock solid, up on his right toe, and he held his pose with his arms wrapped around his shoulders like a scarf. His dad always lost his balance and chased after his ball, but Ricky looked just like the pros he'd watched on the telly playing in the Open Championship.

His father clapped him on the back.

'So what the hell am I delivering milk for? You're a natural, son. A bloody natural.'

And he was right.

Chapter Two

Richard Randal, ENG +1
Open Championship +14
72nd Place
Prize Money €33,361
2nd Hole
367 Yards, Par 4

The second hole at Muirfield is a par four. The word 'par' in golf denotes the number of shots (strokes) that are allowed to complete any given hole. A par four means that, from the tee, the player has four shots to get his ball into the correct hole. A hallowed feat for an amateur golfer but the bare minimum a tour pro expects and precisely what Ricky Randal needed at this juncture. Anything to end his bogey run.

Each golf hole has a different par and the aggregate of the eighteen holes gives the 'par for the course'; hence the cliché. Par is the yardstick by which all golfers are gauged. Ordinary mortal golfers attempt to get as near to par as possible. But the professional golfer needs to shoot sub-par if he is going to make enough bread to live off. And on the main tour, there's no money in achieving par golf and a career beckons for teaching the game rather than playing it. Another cliché, then; ...and *those who can't...*

On the tee, Ricky fidgeted. He still had one eye on the match referee who was every bit as animated as before, chattering into his radio, and now looking even more flustered.

Late as ever, Marshall plonked the golf bag down and groaned loudly. Either he was exhausted or upset that his great read on the first green hadn't been acknowledged. Ordinarily, a caddie would have studied the pin placements issued each morning and would advise his player on how best to confront the hole; which part of the fairway to attack the green from and ideally, on which part of the green to land his ball in order to make a putt. Ricky consulted his stroke-saver booklet.

The safe play was to hit three wood, but safety was yet another luxury that Ricky couldn't afford right now. A high-risk, high-reward strategy was called for. With his par at the first hole, Lee had the honour of hitting first, and was already swinging his three wood.

Pussy!

Ricky pulled out his driver, or one wood. The driver is the biggest and longest club in the golf bag, colloquially known as the Daddy, The Big Dog or The Gun, and very often, after a poor shot, a Piece Of Shit. The driver offers the greatest reward and the greatest risk. It's the club for the confident player and the desperate one alike.

Once again, Marshall did not approve of his player's club selection. He waited patiently to catch Ricky's eye, and then shook his head. It was better than a tut, but not by much.

'What?' Ricky spat, annoyed with himself for even asking a man who was until an hour ago, a freaking toilet attendant.

'Well...' Marshall began.

'Oh, shut up.' Ricky spat. He had no time for his explanation.

'OK, but unless you cream it, you'll be in sand. So better play short, then go in with a four or a rescue and take your par. Good score on this hole.'

Ricky ignored him, pretending that he hadn't heard what appeared to be pretty sound advice. Par on this hole was a very good score, and he dearly wanted to end his run of dropped shots. Par on any hole at Muirfield on Sunday was a good score - and he reminded himself that he shouldn't get greedy. Greed can be very costly in golf.

Lee teed off; his ball sailed gracefully away and landed short of the bunker that Marshall had just flagged up.

Risk and reward, Ricky repeated to himself. He waggled his driver to and fro, avoiding Marshall's disapproving glare. He noted that the young boy was still watching; apparently undeterred by the previous bogey, he stood outside the ropes and observed Ricky closely.

Ricky liked the idea of being within the ropes; like a boxer fighting for his life. It felt entirely apposite. And with this image in mind, he decided that he would put his driver back in his bag. But not until he'd crunched his ball down the middle of the fairway and over the bunker.

His ball hit the sand very hard indeed. A brilliant tee shot, matched only by the brilliant positioning of the bunker. A few yards to the left and Ricky's ball would've scooted on fifty yards and into birdie territory. But now his prospects were bogey at best.

Fuck.

Ricky closed his eyes and snapped his tee peg out of the ground. The worst possible start to his round. He heard a wolf whistle from somewhere behind him; some wag was referencing his skirt, and very funny too. The match referee too, was trying to catch his attention, but he ignored it and got on his way down the fairway, muttering angrily to himself.

On the long walk to the bunker, he and Marshall argued about blame, and Ricky's mood darkened even further when he saw his ball had plugged. He had no alternative but to hit out sideways, and he quickly grabbed his sand wedge, clenched his jaw and made sure of the shot without saying a word to his caddie. He swung hard and angrily and his ball with a chunk of sand flopped on to the pristine turf. *Fuck it.* Two shots down. Two shots left for his par, and he would need three at least. Another bogey then?

'Well out,' Marshall assured him, rather pointlessly, and then handed Ricky his wedge, apparently feeling no need to add anything further. Nothing about pin placement? Exact distance? Wind or anything else? Ricky gave him a needy look. Some encouragement, at least, or even better, some advice - because his calls so far had been unerringly accurate.

Marshall pursed his lips, thought for a moment, and then nodded briefly.

'The green is running away, so anywhere right of the flag and you'll make double. Left of the pin and you'll make two putts. Bogey will be good now,' he said, economically and expertly. The 'now' might have been loaded with meaning, but the advice was sound - and his confident manner was as welcome as it was surprising.

He certainly wasn't orthodox or predictable. Ricky nodded as he processed this information, then thanked him quietly with a renewed sense of bewilderment.

'Imagining the shot' is a technique frequently used by the golf psychologists, many of whom make a greater income from the game than Ricky had ever managed for himself. And consequently, the very top players now count psychologists as key members of their entourage. Golf is unlike the frenetic and instinctive team games, football and rugby, where there's little time to plan. Golf is about playing a stationary ball, with plenty of time to think and dwell and panic.

Ricky's iron cut into the back of the ball and then crunched through the pristine Scottish turf, creating an explosion of energy, propelling the ball high in to the air and towards the green with a languid snake of turf following behind. But which side of the pin would his ball settle on? Ricky leaned his torso leftwards to encourage its flight, while Marshall stood stock still. Either he already knew or he didn't care.

The ball pitched onto the green, right of the pin, but its trajectory took it across the pristine surface to finally settle fifteen feet to the left.

'Good shot,' Marshall said casually as he heaved up his golf-bag, slotted the club back into place, and got on his way. His playing partner, Lee had made it onto the green in two shots, but was right of the pin and would struggle to make his par.

Marshall had him down for a bogey as well - the same as score as Ricky, hopefully.

'That was a good call,' Ricky said as they got on their way.

'Er, is that a thank you?' Marshall asked cheekily.

'Sure, if you like. But more of a question.'

'Oh, really. How so?'

Well, you don't play golf. You don't caddie. And yet you're almost an expert - how come?'

Marshall thought about this for a moment and then just shrugged, looking genuinely puzzled.

'Dunno, really. But isn't it fairly obvious? How many shots and which direction to hit it?'

'Yeah, and the wind and the rain, and the terrain, and the wet and the dry, and the borrows and the rough, and the direction of the grass...'

Marshall shook his head. 'People complicate everything.

Not just golf. I mean everything. Even simple things. It's a sure-fire way to make sure that they're needed.'

Ricky shook his head. The explanation was as thin as his last chip shot and just as unsatisfactory, because what was required of him today was anything but simple. 'Impossible' more like, and so he got back to the task in hand.

At home in Berwick, a little south of the border, Maggie Randal stared at her television, unable to take in what she was seeing. Her phone was buzzing incessantly; friends and family, no doubt. She ignored them all.

Ricky's mum Tess was over to help with the kids, as per usual when Ricky was playing a tournament - or working, as he called it. And watching him on the television now, Tess was every bit as worried as her daughter-in-law. Live coverage of the Open wouldn't start until 9am, but Ricky was already featuring prominently on various breakfast TV programmes - and not for his golf.

Maggie looked a little closer at the screen. It was definitely her Ricky, but what the blazes was going on? While it was exciting to see him on the television, but not in such circumstances.

She replayed their most recent conversations over in her mind. He'd sounded fretful. He'd mentioned feeling frightened and peculiar, which they'd put down to the pressure. But on the course now, she could see that he looked troubled and bewildered even without the distraction of his attire and she worried for him.

'Jesus. What is he wearing?' Tess repeated.

This year's Open Championship had already been something of an earthquake for the Randal family, just as Ricky had warned them. To begin with, he'd actually qualified, for the first time in twenty-four attempts. Most professional golfers at Ricky's level didn't bother trying, but Ricky had no option. Way back when, he and his dad had promised themselves that one day Ricky would take on a famous links, and it had become his thing.

He'd come close once. Eight years ago, with his dad caddying, and he'd missed a putt on the eighteenth green which nearly killed them both. But this year it'd all gone according to plan and he'd qualified by a single shot to deny the illustrious and much-loved José Maria Olazábal. The Open's loss, perhaps?

As soon as Ricky had qualified, Maggie had quietly decided that it was fate; she'd started to dream, wondering even if he might win the darned thing. She even checked out what the first prize was. Ricky, though, was more realistic.

He knew he couldn't win the event. Not possible. He just didn't have the game. Not over four rounds, anyway, and he'd set his sights on making the cut - which would be a magnificent achievement, but highly unlikely. The entry field for the Open consists of the world's elite golfers, and only the top half would qualify to play the final two rounds.

Naturally, Maggie had wanted to accompany him to Edinburgh - but she knew the drill by now. She hadn't been to a tournament since their first child had arrived, and the Open was not the tournament to break habits and try something different. Ricky had a thing about his routine. He was meticulous and he didn't like change. Which was, of course, why she was now so worried about him; for a golfer, dropping his caddie and donning a kilt is change on a seismic level.

Normally during a tournament she confined herself to following his progress online but after his brilliant second round on Friday, she'd listened to him being interviewed on BBC Radio 5 Live.

'Ricky Randal, congratulations. A sixty-eight today to go with your seventy-four yesterday, making you even par for the Championship and set to be here for the weekend.'

'Yeah, I'm delighted. A real career highlight for me today. The conditions were kind and I was able to take advantage. Thrilled. I'm absolutely thrilled to make the cut. Thank you.'

'So what happens now? This is your first Open. Do you start to think about what comes next? Another round like today and you could put yourself right up there with the big names.'

'Oh, I don't know. I'm not getting ahead of myself. Just happy to be here for the weekend - and from here, take things as they come. Just one hole at a time.'

A live interview on national radio was another first for Ricky and so he could be forgiven for leaning so heavily on clichés but this was not even noticed by the adoring Maggie.

Making the cut was mission accomplished, and she'd really started to believe in her man - what he could achieve, and what they could buy - after two more solid rounds. A new kitchen? Her own car?

'Blimey, Mum, what if he wins the bloody thing?' she'd dreamed aloud. 'We'll be able to move house.'

'Yeah, with a granny flat, I hope,' Tess had replied; they both laughed.

Maggie had studied the European Tour website. This year, the player in fifth place would trouser four hundred and seventy seven thousand Euros! At this, she'd felt her baby kick inside, which she took to be a warning sign, and so she turned off the website in-case she got over-enthusiastic and went prematurely into labour. Ricky had enough on his mind already.

She'd suffered a great deal over the course of her husband's stuttering career. His constantly being away from home was difficult enough; handling his disappointments and dashed hopes was worse. But she'd never complained or lost belief in him, and now she was about to be repaid. She'd chosen well and her Ricky was about to come out on top.

But then round three happened and she put the catalogues away and quickly revised her dreams downwards – to, perhaps, a slow cooker. She'd followed Ricky's demise online as bogey followed bogey, and then on the telly, when Ricky and Paddy arrived at the 16th green.

It made for difficult viewing; he was crestfallen when they spoke on the phone immediately afterwards. He talked about a strange feeling - only to be expected, given what had happened. But quickly enough he'd changed the subject and moved on to the boys, who were fine and missing him. He rang off promising to get a good night's sleep and hit the course hard tomorrow.

That was about it and he certainly didn't mention a bloody kilt.

This morning, the television shot narrowed; her husband's face filled the screen as he marched towards the green, and suddenly she felt a burst of pure love. Because there he was, all on his own and fighting against the world's best players, and she felt so terribly proud of him.

A tear formed, bulging in her eye - and then, in that instant, something changed. It was peculiar, but her fears for him suddenly eased. She didn't know why. It was just a feeling she had; a sense of contentment that washed over her, allaying her anxieties. Whatever happened to her Ricky today, he would be coming home tonight and she loved him.

Now the television picture cut to a wide shot, and she smiled. It was lovely seeing him on the telly, no matter how silly he looked. Her only remaining sadness being that his dad was not here to see him. She smiled again, and wiped her wet cheek, and cradled her swollen belly.

'You all right?' Tess asked her daughter-in law.

'Yeah, Mum, I'm fine.'

'Hey - maybe he's doing it to get on the telly,' Tess reasoned.

This was a thought that had already occurred to Maggie, but quickly she'd dismissed it. Ricky would never hatch such a scheme. He was too proud. Playing in the Open had always been his dream. He'd talked about it endlessly with his dad, and he'd just want to play well, like he knew that he could. And anyway, he'd have told her if he'd had such left-field plans, surely?

'Hey, maybe it's a good plan,' Tess continued, warming to her theme. 'Do you remember that Eddie the Eagle bloke?'

Maggie shook her head. 'No, that's not it. No way. Ricky would never do that.'

'Well, what, then?'

'I don't know.'

Tess looked at her a little oddly. 'Well, you seem very OK about it, I must say.'

'Yeah, I am. I don't know why,' Maggie responded without looking up.

She didn't understand what was happening any more than anyone else. Only Ricky knew what was going on - and whatever it was, he was in control, and Maggie felt safe.

On the second green, Ricky's mind was continuing to swirl. Marshall hadn't said anything to him this time, so presumably the putt was straight at it.

It was a makeable putt - but only in the hands of a confident golfer. Someone who could trust his line and give the ball enough speed. Ricky was anything but confident, and struck his ball tentatively, finishing three feet short. Another bogey. His ignominious run continued.

Lee's birdie putt scooted by the hole and ran on into bogey

territory, just as Marshall had predicted. The old man smiled broadly towards the young spectator, who was still looking on at their match intently.

It was just after 7.30am. Other players would have teed off in the final round already, players much more illustrious than the two golfers involved in this match, and yet this boy was sticking with match number 1.

'Looks like you have a fan,' Marshall murmured, but Ricky wasn't particularly excited.

'Yeah, but for how long, I wonder?'

'Oh, I don't know,' Marshall said. 'I think this kid is a stayer.'

Chapter Three

Richard Randal, ENG +2
Open Championship + 15
72nd Place
Prize Money €33,361
3rd Hole
379 Yards, Par 4

Michael Landale was pure old school; a forthright and forbidding presence in the world of golf. An old Harrovian and Oxbridge Blue, a lawyer and scratch golfer, he could be genial when the mood took him but he did not suffer fools gladly - and his incendiary temper was legendary.

As the Championship referee for the Royal and Ancient, Landale had been enjoying his Open - right up until the start of the fourth and final round. His Championship had been on time, with no breaks for weather or anything else unforeseen. Nothing controversial had happened. No idiot player had signed for the wrong score. In fact, he hadn't been called to adjudicate on anything at all, which suited him perfectly. He had an impressive leaderboard with an array of star names, and the required smattering of upstarts as well. Fine by him; just so long as they didn't go on to win the damned thing.

Two amateurs had made the cut, making the contest for the silver medal competitive, and the Muirfield links was enjoying the better of the players, with three under par being the leading score. All good. Until some idiot turned up in a fucking kilt. Landale almost died choking on his Danish pastry? when he received the news.

All sports have their rules and their governing bodies, but none are revered and quite so strictly observed as the rules of golf. Practically biblical in length, they are applied rather appropriately with a religious fervour by the authorities and, to a commendable degree, by the players themselves.

In other sports, cheating has become part of the game; a perfectly legitimate, if not legal, way to gain a competitive advantage. Not so in golf. Football players will dive for a penalty or feign injury to have an opponent penalised. Crick-eters will refuse to walk and athletes will gorge on hormones that might kill them - but so what, so long as they can be buried with a gold medal?

Such things simply do not happen in golf - whether or not because the game is recorded by television cameras and the player's actions can be scrutinised later.

'He's wearing a what?' Landale screeched into his radio. 'A kilt? He's wearing a kilt? As in, a fucking skirt?'

As soon as the news got through, metaphorical claxon horns were sounding throughout the walnut-panelled offices of the Royal and Ancient, the esteemed body founded in 1754 to enforce and preserve the integrity of the great game.

At first, Landale was more confused than angry. He pinched the bridge of his thinly-cut nose and tried to make some sense of what was happening. Certain rules of golf are more vaguely worded than others, and as such they are open to interpretation. These rules are subjective and call for opinion and nuance, whereas others are unequivocal. Like, for instance, playing in a kilt.

'He hasn't teed off yet, sir,' the match referee gabbled into his radio. 'What would you like me to do?'

'Well, fucking stop him, of course,' Landale shrieked as he fumbled with his mouse and bashed at the keyboard of his laptop.

This was the answer that the match referee had feared; he asked for clarification. 'So you want me to disqualify him from the Championship?'

It was a big question and a big call - and it could well become a world sports story. Preventing Randal from teeing off would mean missing his tee time to retrieve appropriate clothing, and this would result in instant disqualification.

The colour drained from Landale's face. A disqualification was never good news. It would bring adverse attention to the Royal and Ancient, and their showcase tournament, not to mention a media frenzy around the player himself - which was presumably his intention. In last place and with no prospects of finishing in the money, this was clearly a bid for infamy by a journeyman who did not have the game to garner headlines for his golfing prowess.

'He's about to tee off, sir - what would you like me to do?' The match referee was desperately repeating himself and delighted that he could defer responsibility.

Landale recognised the player now. The idiot from the 16th yesterday; he'd been sure his name was familiar. Sat at his computer screen yesterday, he'd watched Ricky's third round collapse with particular interest and some relief.

He thought rapidly about his options. The first match out

and with no traffic ahead; Randal might scoot round the links in three hours. So by the time the live television coverage started, his round might have already collapsed and his tournament effectively over, especially if his bogey-run continued with the Sunday pin placements. People would soon lose interest in the crank in a skirt. He would finish his round in obscurity... whereupon Landale would enjoy tearing him apart.

'Sir?'

He bit at his lip as his mind flitted between his two options. 'Fuck sake, let him tee off.'

'Really? That is your decision? You want me to let him tee off?'

'Yes.'

He was seething as he slammed his radio onto his desk. It was a decision that moments later he would regret, as an assistant warily entered his office, turned on the television, and then quickly vanished. Landale stared at the screen in disbelief. A full shot of Richard Randal, ENG, looking resplendent in his kilt. And the true horror of what had landed on his desk began to dawn on him.

Out on the course, just beyond the green at the first hole, the match referee's radio buzzed. He knew who it was and he answered it immediately.

'He's on the television!' Landale snarled.

'What? Who is?'

'Him. Him in a kilt. What the fuck is he doing on the fucking television? It's only 7.20...'

The match referee didn't know how to respond.

'I don't know, sir. He's on the first hole and he's has just thinned his chip...'

'I don't give a shit what he's thinned. Why is he on my fucking television?'

The match referee had already thought to turn his radio's

volume down, such was Landale's fury - not to mention his invective - but even so, he was mindful to take refuge beyond the green, away from any pricked-up ears.

With his remote control, Landale was flicking through the television channels now and there, on numerous news programmes, were the same pictures of Ricky Randal. He almost bit through his lower lip.

No doubt the head of BBC Sport was enjoying himself, and Landale didn't relish the prospect of suggesting that such images should not to be made available for broadcast. Journalistic and editorial integrity would be waved in his face – abstract concepts which Landale would dearly love to shove up the BBC man's pinko arse. His mind racing now, he wondered about instant disqualification. *Yes, good. Best to nip things in the bud?*

But quickly he relented as his panic surged. It was all so public now; and the man's round had already started. He could only imagine the opprobrium that would be hurled his way. It could get pretty ugly - and the media would feed off it, of course.

After a moment's reflection, he began to consider the idea of sending out a pair of 'regulation' trousers from the pro shop, but he worried about the inevitable shots of the player going off to get changed - or even worse, dropping his skirt on the blinking fairway. But what other choice did he have? Let him continue playing and defile the world's greatest tournament?

Only one thing was clear and as yet certain in his mind. Michael Landale was going to kill Richard Randal.

'I'm going to have some trousers sent across from the pro shop,' he spat. 'And find out what the story is with his bloody caddie, as well.'

· · ·

On the third tee and already +2 for his round, Ricky was unaware of the furore that he was causing elsewhere; he did not hesitate to reach for his driver and this time Marshall approved.

'Hit it straight, 285. Leave yourself just a flick with a wedge,' the old man suggested helpfully.

Hit it straight!

Yeah, thanks, Marsh. It made him smile anyway - it was the sort of thing his dad might have said.

Still with the honour, Ricky waited for Lee to hit first. On the outskirts of the hole, the match referee was still chattering into his radio. He hadn't taken his eyes off Ricky since he'd stepped onto the first tee. It was all very off-putting and he had enough pressure to contend with as it was. He'd apologised already, hadn't he?

He would hit his third tee shot first, he decided, and then he'd have a quiet word with the official and they could try to put the matter behind them.

Lee's tee shot found a bunker, which buoyed Ricky a little. Cruel, perhaps, but there we are; human nature.

The crowd following his match remained very small; just a handful of people. Ricky noticed that the young spectator had now been joined by an older man - his dad, perhaps?

Ricky took up his position, settled himself with a practice swing, waggled his club a couple of times and then smashed his club through the ball.

'Shot,' a young voice called out almost as soon as Ricky's ball took flight. The tee peg span backwards.

It was called a little too early – after all, the ball can move in the air – but Ricky appreciated the comment all the same and he was grateful also that the lad hadn't shouted out the moronic 'get in the hole.'

And as it turned out, the kid was right; Ricky's tee shot was straight and true. A proper golf shot. What golfers call a peach;

it landed twenty yards short of the two bunkers, where the fairway narrows almost to nothing, and came to a stop smack in between them both. The perfect tee shot. Ricky couldn't have positioned it any better if he'd carried his ball down the fairway and dropped it. It was very welcome; indeed, certainly a nerve-settler, and he breathed out heavily as he watched it land and his shoulders eased a little.

Of all the golfing talent that would be following him onto the course today, no player with the exception of Rory would hit a better shot at this hole and Ricky felt energised. If he could just hit another sixty-odd shots every bit as good as this one, then his fortunes might turn around.

Ben Costello was enjoying his day at the Open more than he could have imagined - although for some time now he'd been sensing an imminent confrontation with his dad.

And then, right on cue, it began.

'Hey, Ben - come on, let's head back to the first tee now before the crowds get too big. Monty will be going out soon.'

Ben's dad, Eric, had enjoyed Ricky's tee shot as well; but not so much that he wanted to stay and see any more of his game. The kilt was funny, but the novelty had waned already, and the golf was never going to be good enough to keep their attention.

But Ben disagreed; he calmly shook his head. Nothing against the great Scottish golfer, but he wanted to stay with the first match.

His dad was understandably miffed.

'What? Are you serious? You want to stay with this match?'

Ben just shrugged.

'Er... why?'

It was a reasonable question, and Ben could not explain. It

was just a feeling he had. A compulsion, almost, to watch a golfer who an hour ago he'd never heard of.

'Come on, Ben - what, really?'

'I dunno. I just like him. And it's quiet. I can see him up close.'

'But Ben, he's last and sixteen over.'

'Fifteen.'

'Fine, fifteen,' His dad said rather testily; immediately, he caught himself and felt a pang of guilt. 'But Ben,' he pleaded, 'Monty is about to go out. This guy is last. He's a nobody.'

'Yeah, I know. So then maybe he needs my support.'

Eric could see he was going to have to concede; this was, after all, his son's big day out.

He felt pretty aggrieved, though. This was such an exciting and important day for them both, their first ever golf tournament. They'd talked about how they could watch the world's best players together - not to mention how lucky they were to even get the tickets. Out of the blue, a chap in their village had announced that he had two tickets for the final round, and would Ben and his dad like to take them? It was such a lovely gesture; especially since it wasn't that he couldn't make it himself. He just said he didn't fancy the long trip north, and he wanted to offer them up, and that was it.

His mum had fretted, of course. Immediately she'd consulted his doctors and they had been dubious, as much about the gargantuan drive from Plymouth as anything else. And with this in mind, his mum had refused and Ben, quite uncharacteristically, hit the roof. He was adamant. He wasn't asking for permission but explaining why he would be heading to Scotland, and again this was most out of character.

'Well, I don't know what's got into you, Ben.' His mum said. 'Eric, you speak to him. You explain to him that...'

'But Mum, you have to understand...'

'Your doctors...'

'Don't know anything.' Ben snapped.

'What?'

'Not really. Not how I feel, anyway. Mum, please.' Ben appealed. 'This is a chance of a lifetime. The chance of my life, anyway - and I'm going to go. I have to.'

Given his circumstances, his choice of expression was particularly unfortunate, and his mum promptly burst into tears.

'Oh, please, Mum, don't cry. I hate it when you cry.'

It was all very dramatic and his dad quickly relented. He suggested that they might fly up; and then, when the lack of flights presented itself, he suggested that they make a road trip and spread the journey out over three days. This panicked his mum even further, but Ben became even more insistent.

'Mum, please. This is great. I'd love a road trip. Dad can look after me, and there are hospitals on sat-navs, and I'm going to see Tiger Woods.'

His mum wiped her wet and tired face. 'But Ben, you don't even like golf.'

'So.'

The back and forth continued, but the outcome was apparent from the outset. The doctors were consulted again, and they agreed - so long as Ben was sensible, remained fully hydrated and didn't become too tired or overexert himself. Ben readily promised, and so did his dad.

A key condition for his mum's final sign-off was that Ben and his dad must remain together at all times. Which was fine, in theory, but now on the famous golf course it seemed a little unnecessary and even unfair; especially having to watch Richard Randal when Monty and Sergio were about to get underway.

Eric pondered his dilemma a little more. Ben had his phone

with him, and he wouldn't be any more than a few hundred yards away, and for only for half an hour or so. So it was no different to letting him take the family dog for a walk, really.

'Right, then, Ben, just a few more holes, - eh?' Eric said warily, still hoping that his belligerent son might see some sense and accompany him back to the first tee.

'Yeah, OK, Dad, no problem.'

His dad sighed, bitterly disappointed.

'So I'll be at the first tee, then. And you've got your phone?'

'Yes, Dad.'

It didn't appear that Ben was going to miss his dad very much - which was a little disheartening, although he was pleased to see his son smiling and looking so happy.

'And it's...'

'On silent? Yes, Dad; now please go, or you'll miss Monty.'

But still he dithered and Ben sighed heavily.

'Dad, go, please. I need to watch Ricky's second shot.'

'Right, OK. I'll just see a few of the other players and then we can meet up in an hour or so. I could save you a spot if you like? Or we could meet somewhere else?'

'Sure, Dad. I'll be fine. And I'm feeling great, by the way.'

'Good. Not too tired, anymore?'

Ben thought for a moment. The drive from Plymouth had been harder than he had expected, and despite his best efforts he hadn't been able to hide his fatigue - which was inevitably fed back to his mum. And as tired as he'd been when they arrived in Edinburgh, he'd been so excited that he hadn't managed to sleep very much last night - and yet now he felt fine. A second wind of hurricane proportions. He smiled broadly.

'Yeah, Dad, I feel great.'

'Good. See you at the first, then, or somewhere ahead?'

'Yep.'

You still here, Dad?

'And you've got your kit?'

Ben glared at his dad. At fourteen, he was still short of puberty, perhaps delayed by his treatment, but he could still assert himself when he needed to.

'All right then. And if your mum rings, don't answer it.'

'She won't ring. We made her promise, remember?'

'Yeah, right...'

Ben smiled wryly as his dad headed off, unaware that he would be back to his son well within the hour.

After his dreamy drive, Ricky ploughed down the fairway with something almost approaching a spring in his step, and for the first time since yesterday morning, he was aware of enjoying a sense of calm. Of course he'd prefer to have Patrick on his bag - and to be wearing a pair of trousers - but it hardly mattered now. He just had to just get on with it and his latest drive was a good place to start. He just had that 'flick' with a wedge to come and, who knows, he might even get a shot back.

Marshall was again struggling to keep up but remained close enough to say the wrong thing and still be heard.

'Hey, Ricky, why couldn't you have hit that shot on the second hole?'

Sitting mid-fairway, Ricky was feeling relaxed enough to smile at his caddie's ridiculous question. He was also aware that he hadn't yet spoken to the referee as he'd intended. If only the man would ever get off his radio...

Ricky quickened his step. He wanted to appear business-like, but was also mindful of his slow play so far.

Golf is a long and slow game anyway, but championship golf is drawn out interminably, with some rounds taking six hours and more. To combat this, players are allocated a strict amount of time to complete each shot and any player falling behind the schedule can be penalised with shots being added to their score. One of the only thing that millionaire golfers cannot afford.

And, being the first match out, he also dreaded the thought of holding up the cream of world golf behind him. Tiger leaning against his club and tea-potting him was too painful to countenance and so he charged into the gentle breeze that had recently picked up - and he noticed a clutch of angry-looking clouds gathering to his left.

'...and on he goes. Still chattering away to himself, more calmly now though after his great drive. But he still cuts a lonely and somewhat vulnerable figure, and his attire makes for a sight we have never seen before at the Open Championship. And who would doubt that there are not more surprises to come? Now, back to the first tee where Scotland's first golfer, Colin Montgomerie, is about to tee off...'

Anna Wade sat in the media centre at The Open Championship, fretting. Her dad's sage words of warning were quietly, constantly, nagging at her.

He had a habit of being right; her barren three days of golf coverage had provided her with no story and zero income - and today's prospects didn't augur well either.

It was a better time than ever to be a woman in sports journalism. No doubt about it. Years of male dominance had reached its watershed, with broadcasters and print desperate now to be seen as inclusive and accessible. Despite unofficial quotas and female-only roles in broadcast, the odds remained overwhelmingly against female reporters. Professional sport is almost exclusively male - and this extends to the journalists covering it. The atmosphere in the media centre was overwhelmingly masculine and a knowing, blokey banter prevailed, underpinned by the familiarity that came from travelling the world together and sharing in raucous, scandalous experiences that will never be reported. *What goes on tour...*

The centre was already busy, and unexpectedly excited thanks to the story that had taken everyone by surprise. Journalists from all over the globe were all keen to fill their boots with the novelty kilt story before the big guns teed off and the proper sports reporting got underway.

Anna sat at her desk and mulled over her father's advice that this Open might need to be her last roll of her journalistic dice - at least exclusively, anyway. She was thirty-three and to date had managed almost no traction as a journalist. She barely scraped an income, and she was heavily subsidised by her parents who still kept a room for her. Her first-class degree in media studies from Portsmouth University had not delivered what it had promised and her very expensive MA in journalism from Leeds had been equally unproductive. She had a mountain of debt and a distinct lack of column inches. And now her dad's encouragement to consider teacher training was sounding ever more sensible.

Only in politics is the Oxbridge degree more prevalent than in the media arena. There are more opportunities in female sports broadcasting, but they tended to skew prejudicially high on the 'phwoar' scale, and Anna couldn't imagine hopping into that particular bear-pit.

She was attending the Open as a freelancer, which meant she was living off scraps, hoping to get lucky eking out a story that no one else had noticed and selling it to one of the networks. The story of the player in a kilt might have been a good one, but it was already being devoured by the hacks - every possible angle exhausted. Journalists with deadlines and outlets already were all over Ricky Randal.

Anna stared at Ricky on her computer screen. It seemed to her that he had settled down a little from when he emerged on the first tee. On the third hole now, he looked a little less lost and bewildered, whereas at the start he'd appeared like a small boy in a shopping centre without his mum - not dissimilar to how Anna felt amidst the world's sports journalists.

If only he knew how much chaos he was causing outside his game of golf. All around her, keyboards were clicking furiously.

She smiled. She liked Ricky Randal, the underdog with the kind face, even if she wasn't quite certain why.

Already having a better day in the world of media was Daniel Colindale, a trainee cameraman - or 'operative', as they called him nowadays to comply with equality standards.

His boss had given him the opportunity to record the first shot of the final round, which might be used later in a compilation piece for broadcast. It had been his first big chance; and so he'd been thrilled at the opportunity even before he set eyes on Ricky and his kilt.

An hour into the final round, the BBC director of Outside Broadcasts (Sports) was sitting in one of his enormous television trucks, staring at his single TV monitor. In front of him was a bank of further screens, most of them showing a holding slide of the Muirfield clubhouse. Three screens were showing live on-course pictures, which were all available to various news feeds across the world. But as yet, only the images from Daniel's feed were of any real interest.

Last evening, he'd studied the roster of forthcoming matches and naturally his attention had focused on the leaders who were going out later in the day. Justin Rose against Tiger Woods would be the biggest draw and as such, would require his best technicians.

He watched Ricky play his wedge shot onto the third green. The picture was nicely in focus. *Good job, Daniel,* he thought, and the golfer of the moment looked good too, with a smooth and efficient swing. The screen cut to the green and captured the ball landing softly and stopping within fifteen feet of the pin.

A bloody good shot. He made a note of the time code, should he need the footage later. A birdie opportunity - possibly the first of the day.

He got onto his radio and told Daniel to stay with this match for a little longer.

'You might gain some more experience,' he said mildly, 'if nothing else.'

Once again, Marshall said nothing at all on the green. There was no need; the putt was straight, and Ricky had the luxury of two putts to make his par. He didn't need any reminding that par on Sunday is a fine score indeed.

He softened his hands on the putter's grip, and then drew the flat blade back slowly, his head rock-solid as he struck the ball.

The speed was good, but it was never on-line, so never had a chance. But no matter, because Ricky was not going to miss the two-footer coming back and finally he would end his long-est-ever bogey run as a professional golfer.

He could hardly wait to slam his ball home, but he had to wait first for his playing partner to finish off first for his consec-utive bogey.

Ricky quickly replaced his ball and without hesitation he drained it for par; a wave of sheer relief washed over him. Finally, a par and something to cling on this most dramatic and confusing day.

Chapter Four

Richard Randal, ENG +2
Open Championship +15
72nd Place
Prize Money €33,361
4th Hole
229 Yards, Par 3

The female presenter of BBC Breakfast chuckled along with her male co-presenter, although she didn't understand his quip.

The joke, referring to their last news item, probably wasn't even very amusing, but on morning television laughter is the default position and especially so on the weekend. It's what the viewers tune in to see; people who are easy on the eye, in shiny studios, looking lovely and happy.

Her autocue scrolled up; a red light on top of the camera began to blink. The next item was ready. A piece hastily put together, aping a radio broadcast that had just gone out on BBC 5 Live.

'A big day of sport ahead, with the conclusion of The British Open at Muirfield in Scotland. The final round is already under way, and it looks set to be a cracker as always. Now...a little earlier we were showing you the British golfer, Ricky Randal, resplendent in his kilt. Well, here he is again.'

'This is Ricky just a few moments ago, on the third green, facing only a very short putt for his par. And... well, have a look at this...'

The studio vanished from view, replaced by recorded footage of Ricky Randal holing his tiny putt for par and followed by his exultant celebration.

It was a reaction, more in keeping with a player winning the Championship than achieving par on the third hole, and it looked ridiculous. As soon as the ball began to drop, Ricky bent forward at the knee and pointed his stiffened index finger at the hole. It looked as if he was angry and was giving the hole a damn good telling off. The only thing missing was a look to the heavens and a 'thanks' to his dad.

And then our effervescent presenters were back onscreen, both of them laughing wildly.

'... and that was for his par! Which goes to show how difficult this golf course is, if that's how the world's best golfers react to a par!'

The male presenter pointed his index finger in imitation of Ricky; his colleague laughed again.

'Do you know, Harry, that putt was so short, I think even I could have slotted it home.'

She laughed wildly at her own quip, but the more experienced Harry was instantly poker-faced. Media-trained to the hilt, he was savvy enough to recognise even the slightest career-affecting pothole, which this remark was, because it could be interpreted to infer that his colleague (ergo, women) were not terribly good at golf. And therefore, nothing funny about her remark whatever.

He protected himself further by looking even a little bit offended by it - no such thing as overspending these days in fending off a charge of sexism. And quickly, he moved on into calmer waters.

'So do keep those texts and emails coming and let us know what you think about Ricky's outfit. Doris Debnor has emailed us. She says,

'My husband used to wear a kilt playing golf, and he always looked very smart and I think Ricky does too.'

Ahh, that's lovely. Thank you, Doris.'

With news bulletins now required to fill twenty-four hours, it follows that viewers are encouraged to get involved - and fortunately the public are only too willing to oblige, hungry for their fifteen minutes of fame. Please, get in touch. Help us. Text us your thoughts. Get involved. Phone us. Email. Tweet. Send us your pictures and videos. And they do and why so many ordinary Joes can find themselves as unlikely broadcast correspondents.

'...the helicopter came down about a mile from where I live. I heard a loud bang and then I saw flames and a plume of smoke in the sky...'

No shit. Thanks for that.

'...and joining us now in the studio to discuss Ricky Randal and his infamous kilt is the secretary of Holmes Chapel Golf Club and chair of his regional rules committee, Mr Mike Harrison. Morning, Mike...'

Mr Harrison was one of the many experts who were having their Sunday morning disturbed by a frantic media chasing an unlikely and ever-evolving story, with cars being dispatched and interviews being hastily arranged.

The story had taken an unexpected, even feverish turn when an Edinburgh lawyer announced on local radio that the kilt predates the game of golf and therefore its rules, since there are constitutional safeguards to protect an indigenous culture and which might include the wearing of the national dress. It was a Scotsman's right, wasn't it?

Only Ricky Randal was not a Scot. He was English and so the new charge of cultural appropriation might be laid at his door? Hang on, but wasn't the kilt invented *by* the English? And inadvertently Ricky had opened up a can of Scottish nationalist worms. And what a can this is; when calls for a second referendum on Scottish independence are continuing with hungry lawyers circling and as per, the only sure-fire winners.

Mr Harrison droned on about the proud traditions of golf for a drab few minutes before the floor manager began frantically waving a circular hand to wind things up.

'...well thank you, Mike. Fascinating stuff there. A little later in the programme I hope we can speak to an apparel historian about the origins of the kilt, which will be very interesting indeed, so stay tuned for that... and we'll also have a psychologist in the studio to discuss our golfer of the moment, Ricky Randal. Who I hope continues to play well, because if that's how he celebrates a par, then I'd love to see him sink a birdie or, dare I say it, even an eagle...'

He wouldn't have long to wait.

The fourth hole at Muirfield is the first of four par-three's on the course; golf holes where the player is expected to hit the green with a single tee shot, and then complete the hole with two putts for par. As such, par-three holes can be very short indeed. The Postage Stamp, just along the coast at Royal Troon

Golf Club is one of the most famous and formidable holes in golf and yet barely stretches a hundred yards; a distance that all golfers, even novices, can manage. But the fourth hole at Muirfield, at two hundred and twenty nine yards, is a bloody good thump for the ordinary golfer and a solid hit even for a professional.

Ricky caught the referee's eye again; buoyed after his par, he decided that now was the time. Moving to the left, he gestured for the other man's attention and the two of them moved to one side.

'Look, I'm sorry about the kilt. I really am.'

'Right - well, can you explain it?'

Ricky faltered. He wasn't sure he could bring himself to explain the intricacies of his bowel movements to a man who was already at the end of his tether.

'Er, no, not really. Not now, anyway – I'm sorry,' he offered lamely. The official looked distinctly unimpressed.

'Well, that might not be good enough, I'm afraid. It's out of my hands. You do know that you're all over the television?'

Immediately, Ricky thought of his wife and his mum glued to their television at home.

'Look, Ricky, I'm sorry, but I'm under huge pressure here. The rules committee are freaking out, as you can imagine...'

'OK, fine...' Ricky interrupted. 'I had white trousers on this morning and I had an accident. You know? An *accident*?'

'Oh.'

'Yeah. I shat my pants. How's that?'

The referee would have laughed if it hadn't been so serious and quite possibly caught by the television cameras also.

'Right. Well, that's pretty much bang on... because you and your kilt are causing a total fucking shitstorm. Michael Landale was an inch away from disqualifying you.'

'I know, I can imagine. I'm sorry.'

'No, Ricky, I don't think you can imagine, and you'll need to be really, really, sorry once you finish your round. If you're allowed to finish, that is. You have no idea of all the shit that you've caused.'

The pun was unintentional. Neither of them laughed.

'They're having some trousers sent over from the pro shop. They should be here soon enough.'

Ricky nodded enthusiastically. 'Great, thanks. I'll be delighted to get this bloody thing off.' He hoped that this might be the end of it, but the referee still looked fretful.

'Anything else?' Ricky asked.

The referee pulled at his face and sighed.

'What now?' Ricky repeated.

'Well, your pace of play is borderline, which...'

'Because my caddie was a no-show. What else could I do?'

'Well, you could have got a young pro to caddie for you.'

'I thought about that, but Marshall is fine. I like him, and I'll get him to pick up the pace - OK?'

The referee stared at Ricky, agog. 'Er...'

'Right, so that's the trousers covered and my caddie dealt with. Anything else?'

The referee tilted his head a little but said nothing. This whole thing was all too confusing and outside his sphere of expertise and better left to professionals with letters after their name. After this little exchange, he needed to speak with Michael Landale again and slowly he began backing away. This was a welcome sight for Ricky, who leapt onto the tee and grabbed his five iron from Marshall – a good choice.

'Ricky, the wind's getting up, so I'd give it a really hard belt. Don't leave anything on the tee.'

Loyal as ever, the young lad was still looking on, no doubt having enjoyed his par at the previous hole and hoping it might be the start of things to come. A par run, perhaps? Par golf from here on in would be a marvellous final round and might even see Ricky crawl himself up from last place.

Ricky smiled at his young fan. He could sense that the boy was taken by him - and it flattered him. He was unaccustomed to having fans and was heartened to have picked one up today. He noted that the boy was on his own again now. Ricky winked at him and the lad beamed back, seemingly thrilled at their connection.

And then to business. After his chat with the referee, and knowing that trousers were on their way, Ricky was enjoying a renewed sense of enthusiasm. He felt almost normal, in fact. Finally, his bogey run was behind him and he waggled his club with a defiant sense of purpose.

Standing over his ball now, he took his eye up and glanced left towards his target. The tiny flag was fluttering a long way off in the distance and once again, he visualised his shot.

Ricky eased his fingers on the grip of his club, breathed in calmly, and then slowly drew his club back; his shoulders pivoting against his fixed hips until his body could rotate no more. His head remained perfectly still and then, just before his downswing, something most peculiar happened. Everything stopped; as though for a split second, time slowed and then stood eerily still.

All external sound died to a muffled hum and Ricky was able to remove himself and observe his situation as if he was standing outside it.

Another first and highly unusual, the sort of thing he had heard about happening to other people - before an accident, for instance, when one is mid-air and about to hit a tree or another car. Ricky wondered if there was something incoming waiting for him, although this moment felt extended and unrushed. He could almost relax, soaking up the scene before him. It was as though a giant pause button had been pressed, and so the Open Championship and the world's elite golfers could wait.

Ricky took a second to observe himself at the top of his back swing. He was in a good position. Right knee a little flexed, but firm and nicely tucked in. His weight on his right side, his hands in perfect line with the target, and his left shoulder nestling against his solid chin. Ben Hogan would have approved. A text-book back swing, even if he said so himself.

And then he took in Marshall, with his dreamy nonchalance - a stark contrast to the excitement of the spectators looking on. And in particular, his only fan, the young boy staring up at the golfer, his face a study in pure concentration.

Now he looked into the lens of the television camera and thought of Maggie again. She'd be watching with his mum, Tess, glued to their telly and asking themselves the same question he was asking himself. Just what the hell was going on?

And then the bubble burst and reality was all around him once again. The noise hit him first. The sound of the breeze, and the noise of the hush that envelops a tee. Back in real time at the top of his backswing, and without taking even a beat, he ignited an explosion of energy as he began his aggressive downswing. Both eyes glaring at his ball on its wooden plinth about to be crushed by incoming iron, his concentration steely and complete, his club accelerated downwards, faster and faster.

His club struck the ball at well over one hundred miles an hour, and yet he felt nothing in his hands. There was no impact at all as the ball fired away, and he wrapped both arms around his left shoulder like a scarf against the breeze, and he stood perfectly balanced on his left foot and right toe.

His ball fizzed away, zoning towards the target and narrowing all the way. Certainly a good shot and definitely green-bound. Another par would be fabulous. Or how about a birdie, even?

Marshall was watching the ball as well but with the look of a man without a care in the world.

The ball landed on the front of the green, skipping forward and left as it started to run out in the direction of the pin. From Ricky's perspective, it was looking very good indeed, which came as an enormous relief. Left of the hole and within range made a par a real possibility on one of Muirfield's most frugal holes.

His eyes narrowed at he watched his ball rolling out, until quite suddenly, it vanished from view. Obscured by a swale perhaps? But wasn't this a flat green?

There was no crowd at the green to applaud and indicate just how close his ball had finished, but Ricky was exhilarated just to be on the green. He handed his club to Marshall, who was now beaming from ear to ear, and suddenly, there was a commotion from the right of the tee box. The referee was chattering into his radio again. *Fuck's sake, what now?* Maybe they had a pair of trousers, but not in his size?

The cameraman was also speaking into his headset and he smiled too and raised his thumb into the air and then began pointing down to the ground, like Caesar at the amphitheatre - only this downward thumb was very good news indeed.

It could only mean one thing. An eagle. An ace. Or, more conventionally, a hole-in-one.

It took a split second for this to register with Ricky; and then when it did, Daniel was poised, ready with his television camera to get the shots that would go around the world and make an unheard-of golfer very well-known indeed.

Bernard Gallacher was taking his turn in the commentary box, and he was delighted at his fortunate timing.

'...he'll be feeling absolutely elated, and it's things like this that can change someone's round. Because that ball could easily have rolled on past the hole and then he makes just a par. But if Ricky Randal can use this to kick on, then who knows what lies ahead for him...'

Chapter Five

Richard Randal, ENG Even Par
Open Championship +13
67th Place
Prize Money €34,132
5th Hole
561 Yards, Par 5

'... **O**ver the pond now to Scot-Land where the British Open final round is underway, and where ACNBC will be live today from 12am Eastern time. Always an exciting day for American golf fans, with Tiger, Phil, Jordan and Bubba all in the hunt, but after an hour's play already this morning, the player making all the headlines is Richard Randal of Eng-Land.

'This is Ricky on the first tee wearing, yes, would you believe it, a Scottish kilt - which is a skirt to you and me. He opened bogey, bogey, but how about this at the long par-three fourth hole? Hitting five iron, he fires off... and as you can see... in for an ace.

'How do you like that? Right there. Boom. That's one way to get back those dropped shots? Randal now level par for the day. They say that putting is the hardest shot in golf... so best, then, just avoid it altogether.'

Now on the television screen was a shot of a beaming Ricky Randal, picking his way across the green to scoop his ball out of the hole, which evidently had excited the American news anchor as much as everyone else.

'And a nice touch coming up here... Ricky Randal, certainly a golfer with an eye for the headlines. Instead of tossing his ball to the crowd, he walks over and hands it to a young fan who's looking on.

'Naturally, the kid's thrilled, and the player even stops to have a little chat with him as well. Nice touch, Ricky - but come on, seriously dude, lose the kilt!'

Ricky's hole-in-one was picked up by newswires across the globe with a combined audience of many millions, all of them marvelling at the shot and chortling at the golfer's unique look. It was the sort of exposure that all professional sports stars craved - and what Ricky needed now, even more than another par, was a manager to exploit his newfound and most likely fleeting fame.

Needless to say, Ricky did not have a manager.

At 3am, in New York City, unable to sleep, Jago Silver sat watching the news bulletin on ACNBC with a keen and gathering interest. At such an early hour, the current television audience in America was not only insignificant but also an unattractive demographic; drunks, students, and the unemployed who don't have to worry about getting to work the next day. With the exception of Jago Silver, that is, who was watching on his laptop in his enormous and opulent office.

A bank of financial screens covered the wall to his left and in front of him were three large television monitors, each tuned to various business and trading channels from markets across the world. Jago Silver had grown into his surname in more ways than one. In his late forties, he was famed for his thick silver mane, which he spent many thousands of dollars on maintaining with real hair weaves to bulk it out. It contrasted beautifully against his perma-tan and his preposterous and hideously expensive white teeth.

Jago had no interest in golf, outside the corporate shindigs that he lavished on his clients. He didn't play the game and would never watch it on television, but the man in the kilt had caught his attention - and very quickly, he became transfixed.

He never tired of explaining to anyone who would listen that his success was based on his ingenuity and inspiration. 'Being ahead of the curve' was one of his favourite expressions.

His antennae quivering, he called out, loudly and precisely, "TV, screen three. Go to channel eight-sixty-two."

Television monitor No. 3 got to work, and the screen flickered momentarily before Ricky Randal filled the biggest screen in the cavernous office of one of Wall Street's biggest hitters.

And then it occurred to Jago, and he chuckled to himself as he clapped his hand down hard on his ebony desk. 'Thinking outside the box' was another of his mantras - and how had it taken him so long to see this glaring opportunity? It was perfect, but it was a rapidly closing window, and he needed to act quickly. And it was particularly appetising because it would be yet another gift horse from Scot-Land. He really should visit the place someday - because who would have thought such a small country could be so bountiful for him?

It was perfect, goddamn perfect. He grabbed at his mobile phone and snapped loudly, 'Ring Noah.'

. . .

By the time Ricky had reached the fifth tee, there was a small but enthusiastic crowd waiting for him and they made plenty of noise greeting him. Being a player without a reputation - one that nobody had even heard of, in fact, before this year's Open - he apparently came across as less intimidating than the famous golfers, and so some spectators felt sufficiently emboldened to try a little bit of banter with him.

'Can I have your putter?' one wag called out. 'Seeing as though you don't use it anymore.'

This got an appreciative laugh from everyone, including Ricky.

'You can keep your kilt, though,' someone else cried and this got an even bigger laugh.

It was all good-natured stuff, and very welcome. Ricky was certainly feeling more at ease now, and he reminded himself that pretty soon he would be back in a pair of trousers and then all would be well.

'You'll need to win it now, Ricky, if you're going to get everyone a round in,' another spectator or 'fan' shouted. This was a reference to the tradition that the golfer holding an ace should buy a drink for everyone on the course. Seventy-two golfers at Muirfield prices and during the Open Championship would be an eye-watering bar bill indeed.

Ricky added to the mirth by handing over his putter to a delighted onlooker, which Daniel recorded and immediately flagged up to his editor over his radio. Humorous and human interest footage was most welcome; ideal for closing montages, and more material to feed into the media sensation that Richard Randal was fast becoming.

It was all a great release and distraction for Ricky. *What an extraordinary bloody day*, he thought.

Marshall glanced back in his direction and nodded as if to reassure him. He still had a calmness to him which was

extremely welcome, and Ricky thanked the Almighty that he
had run into such a thoroughly useful toilet attendant. The kilt
aside, were it not for Marshall, he would most likely be in his
car now and on his way home in ignominy.

Instead he was on the course and had just hit his first ever
hole-in-one in competitive golf. And what a time to do it. In the
Open. The final round, and recorded on TV to boot. Maggie
would be leaping about their lounge, and he smiled to himself
at the thought of it.

Briefly, he wondered how many places his shot might have
nudged him up the leaderboard. In his starting position of last,
the only way was up.

On making the cut, Ricky had studied the increasing value
of prize money for each place above him. To begin with, it was
only increments of only €150 per place - which seemed a little
stingy - and it wasn't until the mid-sixties when prize money
jumped to €900 per place and built on steadily from there.

Fiftieth place was the best that Ricky could hope for, and
was his private target. It was worth €43,281 and he reasoned
that he'd need to shoot par to achieve it, the mark he currently
stood at thanks to his remarkable previous shot.

Ricky Randal's attire had become the talk of the course, and
players and spectators alike were keen to witness the golfing
fashion crime for themselves. For now, at least, Ricky was the
star attraction, the giant panda at the zoo - and Ben was still in
the prime position to take it all in.

He was the original fan, he thought with a burst of pride;
and the fan with the most credibility because, although he
didn't know why, he had followed Ricky before it was fashion-
able to do so. Before the rest of the world had caught on to him.

And of course Ricky's newfound fame had already shone

brightly on Ben as well, when he'd handed him his golf ball. It had immediately become Ben's most prized possession - even above the Roger Federer autographed photo that he'd received in the post after his dad had written to the Lawn Tennis Association.

As soon as his round of golf was complete, Ben thought, he'd ask Ricky to sign the ball, and he'd get his dad to photograph him with Ricky right there on the 18th green.

Barry Singleton sat in front of his television with pictures of this new and unlikely golf hero, completely motionless and unable to speak. Slouched in his pyjama bottoms and his string vest, he hadn't moved all morning. He was jubilant, of course, but also terrified.

Presently he was particularly nervous, because his fearsome wife was sitting opposite him, eyeing him suspiciously while she breastfed their brand new arrival.

She didn't trust her husband at all - and with good reason. Having been married to Barry for so long, she'd developed a highly sensitive sixth sense for mischief, which was now setting off alarm bells despite Barry's best efforts to appear nonchalant.

Barry smiled weakly as her doubting gaze burnt into him. He needed to get out of harm's way.

'Cup of tea, love?' he asked.

His wife didn't reply. Her eyes narrowed as she watched him get up and move shiftily across their tiny lounge, heading quickly for the kitchen.

Barry had already been up for hours; he'd woken at 5am with a start, feeling worried and anxious; and straight away, drenched in a cold and sinister sweat, he'd known there was no chance of getting back to sleep.

It was a moment of rare quiet in their tiny terraced house in

Bromsgrove, Birmingham. His wife was still asleep next to him, and, remarkably, so was their new-born child, and the twin boys in the adjacent bedroom.

Normally, Barry would have lazed in bed until baby Bethan started screaming, closely followed by his wife. But this morning he'd felt a chill of unease as he picked his way gingerly downstairs and turned the lights on in their cold kitchen.

On reflection, he'd gone to bed feeling peculiar, although perhaps he hadn't realised it at the time.

Now, though, he knew that his own state of mind was going awry - and most worryingly, tumbling out of his control. It was a feeling of helplessness that he knew only too well. A compulsion that he recognised immediately; and he knew where it would end.

His hand was trembling as he dunked his teabag onto the drainer and stirred in three sugars, down from four as the result of a successful Lent.

Barry sat on his sofa - which he did not yet own - and tried to employ the exercises and mental techniques that his counsellors had provided him with. Techniques that had kept his urges at bay over the last four years.

Until today, at least; because he knew that he was about to succumb. The only thing that could save him now was baby Bethan waking up - but she didn't. Not a peep. It was bloody typical, he thought.

Barry fired up his laptop, automatically, staring into the middle distance as if he was now being controlled by something else and his actions were no longer his own. That was how he'd explain it to his wife later.

'There was nothing I could do love. I was impotent.'

'Yeah, I wish you was.' And she'd cry even harder and hate him even more.

His mouth was dry now; his hand quivered as he clicked

his mouse and waited for the page to load. Fear and excitement surged through his body. His wife was going to find out. He could delete his web history, but he would not be able to replace the debit from her account.

Horse racing had been his downfall. It had cost him absolutely everything that he owned - and almost his marriage and the privilege of being a father. The internet, as liberating as it is, is also a dark place for many souls and particularly those with a proclivity to gamble.

But this morning Barry ignored the day's racing completely. Idly, his mouse hovered over the brilliantly-lit and attractively-designed home page of his preferred bookmaker. A page created by experts to be reassuring and welcoming, complete with a free bet of £50 for any new account-holder. *How kind.* Bookies welcome everyone - but most especially, the losers. Punters with an edge are quickly identified and have their accounts shortened and even closed, whereas losers have their credit extended so they can bleed out completely.

Golf featured heavily on the home page and Barry noticed the Open Championship.

He didn't like golf. Golf was a posh game for rich people. Barry had never played it, watched it nor bet on it, and yet he found himself clicking through the golf bets and books on offer. He'd never heard of any of the players - apart from Tiger Woods and Rory McIlroy, of course - but neither of them offered any value at all.

So he searched the 'Open' specials. Bets for the final day only, and with much more generous odds. Carrots dangling in the air. One bet caught his attention; a hole-in-one in today's final round. The price was an enormous 250-1 and quickly, Barry was intoxicated by the familiar excitement of the chase and dreams of what might be. And compounded by such long and attractive odds.

He shut the screen and tried to control himself. His heart was pounding, his mouth completely dry despite his flurried slurps of sweet tea.

'Jesus, Barry, not again. I won't do it. No. I cannot go through this again.'

Barry had long shut down all of his online accounts; altogether too risky and unaffordable. It had been part of his healing and his deal to keep his marriage afloat. And so instead, this fateful morning, he went old school and waited on the telephone line while the operator found the price and took the details of his wife's credit card. He shook as he whispered the number, waiting and hoping for a cry from his daughter. He didn't know what he was doing, or why. It was a compulsion he couldn't explain.

His face was wet with tears as he ended the call. He loved his family - and he hated what he had just done. Just what would he tell his wife? He tried to imagine how she'd respond.

'You just had a feeling? Is that it?' she'd scream at him.

Barry grabbed at the phone and quickly redialled the bookmaker but this time he got a different operator. How many of the poor bastards were working at this hour? He explained his situation to the new operator and pleaded to have his bet revoked - but apparently this was impossible.

Really? Impossible how? Most likely they were trained to be immune to any desperate pleas.

His bet stood. £250. Almost a month's rent, and an amount that they could not afford to lose. But he stood to lose so much more besides.

He buried his head in his hands. And, just then, Bethan started crying upstairs, too late for Barry who was crying also in the lounge below.

· · ·

Michael Landale had never, ever been as angry, not in his entire life, as when the news came through from the on-course match referee.

'I don't give a shit if he's having a full-scale mental collapse,' he screamed into his radio.

All manner of things were now being considered regarding Ricky Randal, and in the very highest echelons of the game and with other professions besides - most notably, the medical fraternity. But his mooted mental health frailties cut little ice with Michael Landale, who now saw through Randal completely and was determined to shoot him down in order to preserve the sport that he presided over.

The replacement trousers had duly arrived on the fifth tee, just after Ricky had fired off another beautiful drive. He had a choice of two styles of slacks, but Ricky had refused them both.

The match referee's face fell. He'd tried to reason with the obstinate golfer, but Ricky had been both adamant and apologetic. He swallowed hard. Reporting back this decision was going to be almost impossible - and Landale exploded, just as he expected.

'You tell that little oik that unless he loses that kilt, he is not to play another fucking shot in my fucking tournament. Get it?' Landale shrieked.

'So you want me to disqualify him?' the referee asked, the panic in his voice impossible to disguise. 'Here on the course? You want me to disqualify him live on the telly?'

And so they went around again, the same conundrum as before about adverse publicity and the global TV coverage, all of which enraged Landale even more.

They'd already sustained the usual tsunami of criticism that comes with a Muirfield Open and any other venues that had taken overly long to admit female members. That the club's membership were nonetheless a bunch of anachronistic dinosaurs and the headlines now would be equally unfavourable if he were to haul Randal, the people's hero, off the course. The press would gorge on his backstory - and no doubt, his wife was bloody pregnant, and he was struggling to feed his kids.

His hopes that Ricky's game would disintegrate and that he'd disappear into obscurity were now well and truly up in smoke. His hole-in-one was a world story and ensured his continued coverage.

Landale's phone was running hot - almost as hot as his temper and soaring blood pressure.

Ricky was just as stunned at his own decision as the match referee. It was downright unreasonable – bewildering defiance in the face of both common sense and social pressure.

And he couldn't explain himself, either. It certainly wasn't that he didn't like the trousers that were being offered to him; just that he couldn't lose the kilt, not now. Not after a hole-in-one. Just a feeling he had - sorry.

Golfers don't like change, especially when things are going in their favour, and as ridiculous as it was, he couldn't just change his clothes. It was obvious. The kilt had to stay.

'But you could be disqualified,' the referee pleaded, 'or have shots docked!'

Ricky shifted from foot to foot.

'What do you think, Marshall?'

Marshall was quick to shake his head.

'Ricky, right now you're the most famous golfer on the planet. You're on every news bulletin the world over,' Marshalled murmured.

Ricky looked a little shocked at this.

'They'll never disqualify you. Not now. They can't.'

This was conjecture, of course. It had to be, but it was enough for Ricky.

He gave the referee a mournful look; he felt a little worried for the man, honestly, but what could he do? He'd heard what his caddie had to say, and now Ricky needed to be getting along to his ball which with wind, was over three hundred yards away down the middle of the fifth fairway.

Time was pressing, and the two of them quickly got on their way.

'That stuff about the news bulletins?' Ricky asked casually.

'Yes.'

'How do you know that?'

'I don't,' Marshall said. 'But it wouldn't surprise me.'

'Makes sense, I suppose.' Ricky replied. 'The ace and the kilt?'

The referee dropped back, sighed quietly to himself, and raised his radio again. This was going to be a horrible conversation and predictably, Landale was apoplectic.

'I don't give a shit if he's having a full-scale mental collapse...'

'There's something else,' the referee added mischievously, after a few minutes of having his ear assaulted.

'What? What else?' Landale spat over the frequency.

'He says that he's doing it for Scotland,' the referee announced. His radio abruptly went silent and he chuckled a little to himself as he imagined the unbridled fury he had just unleashed.

Michael Landale's radio crashed into the wall of his office. A piece of plastic flew off, but it didn't disintegrate as he would have liked and so he kicked at the offending device for good measure as it rebounded off his wall.

'Doing it for Scotland. Fuck Scotland. I'm sick of hearing about fucking Scotland...'

All morning he'd seen the First Minister of Scotland on television, being hastily interviewed. Like all politicians, ever the opportunist, she welcomed the metaphorical Scottish flag being waved at this pivotal and politically sensitive time with a Brexit backdrop and her desire to side with Brussels and not London. And by an English golfer, no less, which suited her cause perfectly to become the new Queen of Scotland.

As his tantrum continued, Michael Landale failed to see that his secretary had appeared in his office and was frantically trying to attract his attention.

'... see if England cares. Trot off to Brussels, why don't you? How would we cope without Scotland? Without your short-bread and fucking heart disease...'

Finally, he spotted his secretary, who'd resorted to coughing violently in the hopes of catching his attention and he noticed that she was accompanied by a middle-aged man. He was rotund, with a ruddy face and the remnants of what had once been a thick thatch of wiry red hair.

'Er... Mr Landale, this is Angus McLeish. Editor of The Scotsman.

'I can tell you that flush from his ONE at the previous hole. Ricky Randal is playing the fifth hole and has just nailed a two iron from the middle of the fairway that has him just off the green in two at this treacherous par five...'

Back at home, Maggie and Tess were still punching the air and dancing a jig; Ricky's unusual attire and situation was no longer even an issue. They were ecstatic, and curious, too, to see how many places he'd climbed up the leaderboard. But before Maggie could find out, her phone rang yet again - but this time, she knew who it was and that it was a call she would take.

She glanced at her phone and half smiled to herself. This would be an interesting conversation.

'Bloody hell, Patrick. Talk to me.'

Patrick Pollard, one-time caddie of Richard Randal, was the man everyone wanted to speak to, but his call to Maggie was the first conversation he'd had with anyone since the incident at yesterday's sixteenth green.

'Hey, Maggie. How you doing?'

'Er... yeah... you know.'

'Yeah.'

'Odd day, right?'

'Er, yeah. I'd say it is, yes.' Patrick chuckled.

'I was worried to start with. Mad with you, of course, but now... well, not so much.'

'Yeah, I guess. You're watching it, right?'

'Me? No, I thought I'd cut the lawn. Of course I'm bloody well watching it. Are you?'

'Of course, I am.' Patrick said quite casually, as though everything was normal. He'd caddied for Ricky for nearly four years and never missed a stroke until today, the most important round of his life. It was such a bizarre conversation – the whys were hanging in the air and neither of them were willing to broach the subject let alone attempt to answer any of them.

'Ricky seems OK, then?' Patrick offered gently.

'Yeah, he does. Which is... kind of odd, right?'

'Sure.'

'And what about you? Are you OK, Patrick?'

'Er... yeah, I think so. I feel a little odd, I guess...'

'Yeah, well...'

'I know. Nuts, huh?'

Maggie didn't reply. She didn't need to.

'Anyway, Maggie, look, I need to get on.'

'Yeah, sure.'

They both had a golf match to watch on television.

She ended the call, considering how utterly implausible it was that Patrick hadn't even tried to explain himself, nor offer any kind of apology. And equally strange, she hadn't felt any need for an explanation. It was all so peculiar, and yet so normal.

'What? What did he say?' Tess snapped, her patience and calm finally giving way. 'Did he explain just what the hell is going on and why he's...'

'No, Mum, he didn't say anything.'

'What? What do you mean? He must have said something...'

'No, Mum. He's just watching Ricky on the telly like we are.'

Another person glued to the television was Mrs Jean Costello, mother of Ben, at the same time, the youngest and oldest fan of Ricky Randal. Jean had told the two men in her life that she'd be watching out for them on the television, ignoring their scoffs and their explanations about the huge crowds attending Muirfield.

'Mum, we're never going to be on the telly. We'll be pinpricks in a sea of people.'

The on-course BBC reporter was out of breath when he finally reached the fifth fairway, having been dispatched with the mission of getting an interview with the lucky spectator.

'This is Ben Costello, the lucky fourteen-year-old boy who is now the proud owner of the golf ball that has made a little piece of Open history. Ben, if you could show it to the camera please - so that we can all see it?'

Ben grinned proudly as he held up his treasured possession.

'Now, the question is, Ben, with Monty already on the course and Sergio just about to tee off, what was it about this match that made you follow it?'

It was a good question. Ben thought for a moment and just shrugged.

'I'm not sure, really. Actually we came here to watch Monty, but... I don't know. When I arrived at the course this morning with my Dad, I just felt drawn to this first match with Ricky.'

'And Ricky had a little word with you, didn't he? What did he say to you when he gave you the ball?'

Suddenly, something occurred to Ben; his easy smile vanished and he became a little strained.

'Er... is this on the telly? Like, now?' His eyes shifted nervously. 'I'm on the telly now?'

'Yes. You're live on BBC Breakfast,' the journalist said.

'Oh.'

Ben looked worried, which the interviewer picked up on - and so did his editor, watching from a nearby broadcast truck.

Jean stared at her television screen, completely mortified. Without taking her eyes from the screen, she retrieved her phone and placed a call to her husband. He'd been very specific, insisting that a call could be placed only in the event of an absolute emergency.

She hit the green button.

Eric had a great spot in the grandstand directly behind the first tee, and he reminded himself to buy something nice from the onsite golf shop as a thank-you for the tickets. Monty had already got his round underway, and was sent up the first fairway with a huge partisan cheer from the packed gallery. And now it was the turn of the Spanish favourite, Sergio Garcia.

What a day ahead, he thought; watching the very best

players in the world. If only Ben hadn't been so peculiar - they could have sat here all morning and watched the entire field get underway before fighting with the on-course crowds for a glimpse of the action.

He'd been irked by Ben's obstinance, which was most unlike him - but it quickly passed. It was good for Ben to have a little independence; his son had clearly taken a shine to Ricky Randal and it was wonderful to see how happy he was today, even if he had to keep reminding himself that nothing unto-ward was going to happen.

News of the hole-in-one had spread throughout the whole course by now. Eric hoped Ben had seen it. What a thrill it would have been for him.

Sergio smiled, enjoying some banter with the crowd; then, after a few loosening swings, he put on his game-face and a reverent hush spread across the tee. Sergio considered his ball and briefly adjusted his grip a couple of times - and then once again, as was his way, before he was finally ready to hit.

Slowly and purposefully, he pulled his giant club back and away, drawing it around his shoulders and over his head - and just at the very apex of his swing, a mobile phone chirped into life.

Sergio quit his swing and a groan of derision spread through the crowd.

Eric froze. After being so specific about silent settings, he'd forgotten his own phone. And yet he was *sure* he'd switched the wretched contraption to silent. He sprang up from his seat, apologising profusely but quietly as he pushed past knees turned flat all along his pew, avoiding all eye contact as his phone continued to humiliate him.

He left the stand. How was it ringing? And who the hell was calling him on a Sunday morning? The question panicked him even more. *Not Ben*, he prayed. Or even worse, a paramedic.

Digging the phone out of his pocket, he stared at the screen. "Jean". He should have bloody well known. And what emergency could it be, he asked himself angrily?

The crowd cheered as he finally left the stand and Sergio enjoyed the admonishment. Two frosty-looking officials were frowning at him. He got clear and answered the call.

'What is it?' he barked. 'I told you...'

'Why aren't you with Ben?'

Her question floored him. Only his wife could do this to him. She seemed to know things intuitively but this was an impressive new level, given that she was at the opposite end of the blinking country. She sounded so certain and emphatic; frantically considering which lie to opt for, his available options quickly narrowed.

'Put Ben on the phone now,' she demanded.

How the hell did she know? Instinctively, he started up the course, panicking now because he worried that Ben might be in trouble. That was an awful prospect - but selfishly, he gave some thought to the trouble he'd be in as well. His wife would never, ever forgive him. Never mind the rules of no running on the golf course; Eric broke into a fast stride.

'He's on the fifth hole. I was just with him,' he muttered, panting heavily and rather giving himself away.

'And where are you? You promised to stay with Ben the whole time!'

'Yes, I am. I am. I was just off getting us some burgers.' And so the lying began. 'And why are you phoning, anyway? Have you heard from him - is he OK?' he asked, trying to regain some authority.

'I'm *phoning* because Ben's on breakfast television being interviewed.'

. . .

Ricky studied his third shot at this par five fifth hole. He was in excellent shape. Sixty feet or so, it could be putted - but realistically, it warranted a more risky and difficult chip. He had three shots left to make par, but from this position and flush from his previous ace, par was not what he had in mind.

Presumably sharing his ambition and sensing the dilemma, Marshall forced the issue by having his wedge ready and waiting for him.

'You think?' Ricky asked his new caddie – a voice he was increasingly deferring to.

'Unless you're happy making par.'

Marshall had now even acquired the golf phraseology and vernacular. Ricky grabbed his wedge and quickly paced two thirds of his shot, studying the terrain and the line.

No problem with his timing on this hole. He'd only played two shots.

Daniel, the BBC cameraman, had now been joined by a colleague from radio, and the crowd following the match had definitely swelled. Fifty people or so - plus Ben, of course - and it wasn't Lee Pah they were watching as the young Korean finally found the green with his fourth shot.

Now it was Ricky's turn, and he set about his shot quickly. He brushed the grass a couple of times with a degree of purpose, before edging his club behind his ball and popping it up into the air.

Speed would be as important as the line and both looked good. The ball bounced once, then again, before finally settling on to the smooth surface and rolling out towards the pin where Marshall was waiting patiently. Everyone watching tracked the ball intently, including the radio reporter who could now speak at normal volume into his lip mic.

'*...it's a nice looking shot. It looks good. It looks very good... very good indeed, tracking and tracking towards the hole and... IN! Oh, my word, what have we here?*' the journalist bellowed as the crowd roared their approval.

'*...how about that from Ricky Randal? In for an eagle, three. Would you believe it? That's back to back eagles here at Muir-field. It's not often we get to say that at the Open Championship. Ricky Randal, who stood on the fourth tee at two over par - he now heads to the sixth at two under. Can you believe it? The player punches the air and he has every reason to. Remarkable stuff. Terrific golf.*

'*We have our first real charge of the day and it is Ricky Randal, the man who was making all the headlines for all the wrong reasons. But now his golf is doing the talking. Currently at eleven over par for the Championship, so he will not contest this Open, but who's to say that his charge up the leaderboard will not continue? And what a popular charge it would be. He's a popular golfer, is Richard Randal, and you won't miss a single piece of the drama here on BBC 5 Live because we're going to be here all day.*'

Chapter Six

Richard Randal, ENG -2
Open Championship + 11
63rd Place
Prize Money €37,132
6th Hole
469 Yards, Par 4

Ricky practically floated to the sixth tee, riding on a sea of goodwill and congratulations. The redundant putter joke had even more resonance now and it duly received an even bigger laugh on its second outing.

Nothing could puncture his euphoria; not even the continued attention of the match referee who still had Michael Landale raging at him over his radio. Having failed to order Ricky into a pair of sensible slacks, the referee had now changed tack and was appealing to the player's conscience.

'Ricky, please be reasonable about this. You'd be doing me a huge favour, to be honest. And yourself. There are shots of you being beamed all around the world.'

'Told you,' Marshall chipped in. 'No such thing as bad publicity. Have you got a manager, son?'

Ricky reflected on this for a moment - the referee's appeal, rather than Marshall's question. Defying the Royal and Ancient was foolhardy. At best, he'd look obstinate and at worst, arrogant. It was so peculiar, then, that this was precisely what he intended to do - and because he couldn't explain his decision, he didn't begin to even try.

'Look, I'm sorry...'

The referee threw his hands in the air. He didn't want to hear any more; if Landale wanted Randal disqualified from the tournament, then he could bloody well come onto the course and do it himself.

Ben observed this angry exchange and was pleased to see his dad approaching at a jog from a little way off. But he quickly realised that his dad did not look happy and that something must have occurred. Maybe Monty had doubled the first?

'Hey, Dad, what's up?'

'Shit, son - are you OK?'

'Yeah, I'm fine. Why?'

Eric pulled his hand through his hair, panting heavily.

'Oh, thank God.'

'Hey, Ricky had a hole-in-one and he's just eagled five.'

Eric nodded. 'Yeah, I know. Your mum's been on. She phoned - can you believe that?'

Ben looked a little guilty now. 'Oh. Yeah, and I've been on the telly.'

'Yeah. I know that now. Your mum saw it.'

'Oh.'

Ben tried to imagine how his mum might have reacted – and, worse, how her conversation might have gone with his dad. He smiled.

'Bloody phone, I could have sworn I had it on silent...'

94

Ben, rapidly piecing together exactly what might have happened, began to grin.

'...it was a nightmare. I was in the stand at the first. Sergio was about to tee off...'

Ben burst out laughing. He couldn't help himself; and finally his dad joined in as a sense of relief swept over him. Relief that Ben was OK - and the joy of seeing his wonderful son laughing so heartily.

'You can't believe the trouble I'm in.'

'Oh, no, I can,' Ben giggled as his dad knuckled his head affectionately. 'Blimey, Dad, I'm sorry - but I had no idea.'

'No, who knew, huh?'

'It's Ricky's fault, really.'

His dad chuckled again. Getting caught out in such an emphatic way and live on television; it was a rather beautiful story and certainly comic - and no doubt it would be dragged up by his friends for years to come.

But then reality struck like it always did when they thought of the years ahead and how they would be so different and diffi-cult. Instantly he felt a pang of hurt.

'I'd better call your mum,' he mumbled.

'No, Dad, you don't. There's no need.'

Ben pointed towards the cameraman who'd recorded his interview earlier, and who was now positioned at such an angle that it was highly probable that they were both appearing on television at this very moment.

Immediately, Eric began to feel self-conscious. He could just imagine his wife watching him.

Ben, though, was either a natural or he'd simply become more accustomed to such attention; he gave a surreptitious thumbs up towards the camera for the benefit of his mum watching at home. Not terribly original or personal - but it was the sign he always used when he came around from anaesthesia. He knew she'd like to see it.

His dad checked his watch. Half past eight. The live coverage would start at 9am, and so he fired off a quick text just to be sure.

Back with Ben. He's fine. Love you. Wish you were here!

His phone, now on silent, vibrated immediately with a reply.

I am watching you!

Her reply was probably meant as a joke, but even so a little chill ran down his back and he grabbed Ben around his shoulders and kissed the crown of his head.

Ricky smashed another drive, just as accurate as his last, climbing high and away off to the right before starting its slow drift back on-line, and landing comfortably within the fairway.

'Shot, Rick,' Marshall whispered casually.

'Yeah, thanks, Marsh.'

Wow. Things were going spectacularly well with his golf - and equally well in terms of his ongoing relationship with his new caddie. They barely knew each other and they were shortening each other's names already. Always a good sign.

Ricky's confidence was growing all the time. He still felt peculiar. Certainly, nothing was anywhere near normal. The feeling of uncertainty remained - but at least he didn't feel frightened anymore.

He glanced down at his exposed knees. Two under par and leader on the golf course over the final round. Keeping the kilt had definitely been the right thing to do.

'*...and on he goes, cutting a unique and totally bizarre sight on the links of Muirfield. One Richard Randal - out in the first match this morning - on his own and into the unknown he goes. And let me say just how popular he's becoming. With* *golf fans in general, but in particular with the Scottish fans who are here today in great numbers who seem to have embraced this unlikely Englishman and taken him to their hearts...*

But this was not a sentiment shared by Michael Landale. He'd placated the editor of the Scotsman as best as he could, but he couldn't worry about him right now.

'I blame that smug bastard Simon Cowell,' he spat at no one in particular. All of his gathered colleagues recognised that this was one of his rants, and that they needn't respond.

As far as Michael Landale was concerned, he explained loudly and angrily, the only thing that should ever differentiate one golfer from the next was their score. 'Just be very fucking good at golf. Simple.'

A tactic used by so many golfers and to such great effect.

'Rose, McIlroy, Koepka, Woods, Faldo, Johnson, Thomas, Westwood, Donald... they're all famous and rich, and do you know why? Because they all shoot low - not because they go around wearing fucking stupid clothes!'

His colleagues remained quiet. At this juncture, high-lighting the fact that Ricky Randal had just had back-to-back eagles and more recently split the sixth fairway was not help-ful. Hopefully he might bogey six. It was the hardest hole on the course. He might even make double or triple, puncture his impetus, and bring his round to an end. *Hopefully...*

Ricky chatted quietly with Marshall as he marched up the sixth fairway.

'... ah, well, that's a shame. You'd have been a good dad,' he said quickly, keen to fill the void of awkwardness that often comes when an adult explains the absence of any progeny. Not that Marshall seemed to be put out at all.

'No. Kids were never going to happen for me,' Marshall explained. 'Just never met the right lady, that's all.'

Ricky nodded. 'Ah, well, but you never know these days.'

'What d'you mean?'

'Er...' Ricky dithered. 'Well, look at Simon Cowell. He's just had his first child.'

'Right, and who's he?'

Ricky frowned. 'Are you serious?'

'Is he a golfer?'

Ricky chuckled. 'OK, then, how about Michael Douglas?'

Marshall shook his head again. *Nope.*

'Bloody hell. Where do you live, in a cave?'

Marshall chuckled. 'Anyway, enough about me. What about you?'

Ricky looked a little rueful at this, given he had established absolutely nothing about Marshall. But no matter – they would have plenty of time together after their round.

It was good having Marshall on his bag. He was a soothing presence; and it was peculiar to think that in all the pandemonium of the day so far, the old boy hadn't once looked particularly flustered, not even when the referee had been so rude to him. He had the sort of calm aura which was a vital characteristic for a successful caddie.

Who knew - he might even have a new career ahead of him. Certainly better than attending toilets, no matter how illustrious the people were who used them. Ricky arrived at his ball and immediately his focus changed.

'What do you reckon, Marsh?'

A black SUV with darkened glass drove quickly through the gates of Muirfield Golf Club, swung left and came to an abrupt halt. The driver was quickly out of his seat and running around the muscular vehicle to open the sliding rear door.

A moment elapsed before the world's most famous sportsman emerged. The value of Tiger Woods might have dipped in more recent years, but he was back again with a vengeance and was still the game's reserve currency and the player to whom all others still deferred.

A crowd gathered quickly. Furtive glances from everyone towards the vehicle; all conversations stopped. A reporter with a microphone, standing ready, grabbed his opportunity, lunging forward to fire off a quick question. Tiger had plenty of time to kill and he duly obliged. At two under par, he wasn't due on the first tee for at least another three hours.

'The final day of the Open is always special. But I don't know...' The American smiled as he took in his surroundings, '... something about today feels different somehow. Like - who knows, out there anything can happen. But I'm looking forward to it. To get out there and see what I can do. Because there are scoring opportunities out there, right?'

'So you saw the hole-in-one, then?'

'I did.' Woods chuckled. 'I think everyone's seen Ricky by now and good for him. I'd love to shoot that five iron, but I wouldn't wear a kilt to do it - even if it is magic.'

It was a decent enough joke in anyone's mouth; but coming from the world's most illustrious sportsman, it was hilarious and everyone laughed hard. It was a great sound-bite and it'd be used throughout the morning to indicate that Woods was relaxed and ready to prowl.

Tiger bowed his head as a signal that the impromptu interview was over. He had matters to attend to.

. . .

Ricky had been between clubs for his approach on six, and Marshall just shrugged in a way that only he could get away with.

Dunno. You're the golfer!

Ricky finally went with his four iron and was short, barely making the putting surface – and taking into account the treacherous surfaces of Championship greens, this put him firmly in three putt bogey territory. He marked his ball, surveying what he had left, and still Marshall seemed distracted and said nothing.

'Don't feel like you need to add anything?' Ricky called out to him as his caddie peered out to sea.

Lee Pah was in yet another bunker, his mood darkening with every shot. Lee spoke fluent English, having grown up on a golf factory somewhere in the States - Florida, most likely - but he hadn't said much in that language this morning, relying on his native tongue to vent his anger.

The young Korean swung his club hard into the bunker but only sand emerged and no ball. His caddie closed his eyes and turned away, joining Marshall in taking in the North Sea. It was beautiful - and seemingly more interesting than what was occurring on land.

Finally Lee found the green, and now it was Ricky's turn. With at least forty feet to cover in no more than two putts, his first shot was crucial, and as soon as he struck his ball he knew that he hadn't given it enough. It stopped fully ten feet short of the hole. A poor putt and a cardinal error for a professional golfer. He was likely to cede one of his shots back now, and he was furious with himself.

He turned, expecting a reaction from Marshall, but got nothing. Instead the old man was standing with his hands on his haunches and had a big dumb grin on his face. He looked like a picture of contentment; like an ancient soul watching his grandson walk for the first time.

There was no figuring this guy out, and Ricky decided it was better not to try.

Maggie studied the European Tour website. In his current position, Ricky would be making his second highest payday ever and his highest for a decade. Naturally, her phone was still running hot. As soon as she ended one call, another came through.

I've just seen Ricky on the news! Ricky got a hole-in-one! And, lest we forget, *What the hell is he wearing?*

It was all wildly exciting. To see Ricky playing on television and playing so well - and then to have Tiger Woods refer to him by his Christian name, as though they were buddies?

Tess came through with another cup of tea, even though neither had finished their previous brew. Ricky's youngest son, the five-year-old Patrick or Paddy, was glued to the screen. Every so often he'd shout at the TV, demanding that they show his daddy again, and he screamed even louder whenever they obliged.

'Daddy, there's my daddy,' Paddy would shriek, and leap into the air and go into what looked like a frenzied dance, thrusting his hips back and forth while punching both of his clenched fists to each side. It was a bizarre little ritual, and his granny stared at him, transfixed. Maggie caught her look and smiled to herself.

'Don't ask,' Maggie said. 'He's fighting the Itsy Bitzys - aren't you, Paddy?'

Tess laughed a little and placed a hand over her breast.

'Me and Dad are the only people who can kill them,' the

little boy announced as he ramped up his movements even more. Tess looked enquiringly.

'It's something Ricky came up with. Just one of his silly games that he has with the kids.'

Tess smiled fondly at her daughter-in-law, and thought back to Ricky when he'd been a little boy. She hadn't heard the name 'Itsy Bitsys' nor seen the 'little dance' since her husband had devised it for Ricky when he'd been a similar age. It was heartening to know that her son was continuing it on, and she wondered what would have made her late husband more proud - how his boy was faring as a golfer, or as a dad?

Maggie's phone rang again.

'Oh turn it off,' Tess exclaimed. 'You'd think people would know we're busy here.'

Maggie laughed. This was another phone call that she had to take - and it was about time, too. What an amazing morning it was turning out to be.

Ricky settled quickly over his lengthy par-saving putt. It was a crucial shot to maintain his momentum.

As he saw it, the putt was straight, and Marshall agreed. Or at least, he hadn't said anything, so Ricky assumed as much. Without question, his caddie was the strangest man he had ever encountered.

'...this putt is what they call a tester. A nasty length - a length that all professional golfers look to avoid and certainly so for their par. He does not want to give a shot back here and undo some of the spectacular golf he has already played...'

Ricky held his head statue-still as he pushed his putter head through, his eyes boring into the pinprick of grass which his ball had now vacated. He waited a beat before glancing sideways just in time to see his ball rolling towards the cup. The line looked good - or good enough, anyway, because it dropped from view.

Dead centre. Par - and this time Ricky clenched his fist slowly and shook it gently. The onlooking crowd screamed their approval, but he could barely hear them. The only thing he saw was Marshall smiling at him in his confident and unique way.

On to the next hole. The seventh, was it?

Chapter Seven

Richard Randal, ENG -2
Open Championship + 11
62nd Place
Prize Money €38,219
7th Hole
187 Yards, Par 3

There was some further joking as Ricky got onto the seventh tee - since it was, after all, another par-three. Ben was enjoying himself, delighted that his dad had joined him again, and Eric, too was becoming enthralled by match number one.

He'd had another text exchange with his wife; she felt assured now of Ben's welfare and was enjoying being able to watch him for herself on the television. Conscious of the TV cameras now, Eric stood next to Ben and held him close.

The crowd following the match continued to grow; it now included Anna Wade, who'd mooched over from the media centre to get a look at the man of the moment and the player she was unable to write about.

She'd actually begun to daydream about an angle on the story, but she didn't hold out too much hope for it or for herself. While everything about the on-course Ricky Randal was already being analysed and opined on by anyone and everyone, Anna wondered if people might be interested in the remarkable nature of his life off the course. He was, after all, an elite golfer without an agent or any of the support team that one associates with the professional who rips up the course on a Sunday at the Open.

She'd tried to interest a few press agencies, but so far there hadn't been any takers - besides, it was hardly a flash of inspiration, and no doubt journalists would be hammering on the door of Mrs Randal at this very moment.

Pushing her way forward through the crowds, she recognised Ben immediately, standing at the front, his torso hard up against the rope. Something about him intrigued her. He looked intent and completely focused. And she began to wonder.

There was great expectation on the tee as Ricky drew out his club. He didn't want to disappoint anyone, but making par here would be absolutely fine. Playing par golf for the rest of the round, in fact, would be bloody marvellous; it might even place him just outside the top fifty. Ricky wasn't sure what the corresponding prize money was for such a high place because he hadn't bothered to check – and he still had a lot of work to do if this was ever going to happen.

The breeze had picked up a little and was now a factor, blowing directly into the player's face. It was the choice of a six iron stuck easily or a bloody good wallop with a seven.

Ricky pulled out his seven iron and twisted it quickly over and over in his hand. Right now, with his heart thumping and his adrenal gland pumping, he felt more comfortable whacking something very hard than caressing something softly. He loaded a brand new ball onto his peg and stood back, viewing the target off in the distance.

Just as he was about to take his final set-up, he stopped. Something was not right. He looked about quickly and noticed it immediately. Marshall was not there. He'd disappeared. What the hell?

He scanned the tee again but his caddie was nowhere to be seen. A toilet-break, perhaps?

Anna watched him curiously, sensing the golfer's anxiety which heightened as he became aware of people following his gaze and his eye-line.

Ricky grimaced and clenched his jaw. As peculiar as Marshall was, it would not surprise him if he'd taken himself off altogether and that was the last he would ever see of him. And if so, then Ricky would have to carry his own bag from here. Jesus, wouldn't that be a story? His kilt would be forgotten.

Ricky glanced at Ben briefly and then he turned to look directly at Anna. He stared at her for a second; she even felt a little awkward, and was pleased when he looked away and back to his ball.

Caddie or no caddie, he needed to get on with his game.

Patrick felt a huge surge of relief at having spoken with Maggie. Under the circumstances, their conversation had gone well.

Once word had spread that Ricky's caddie was a no-show, his phone had rung constantly; and shortly afterwards, his door was being pounded on by other caddies, all of them worried that he might have croaked in his sleep or even worse; topped himself. He sent them packing and without an explanation either. A firm and resolute no comment.

The consensus across the media was that his career as a caddie was over. It made good sense. What golfer would ever employ him now? Not Ricky Randal, anyway - and who could blame him? No-one had a kind word for the absent caddie at all, and Patrick didn't care a jot.

Yesterday's incident on the sixteenth was being continually replayed on television by way of explanation; Ricky shouting angrily and gesturing towards the ocean and then Patrick's response, returning the invective and throwing a golf club to the ground before the two men squared up to each other like little kids in a playground. Such a thing was never an edifying sight, even on a football pitch - let alone on a golf course. Patrick shuddered at the memory.

The rest of their third round had been played in absolute silence, and they hadn't spoken since. And it had all flared up out of nothing, as well. Of course, the third round hadn't gone well. Ricky was effectively out of the tournament, but both of them had been coping with it reasonably well. But then a spark from nowhere - and matters had taken on a life of their own.

It had been doubly unfortunate that a television crew had been present to catch the whole thing. They were in place on the adjoining fairway to pick up shots of Ricky Fowler and Zach Johnson, and only chanced upon the incident by accident. More perplexing was how they had not resolved matters after the round and as such, how Patrick came to be watching the golf today rather than taking part in it.

Later into the morning he'd switched off his mobile phone; he didn't want to be disturbed anymore and he had nothing to say to anyone, anyway. He'd taken particular joy in seeing Ricky save his par on the sixth with a brave putt and which under the circumstances he had expected him to miss.

So when the ball dropped, he felt a pang of pride – but then a sudden and tremendous sense of hurt that he wasn't with his friend. It was most peculiar; like a giant hand had emerged from within his television and slapped him hard across his face, waking him up from whatever stupor he had fallen into. He shook his head quickly as his reality now firmly struck home.

Quickly, he grabbed for his phone and switched it on. Inevitably, it beeped loudly as though it was angry for being ignored. It would be impossible to show up on the course now. Particularly embarrassing for him, especially if Ricky sent him packing - which was highly likely. After all, he was managing perfectly well without him.

But it had to be worth a chance, and not trying would be something he'd regret for a lifetime.

Patrick pulled on his shoes. His hostel was a stone's throw from the course. He still had his pass, and he could be there in ten minutes. He might even get to Ricky on the eighth tee if he was quick. But then his phone rang - and he knew he should answer it.

'Hello, Patrick speaking.'

Patrick sat down as he listened to his phone call and said nothing. He untied his shoelaces. He wasn't going anywhere after all.

Ricky walloped his seven iron, but evidently not hard enough, his ball barely finding the front edge of the green. It was a decent shot, albeit a pale shadow of his effort at the previous par-three; a disappointment for the spectators, perhaps, but not for Ricky, who had two putts for his par. That suited him just fine.

'On the green? Good lad.'

Ricky turned quickly on hearing Marshall's voice as Lee

readied himself for his tee shot. Ricky stepped to one side and took his caddie with him.

'Where the hell have you been?' he whispered; more than a little put out.

'Er... I needed a quick word with someone, that's all.'

Ricky looked worried now and searched out the match referee. 'What? Like who?'

But Marshall ignored the question, using Lee's impending tee shot as cover, as he shoved Ricky's phone back into his golf bag. It was all very suspicious - and completely out of order.

Taking his phone and using it without permission and on a golf course during an event - the Open Championship, no less? How many rules had he just broken, Ricky wondered? Jesus, what if Marshall was getting advice on forthcoming greens? It could even see him disqualified.

He glanced at the referee again, but the man seemed unperturbed. So maybe he hadn't been seen and had got away with it, but this could never happen again.

Lee fired his ball away, and Ricky immediately took off from the tee box with Marshall skulking alongside him.

'Hey, Marshall,' Ricky stated firmly.

'Yes, boss?'

'No more phone calls.'

'Yes, boss, sorry. Absolutely.' Marshall heaved up the golf bag as Ricky fished inside it for his phone. He looked at his device and then again at Marshall, who apparently didn't feel any need to explain himself and was now grinning again.

Lee's ball dived into yet another bunker and the crowd reacted disapprovingly when he slammed his club hard against his golf bag. Ricky turned around to see the commotion. He understood the kid's frustration and he felt sorry for him. Marshall continued to smile happily and soak up his new work environment.

'Marshall, you're a difficult guy to figure out.'

'Really? How so?'

Ricky took a moment. 'Have you ever caddied before?'

'No, I've already told you that.'

'Right - then explain to me how you know the game so well.'

Marshall sighed. 'Haven't we done this already?'

'Yeah, I've asked you but you never answered.'

'Well...' Marshall began. 'It's either bloody obvious or I'm having some beginner's luck.'

Ricky shook his head.

'What?' Marshall protested as he chuckled happily.

Ricky's phone was security-locked, but he didn't bother to point this out. It made no sense, but nothing about his day so far or Marshall made any sense, and he had two putts to be getting on with.

Noah Edwards checked his phone to make sure that his conversation with Jago Silver had, in fact, ended. Jago didn't do phone conventions like goodbyes and thank you - he ended his phone calls with just his thumb.

After a year of working for the man, Noah had grown used to this brusque manner – and to the phone calls at ungodly hours. Like some of the world's most committed workaholics, Jago Silver hardly slept and he didn't bother with time zones. His employees could expect his phone calls at any time of day or night, and nothing they were doing was ever more important than the reason for his call. Not even child birth with Jago Silver. Whenever he hired anyone new, he'd leave them with the same words.

'Leave your freaking phone on.' And he meant it.

Silver had emerged from the financial crisis of 2008 with his billions intact and his reputation only enhanced. For six years beforehand, he'd been a senior trader at the Royal Bank of Scotland, working out of Greenwich, Connecticut. With prophetic timing, he cashed in his entire stock holdings nine months before the infamous crash of Lehman Brothers and resigned his position shortly afterwards at RBS, leaving him out of the game and out of the firing-line when the hole in the Edinburgh mothership was eventually exposed.

And since then his star had risen even further. Jago was the financier who could see the future - and quickly he launched his own financial platform, the aptly named Silver Linings, which became an instant success, attracting many billions of dollars from across the world.

As a result, Jago was gigantically wealthy and allowed himself all of life's luxuries, except for a day off, because there is always more money to be made. The only thing that he could not afford was distractions. Certainly no wife and children – the latter being something which he had needed to prove in court on two separate occasions, and which had finally prompted his vasectomy. Who would have thought high class hookers could be so scheming?

One of Silver's many mantras was that everything happened for a reason. Like, for instance, the fact that he'd happened to be watching the golf in the middle of the night. What interested him about Ricky Randal was not his kilt but his golf cap, or lack thereof, and his sudden exposure to a worldwide audience. It was a great opportunity and Noah Edwards was his man in the UK and the man to get it done.

Jago and Silver Linings had already gone large at this year's British Open. Noah had booked eight suites at a range of top Edinburgh hotels, complete with full hospitality at the Championships for all four days with flights in private jets for London's elite City boys. And hadn't they let their hair down? The whole soiree, including escorts and a mountain of various powders, was in excess of $1.6m - but this would be dwarfed by the funds that would flow back in return once the brokers were back at their desks and their heads had cleared.

But now, in addition, came an unexpected and most welcome silver lining; an opportunity to plonk one of his golf caps onto the head of a man who the whole world was watching. Jago had given Noah a budget of a hundred grand to get it done, and he would watch his plan play out live on his television. It was genius, sheer genius, and Jago congratulated himself warmly.

Noah, however, was less pleased with his new assignment. Not for the first time this morning, the name Richard Randal was typed into Google and scant information of any real use was available.

Quickly, he established that Richard Randal did not have 'people' he could simply call and negotiate with - and his first mistake was to assume that this meant that this window of opportunity had closed. A mistake he compounded by calling Jago to explain his findings.

'Jesus, you schmuck, what the fuck do I pay you for? He hasn't got a manager. Who gives a fuck? It'll be cheaper then, right?'

'Yes, but Jago, how am I going to get a cap on...'

'Use some guile, you pussy.'

Noah was still confused.

'You're there, right? You're in Scot-Land?'

'Er...'

'And you've got legs?'

'Er... as in...'

'So, you use your fuckin' legs to walk up to this guy, Randal. I want Randal in one of my caps for the whole back nine. A hundred grand, he'll fucking snap your hand off. Just make it happen. I'm watching here.'

. . .

The impromptu BBC TV studio was a hive of frenetic energy as it prepared to go live and begin its comprehensive all-day coverage. He didn't know it yet, but Ricky Randal was about to go truly global.

Assistants with mops and rags rubbed at every surface that would appear on screen, including the show's anchor, Hazel Irvine, who had her hair pushed up by one lady while another tended to her make-up and another hovered on clothing detail. Technicians and camera operators fussed with their kit and made final checks, all of them with an eye on the digital clock on the studio wall.

'Checking Hazel's talk-back. You hearing me, Hazel, darling?' the producer asked through her earpiece, and he was happy to see his anchor hold her thumb in the air.

There's always a special feeling on the morning of the final round. Everything that's gone before is a mere qualifier for today; already it felt special and the place was humming. Everyone could feel it. Maybe Rory would roar or even better, Tiger and Justin would take it down the eighteenth for one of the great finishes of one of the great sporting events.

A television monitor on the floor showed live pictures from the course, which Hazel kept a close eye on, keen to see what else Ricky Randal might have in store for her. The wise pundits, Wayne Grady and Peter Alliss, were already seated and ready to offer their musings on the day ahead.

'One minute, everybody.'

The TV camera with a large auto-cue facility was wheeled into position. A script prompter sat with her fingers hovering ready over her keyboard. The way the morning had gone so far, it was unlikely that the narrative would remain the same, and the anchor might need to go off-script with millions watching.

No pressure, then - and regarding the seventh green; two putts please, Mr Randal.

Just a few hundred yards away, Ricky settled over his first putt. Two putts for par. Come on, Ricky. Soft hands. Easy and relaxed. Piece of cake.

At a moment before 9am, Ricky sent his ball on its way.

'Stand-by, everyone. Live in 10...'

Like everyone else, Hazel was glued to the TV monitor at her feet, a close shot tracking Ricky's rolling ball. The flag-stick had been removed, making it difficult to pick out the hole.

'We are live in five, four, three, two...'

Just as Hazel was cued live on-air, Ricky's ball vanished from view.

'Stone me... another birdie.'

Her script was redundant; a further surge of excitement and energy spread through the studio. Immediately, people tapped into their keyboards and cameramen listened on their headphones to their new instructions. Today was definitely going to be special.

Peter Alliss rocked back in his chair and chuckled to himself. Three under after seven holes - but what did that make him for the championship?

Chapter Eight

Richard Randal, ENG -3
Open Championship + 10
51st Place
Prize Money €42,092
8th Hole
445 Yards, Par 4

T he BBC floor manager pointed to his anchor.
   'Good morning, and a very warm welcome to all of you watching the 145th Open Championship here at the truly magnificent Muirfield, on the east coast of Scotland, for what is set to be an enthralling day of golf. The best players in the world will battle it out to see who will be crowned the Champion Golfer of the Year. All the big names you might expect are on our leaderboard - Woods, McIlory, Watson, Rose, Fowler and Koepka of course - all of whom will be heading out later today. But today's round is already very much underway - in fact, our early starters are almost at the turn already and it's a

player in the very first match this morning who's making all the headlines - a certain Mr Ricky Randal.'

Hazel took a brief moment to add a little drama before continuing.

'Okay... I hear you. Right now, he might only be a household name in his own town... but perhaps that will change after the extraordinary round he is having today...'

Her producer continued to jabber away into her earpiece with salient information as she read her monologue. And having completed the first paragraph and repeated his name, Hazel now took another deliberate moment.

'...where to start with Ricky Randal? Because, let me tell you, he's something of a one-off and certainly a golfer to gladden a Celt's heart. If you've been watching BBC Breakfast this morning, then you'll already know exactly what I'm talking about. He is 'The Golfer in a Kilt'; but don't let that distract you, because his golf isn't too shabby either. After just seven holes, he's three under for his round today, which for the Championship, makes him...'

'Ten,' the producer muttered into Hazel's ear.

'...ten under for the Championship.' Hazel continued.

'No. Ten OVER. Shit. Ten OVER,' the producer screeched.

'Oh, I beg your pardon - that is ten OVER for the Championship. Not ten under. I just cut Ricky Randal by some twenty shots there and gave him an unassailable lead. My apologies for that...'

'51st place,' the producer advised, enunciating more clearly now. 'Up 19 places today, already.'

'...which puts him just outside the top 50 after back-to-back eagles that included a hole-in-one at the par-three fourth hole, which is almost as noteworthy as his kilt and the fact that his regular caddie has not shown up for work either, which people have also been speculating on all morning...'

'Roll VT,' the producer directed. 'Well done, Hazel, my lovely. 60 seconds on the VT...'

Michael Landale could probably have powered the golf buggy he was sitting in with his own nervous energy. Conscious that he was no longer in the confines of his office, particularly after his faux-pas with the editor of the Scotsman and with cameras all around, he was anxious to appear calm.

Randal's game was holding up as no one had expected it to; the spotlight on the golfer was intensifying and not diminishing as he had hoped, and so Landale needed to attend to the matter himself. The buggy driver, a volunteer marshal, jumped into the driver seat and had no idea who his passenger was.

'Right, where to then?' the volunteer asked chirpily. 'To see the Flying Scotsman, is it?'

Landale sneered at the man. 'The eighth.'

'Okey-dokey. The eighth it is. Where are you on the kilt, then? I love it, myself.'

Landale said nothing as his mood darkened even further; and, appropriately enough, the first drop of rain hit the windshield of the buggy. *Forecasters, wrong again?* A couple of opportunistic journalists recognised him and tried to get an impromptu statement as the buggy eased through the crowds but he gave them nothing.

This morning the entire world's media were keen to get his opinion on Ricky Randal but he had refused to say anything at all. Actions speak louder than words, and Michael Landale was on the golf course and about to head the player off at the turn. His buggy finally got through the crowds and quickly gathered speed.

· · ·

Peter Alliss is particularly well qualified to commentate on golf. Having played in umpteen Opens himself and commentated on even more, having grown up with a dad who was a pro and fellow Ryder Cup player, it's fair to say that he knows the game intimately and as well as any. Add a natural wit to this wisdom and experience, and you have the perfect commentator - but even Peter Alliss had never seen anything like the exploits being served up today by Ricky Randal.

In the television studio, Hazel went to Peter straight out of the video footage. He smiled broadly and feigned being speechless. Peter Alliss is rarely short of a word or two.

'Well where do I start with young Ricky? He's not that young, to start with – unless you're comparing him to me, of course - so we can't blame his youth, and before we discuss his golf and his ball-striking which has included some extraordinary shots - what to say about his caddie and his outfit, of course, which seems to have the entire Championship in a complete frenzy?'

'Especially with us Scots,' Hazel added.

'Well, quite. And believe me, we all love the kilt. It's one of the great pieces of clothing, it really is, but in the right place and at the right time.'

Hazel laughed. 'So you don't approve, then?'

'Well, you see, I love the tradition of our great game. And, of course, the Scots love their traditions too. And, yes, there is some debate about whether or not any rules have even been broken, because after all, this is Scotland. But that aside, let me say right here, right now, that the officials of the Royal and Ancient will be having kittens over this offending garment. Michael Landale - a man I know very well - Michael is the Championship referee and he's a traditional type, is our Michael. I haven't seen him yet this morning but I shouldn't wonder if he isn't lying down somewhere in a darkened room with a cold flannel.'

'And what about Ricky's golf?' Hazel asked.

'Oh, magnificent. Look at his score. In parts awful but there's been some brilliance as well, undoubted brilliance. But as yet still overshadowed by other matters, I'm afraid.'

Wayne Grady, former major champion and jocular Aussie chuckled at this, which Hazel was quick to seize upon and bring him into the conversation.

'And Wayne - Wayne Grady, good morning to you, sir.'

'Good morning, Hazel.'

'And where are you on all of this?'

'Well I'm with Peter, of course, on the kilt.'

'There's a time and place?' Hazel suggested.

'Quite. But I'll tell you one thing. Our Ricky might be wearing a skirt, but he's definitely not playing like a girl.'

Wayne smiled broadly at his quip, but he was all alone. Hazel's face registered alarm immediately and Peter Alliss too was sufficiently experienced and media-savvy to realise the folly of such a remark in such sensitised times.

Immediately, Peter's self-preservation instincts kicked in; he skilfully composed his face into an expression of distaste at the possibly sexist and cruel remark. Wayne, though, didn't have a clue and pressed on; rather pleased with his little angle.

'And I was wondering what he might shoot if he was allowed to play off the girls tees?'

In the gallery, where the director, producers, editors and other television suits resided, a metaphorical claxon was now blaring.

'Jesus Christ. Did he just say 'girls'? Oh, my God. Kill Wayne's mic. Now. Do it now. Don't let him say another word.'

The producer was frantic now. He stabbed at a button on his console and summoned his gravest voice and tone.

'Hazel. Wayne needs to apologise now. He said girls. Make him apologise NOW.'

Live television is always fraught with danger and one of the greatest perils is to upset the sensitivities of the viewers. Timing was absolutely key to containing and defusing what could be a sexism situation. A fulsome apology needed to be issued before the switchboards lit up with calls from the offended. Fortunately, the director in-situ had just returned from a week-long course on 'inclusion and awareness' in Tuscany and he had a contingency for just such a crisis.

Wayne Grady was not wearing an earpiece and was completely unaware of the furore that his quip had caused and continued to smile urbanely.

'Cut from Wayne. Jesus Christ. Get off him. Why isn't he wearing an ear-piece. Fuck. Don't show him smiling like that. Stay on a single of Hazel.'

Wayne vanished from the screens and might never be seen again depending on the next ten minutes or so. It was likely that complaints were already coming in and not just the women's lobby, but the women's sports fraternity, and possibly the Scots as well, and so timing was critical.

He was Australian, of course, but this was no excuse, and such a defence being offered might itself even be racist. The executive producer shuddered at the thought of the 'R' word and his eye wandered to his laptop and his all-important Twitter feed.

A floor manager had hastily scrawled on a whiteboard in thick black felt which he was holding up behind the camera in Wayne's eyeline.

'Wayne. You need to say sorry for the 'Girl' comment. NOW.'

The 'Now' was underlined twice. By now, Wayne had become aware of some commotion but he couldn't discern it's cause and added squinting his eyes to his look of confusion.

'Fuck sake, he's blind. He can't read it. He can't fucking well read it. We're fucked...' The director screeched.

The floor manager was aptly named, because he was forced to crawl on his belly with the sign held aloft to get near enough so that Wayne could read it. It was physically exhausting, but worth the effort because as Hazel floundered on-screen, finally Wayne could just about read the whiteboard and knew what was required of him.

'And can I just say...' Wayne began.

'OK, good, he's got it. Back on Wayne. Single shot of Wayne.' the director barked.

Wayne re-appeared in full frame for his full mea culpa as Hazel Irving reached for her water.

'... I said just now that Ricky wasn't playing like a girl. Which I apologise for...'

Peter Alliss, off-camera, could be heard to murmur his approval and agreement.

'Yes, good, good Wayne... you stupid bastard.' The director breathed out heavily.

'Because what I should have said...' Wayne continued. 'was that Ricky was not playing like a woman.'

The studio and the gallery fell silent for a split moment. And then all hell broke loose.

'Fuck-a-duck,' the producer screeched. 'Hazel. Go live. Throw to live. Now.'

The camera jiggled a little, presumably because the operative was laughing, and finally, Hazel appeared in a close shot on her own.

'And the man himself is just getting ready to play his

second shot on the eighth, so let's go there live. You never know with our Ricky. He might even hole it.'

Peter laughed, and so did Wayne, although he would not be laughing for too much longer.

The ex-tour golfer Phil Parkin was out on the course reporting for BBC Radio 5Live.

'...the distance is not going to be a problem. After a decent drive lengthwise, he can reach the green from here but it's controlling his ball out of this semi-rough that could be the issue. Dangerous spot here. If he goes long and left, then he could make double bogey in a heartbeat. He doesn't want to be too greedy. Might be better to lay up and then try to get up and down for his par.'

But Ricky had other plans. With a determined look, he pulled a club from his bag and the crowd that was gathered tightly around him murmured their approval and encouragement.

'...well, what do I know? Because Ricky Randal is going for the green here, which I fear could be a mistake and possibly an expensive error...'

Ricky steadied himself before making his swing. His club scythed through the grass and made an excellent connection with the ball, which fired out of the rough and climbed steeply. Ricky liked it immediately and so did Ben, who was the first person to clap. Marshall brushed by and muttered his approval.

'...he's made an excellent connection and this is a fine shot... the first bounce will be key to letting us know if he has managed to put any grab on the ball... and, oh, yes, he has indeed. Twenty, twenty-five feet from the pin. That is a truly magnificent effort from here. If he hit thirty identical shots today, one after another, he would not get any closer than that. He'll make his par from *there, no problem. Ricky Randal is fighting and it is thrilling to watch.'*

The match referee approached the eighth green with mild trepidation, knowing that Michael Landale would be waiting for him and the two players - although it was only one golfer that he was interested in. Buoyed by his second shot, Ricky was walking just ahead, and the referee wondered if Ricky realised what was waiting for him.

Ricky was clapped onto the green by everyone present - with one exception. Landale was experienced enough to know not to approach a player within the glare of the putting surface, especially when the bloody media were swarming like flies around the little shit clad in tartan. His radio beeped and he opened the channel.

'What?' Michael spat.

'Just to say, sir - that you are currently live on television. A close up, actually, and Peter Alliss is commentating and is talking about you personally.'

Michael Landale grimaced and his jaw muscle bulged. Immediately, his eyes shifted in search of the lens that was trained on him and when he found it, he summoned all of his energy to form a thin smile. A smile which might have fooled some people, but not Peter Alliss.

'... now, then, there's a little smile, but that is Michael Landale, and I can tell you, that is a smile which is almost killing him...'

Ken Brown, his co-commentator, could be heard stifling his laughter in the commentary box, which was all the encourage-ment that his more senior colleague needed.

'...I'd say that smile is more difficult right now for Michael than if I asked him to do ten chin-ups...'

Ken Brown spluttered now and others present could be

heard hooting, more in keeping with the best traditions of TMS on the BBC Radio 4.

'And I suspect he's not out on the course to see Ricky's golf,' Ken managed to add, mischievously.

'No, no, Kenneth, quite right. It's about to rain and he should be tucked up in his mahogany office with a cup of tea or perhaps a hot toddy... or, perhaps not. It might still be a bit early for that kind of thing just yet. No, no... Michael Landale has been dragged out on to the course by Code Violation... whatever the number is. And as flagrant a transgression as it is, I think even the indomitable Michael will need to stand down on this one. The world is watching, old boy. He'll know that, of course. And he will see how people are responding to the player and what they want from him. I don't like the outfit. I've said that already. But he's on the course now and he's tearing it up, to use the modern parlance. So for now at least, I suggest Michael takes himself off to a darkened room and tries to get through the next few hours with his spleen intact.'

Ken Brown and the others laughed away, all enjoying themselves enormously and added fuel to Peter's fire.

'... and he only has a couple of hours to wait...' Peter went on. *'...but never mind the fireworks on the course, I can tell you, the real ticket here today is going to be ringside in the office of Michael Landale when he calls in Ricky Randal and asks him to close the door...'*

More hoots of joy from his co-hosts.

'...oh, to be a fly... Now, come on, Ricky. This meeting with the R & A is nothing for you to worry about – not just yet, anyway. Right now, you have plenty to be getting on with over the next ten holes or so, and a couple of putts here will do very nicely indeed.'

Marshall had already spent a little time studying this putt, which Ricky was glad of. It was a tricky distance with a small break and was never going to be a single shot. Two putts would be marvellous. Ricky got back to his marker and looked up to catch Marshall's eye.

'Half ball to the left and just give it a good thump,' Marshall said confidently.

Ricky looked at him, surprised.

'What?' Marshall asked.

Ricky approached him quickly.

'You think I should take this on?'

Marshall looked a little confused and just shrugged.

'Sure, why not? Isn't that the aim? To get round the course in as few shots as possible?'

Ricky mulled it over. A three putt was the penalty he might have to pay. He replaced his ball and aimed it a little more left than he had been intending, and then after a couple of smooth breaths and a relaxing of his hands, as instructed, he drew his club back and gave his ball a solid thump.

It raced away and gathered speed as it neared the pin. It was too fast and looked set to roll on by a good distance. A miss-able distance coming back. It would need to hit the hole. *Had* to hit the pin. Ricky could hardly breathe. The line looked good though - but what about the speed? Too fast, surely? The ball hit the cup hard and then leapt directly up into the air, before it dropped and disappeared from view.

'*...well, well, well, just when I thought I'd seen it all. That was either the bravest or the most stupid putt I might have ever seen. But who was right? Because that is yet another birdie and this remarkable, extraordinary round continues. Brilliant stuff from the young man. But I tell you what, though; if he keeps on like this, he'll be in Michael Landale's office a lot sooner than he'd like.*'

The roar from the crowd was the last thing Landale wanted to hear, standing greenside. Even he had to admire the audacity and the skill of such a shot - but he was the only person not celebrating the kilted player's achievement. The match referee had been over for a frank exchange of views, and it seemed that Landale had little choice but to let Randal continue; although he was not ruling out a post-round disqualification or, at the very least, shots being docked.

Ricky punched the air in delight and high-fived Marshall.

'Great read, Marshall.'

'No, not really.'

'Oh, shut up, Marshall. It was brilliant. A brilliant call. You're a bloody godsend, mate.'

Marshall puffed his chest out, clearly delighted to be of assistance.

'Hey - I tell you what. Can you caddie next week?'

'No.'

Marshall answered flatly because he meant it; and somehow Ricky understood and it made him laugh.

Then the old man gestured over to the match referee - because he too was grinning now from ear to ear.

'You see, Ricky? They're all coming round to you, son. Just like I said they would.'

Chapter Nine

Richard Randal, ENG -4
Open Championship + 9
47th Place
Prize Money €46,211
9th Hole
558 Yards, Par 5

W hen Michael Landale got back to his golf buggy, already sitting in one of the central pews was a female spectator who wasn't feeling very well and had asked the driver for a lift back to the clubhouse. He had agreed, and Landale didn't care either way; he barely gave her the time of day. As he sat down next to the driver the rain started to come in harder, mirroring his mood.

'All aboard, then,' the effervescent marshal chirped. 'Another birdie, eh? They love him, this Randal chap.'

'Well, I don't,' the woman behind chipped in quickly and loud enough to be heard, catching Landale's attention immediately.

'I think it's disgraceful that a player should wear such a thing on a golf course - never mind at the Open Championship.' She was well spoken and seemingly very aggrieved. 'Personally, I think he should be thrown out of the tournament.'

'What...' the driver protested. 'Come on, really?'

'Yes, absolutely. He's wearing a kilt for no other reason than to court controversy and at the expense of the sport!'

At this, Michael Landale turned around to get a look at this highly sensible woman. She was attractive enough, shapely and young - and clearly highly intelligent. He stared at her and for the first time today, he smiled.

'I could not agree with you more,' he told her.

'Thank you,' she said. 'At last, a person with a little sense. It is *so* maddening that the entire country seems to be smitten by him.'

Michael Landale's spirits continued to soar.

'I blame the media,' he said. 'Not to mention the great British public, of course.' He spat so that the irony and his distaste were both apparent.

'Oh, yes, I quite agree,' the woman said. 'The great unwashed, you mean.'

'Quite.'

'Excuse my language, but far too many people nowadays arc simply as thick as shit.' The lady stated.

She was becoming more attractive to him by the second.

'I'd like to see him kicked out of the tournament myself,' Michael agreed.

'But they won't, of course. Not now. Not now he's *captured the public's hearts*.' Her last words were laced with heavy sarcasm and illustrated by hand-gestured speech marks.

Landale turned again and smiled at her warmly. A quick fumble in his office might be the upside to this bloody awful day. She obviously loved her golf, and she might be impressed to know that she was talking to one of the game's most influential figures. A man of real power.

'By the way, I'm Michael Landale from the Royal and Ancient.'

'*No*. The Championship referee?'

He nodded demurely, unsure whether to be surprised or flattered. 'Yes, I'm afraid so.'

'Then you have to disqualify him,' she insisted.

'What?' the driver interjected again. 'No way!'

'Be quiet,' Landale snapped authoritatively. It was all his part of his mating dance. 'Just drive the buggy.'

Apparently this woman was unwell, and so they might need to be quick about things. Although she didn't appear to be poorly... and after all, he'd only need five minutes or so.

'I'm serious,' she said. 'You should disqualify him immediately.' She was becoming increasingly anxious, it seemed – excited, even and this suited Michael Landale just fine.

'I came within an ace of disqualifying him earlier this morning, you mark my words. Do you know he actually refused to put on a pair of trousers that we sent out to him?'

'No.'

'Yes. Can you believe that?'

'Such insolence. Disgraceful. So what are you are going to do?' She was almost hyperventilating now, apparently struggling to catch her breath.

The clubhouse was in view and fast approaching.

'Well, for now my hands are tied. So I'm going to have to bide my time. But believe me when I say that all options remain fully open just as soon as his round is finished. I expect he'll be deducted four shots at the very least.'

'Good. Quite right too.'

Finally, the buggy came to a halt and Anna Wade could hardly breathe as she practically fell from the vehicle; giddy with the excitement of her short journey. Such audacity and verve - and so out of character for her.

She wanted to scream at her cunning and to share her coup with someone. Her dad simply would not believe her, and she would never have imagined herself ever doing such a thing.

Wonderful things, smartphones. A quick photo greenside on the 8th, an image-recognising app, a smattering of Google, and the wickedly cunning ploy had presented itself to her. And the very same device had recorded their entire conversation on the way back to the clubhouse.

'Would you like to come to my office to convalesce?' Landale asked. His voice was now leering and loaded with meaning. He might as well have just asked for a good old-fashioned bunk-up.

But this was a call of duty too far for the as yet, green hack that Anna Wade remained. As excited and delirious as she was, she had no problem coming over all queasy now; she told him no with an authentic-sounding rush of sudden nausea and he seemed to believe it.

The world's media had been clamouring for a statement from Michael Landale, and now she had it. If only she knew what to do with it.

Still watching in his digs, as soon as Ricky's ball had dropped on the eighth green, Patrick leapt into the air in exactly the same manner as his friend.

'Get in, you little beauty,' he screamed at his television, and immediately he began to imagine the next hole ahead. A short par five. A hole that Ricky had birdied once already this week, and now he hardly dared to imagine; Ricky could be heading into the back nine at five under par. A championship record, surely?

'...it's more than spitting now. Umbrellas have popped up all around us like early spring daffodils, and I expect the players will be thinking about putting on wet-weather layers for this rain that was not predicted...'

Out on the ninth tee, the wind had now picked up even more and was now hard into the player's faces, making it difficult to pick out a clear line.

The safe play was to hit three wood, but Ricky, enjoying the form of his life, pulled out his driver - to the instant approval of his now-ardent fans. Perhaps as many as a hundred were now following his match, and their number was swelling with every shot and every hole.

Marshall thrust his reddened face into the wind, wincing to make his point; *give it everything you have, son.*

It was out of bounds to the left, and a bunker lay in wait at just shy of two hundred and seventy yards - but it should be out of play now with the wind.

'Marshall, is there a cap in my bag?'

Marshall shrugged. *Dunno.*

'A golf cap? In my bag, for the rain.'

Still Marshall didn't move.

'Take a look, would you?'

'What colour?' Marshall asked facetiously, which Ricky ignored. *I'm wearing a kilt - do you think I care what colour cap I wear?*

'There's one in there somewhere - past the waterproofs, maybe?'

Marshall got about his task, but without much urgency, as Ricky got on with prepping his tee shot. A beat later, the old man caught his eye.

'What waterproofs, son?'

Ricky fiddled with his club and looked at the heavy skies. *Shit.*

Before his round, he recalled lightening his bag to enable Marshall to carry it more easily, but he didn't remember jettisoning his wet gear. And if he had, where the hell had he left it? Occupying the very lowest ranks of professional golf, Ricky didn't receive any equipment or free gear and he didn't relish the idea of replacing it.

With the rain falling and without a golf cap, he made a good connection with his driver. Too good, in fact as his ball was gobbled up by the lurking fairway bunker.

Groans from the crowd. An error. Ricky Randal was human, after all.

Angry now, Ricky snatched up his tee peg and turned, hoping to see Marshall with at least a golf cap and possibly even a jacket as well. But Marshall had neither.

Just his usual carefree smile, which was as warm as ever - but it wasn't going to keep him dry.

The rain was timely indeed for Noah, and so was Ricky's tee shot; because waiting next to the bunker at this very second was a brand new and free golf cap for him, courtesy of New York's Jago Silver and being delivered by his apprehensive employee.

It was all very awkward. Approaching a player with television cameras all around and people watching not least Silver himself, who would no doubt be loving every minute of his latest seize-the-moment bullshit venture. The megalomaniac had already texted Noah twice, his last message being typically to the point.

WHERE'S MY FUCKING CAP?

Noah pulled his marshal bib down square, and made sure that his registration badge was plainly in view. Both items had already cost him five grand.

Using his mercenary instincts, he'd chosen and approached

a marshal who he thought was a likely candidate. With time pressing, he couldn't afford a soft vague opening and so he had to get straight to it.

He explained what he needed and offered a thousand pounds to kick things off, but things quickly got out of hand with the marshal threatening to report him. Fortunately, this only turned out to be a bargaining tool and the price duly headed north.

In the end they agreed on five grand, plus a deposit to make sure Noah returned the items. Reluctantly, he'd handed over his Patek Phillipe wristwatch - a gift from his father, obviously. *And who says advertising doesn't work?*

By now, Noah's window of opportunity was rapidly diminishing and he needed to hurry. Along with his watch, he'd handed over five separate brown envelopes, and for one hour only, he'd become a marshal at the British Open with access to all areas.

By the time Ricky arrived at the bunker, it was raining hard; he was barking angrily to himself, sorely in need of a cap. He and Marshall had argued all the way down the fairway and at one point, Ricky had stopped dead in his tracks and rooted through his bag himself, which was picked up by the ever-present Daniel and was more manna from heaven for the insatiable media.

'It's not my fault, no way,' Marshall moaned. 'You chucked the shit out of the bag, not me.'

'Yes, because you couldn't carry it.'

'Yeah, and? So what, I'm old.'

'You're not that old.'

'Well, I'm old enough. And I'm doing you a favour, remember? As I recall, you didn't have too many options after you'd shat your pants.'

This was a fair point, and it silenced Ricky as he skulked up to the bunker, where a marshal was waiting with a very smart looking jet-black golf cap, emblazoned with the words *Silver Linings* and in silver braid, what else?

'...*well, the temptation here for Randal is to try and advance his ball as far as possible, but you can end up leaving it in the trap. Much better to be sure. To take one's medicine, as they say. He mustn't be too greedy... He doesn't seem to be a greedy sort to me... he doesn't even have a cap, let alone a jacket. You think someone would give him one... Ah, what's this? As I speak, a friendly marshal is on hand to do the right thing...*'

'Golf cap for you, Ricky,' Noah said nervously. He was anxious not just because he was impersonating an official on live television, but because by now he'd had an idea of stiffing Jago Silver out of ninety-five thousand quid. In the circumstances, given how wet Ricky was, he reasoned that the golfer in the kilt would be delighted to be offered a free cap, and they might not even get into the tawdry subject of money. And he was right.

Ricky was as relieved as he was pleased; and very grateful. It was a golf cap, and not a sombrero, which would have been more in keeping with his day so far.

'Bloody hell, mate, thanks. Just what I need.'

Ricky pulled on the cap and looked to Marshall, who seemed to approve.

Noah smiled broadly, unable to quite believe his luck. It was the easiest hundred grand he had ever made, and he would look on it as severance pay - because he was fed up with Silver and looking to leave, anyway.

Peter Alliss was equally impressed.

'...*ah, a nice touch and a very nice cap too. Very debonair.*

What does that say? Silver Linings, and quite right too. A silver lining for them both... now, come on, Ricky, take your medicine and just flop it out.'

Ricky shifted both his feet into the sand, the way that all professional golfers do, and amateurs copy and look ridiculous for doing so. And, as if he could hear Peter Alliss, Ricky did exactly as advised, and popped his ball out sideways onto the fairway.

'...good lad. That'll do.'

Ricky knocked the sticky sand off his feet and handed his club to Marshall.

'...Well done. Now - does anyone out there have a spare jacket, or better still, a pair of trousers...'

For his next shot, Ricky could not consult with his caddie – because, remarkably, Marshall had disappeared again.

Ricky looked about himself in utter disbelief, then completed one more three-hundred-and-sixty-degree circle, just to be on the safe side. He could see the kindly marshal who'd donated the cap who was hurrying quickly away, but not Marshall. His impromptu caddie was nowhere to be seen. Absolutely un-be-fucking-lieveable. Just where the hell could he have got to this time? Another phone call?

He looked enquiringly at young Ben, who seemed to understand, but he couldn't help him, just shaking his head.

Ricky was furious now and it forced his decision. For his third shot, he was going for the green and he grabbed his three wood from his bag. It was a shot right on the limits of his ability and range; but he had a nice lie, it was a par 5 and with the form he was in, why not?

He looked about for Marshall one more time before addressing his ball. He clipped the grass beautifully with his practice swing, but he snatched at the actual shot and his ball squirted forward rather than being propelled. It was a poor shot, more in keeping with a club golfer than a professional.

'...oh dear... that's not pretty, I'm afraid. Definitely not one for the archive, but it hasn't ended up too badly - he's really only where he would have been if he'd been sensible and laid up. So no real harm done, apart from the ego, perhaps, but he can still get up and down for his par. Which is easy for me to say, of course. But who knows? This is no ordinary golfer. This is Ricky Randal - and normal things do not happen to this man...'

Having watched his rather flat and embarrassing shot, Ricky stood for a moment before a horrible realisation dawned on him; without Marshall, he would have to carry his own bag. He glanced over at the match referee, but the man didn't seem particularly exercised.

'Problem?' the referee mouthed.

Ricky shook his head, closed his eyes and heaved his bag onto his back, imagining what the galleries and people at home would make of him now. The first player ever to lose two caddies in the space of two rounds. He was now even more grateful for his new golf cap - which he pulled down low over his brow.

He reached his ball and put his heavy bag down - and still no Marshall, although he hardly dared to look up for fear of catching anyone's eye. Ben was still present, but with the growing crowds following his match, it would not be long before he would struggle to maintain his front-row vantage spot.

Ricky took a couple of deep breaths as he absorbed the shot that faced him. He consulted his stroke saver and calculated that he had exactly one hundred and sixty-five yards to the pin.

And two shots left for par. Up and down required. Something well within his skill-set - and comfortably so - if this had been Bamburgh golf club and he'd been playing with his dad.

But this was Muirfield and he was all alone.

He pulled out a club and spun it over in his fingers. Without Marshall, he was finished. He couldn't carry his own bag anyway; he felt vulnerable and wanted to get his round over so he could get home to the people who loved him.

He was economical with his practice swing, brushing the grass a couple of times, before firing his ball high and towards the green. He stared after it intently. He studied its flight, instantly computing the ball's speed, height, distance, shape and direction, his eyes dancing up and down from his ball to the pin.

All looked well, and he watched it land safely onto the putting surface. The cheer from the crowd from the green was the first good sign - but the roar of encouragement that followed told another story, as did the ultimate enormous groan that travelled back down the fairway.

He must have been close but he wasn't sure where it had finished. Hopefully close enough for another par?

What Ricky could not see was that his ball had stopped within a hair's breadth of the hole. Had it any more energy at all, it would have dropped, and Peter Alliss was as disappointed as everyone greenside.

'...well, would you believe it? How extraordinary. Do you know, I don't think I've ever seen a more strange set of occurrences on a golf course...'

And with this, Peter had spoken a fraction too soon - because Ricky's ball suddenly vanished.

Perhaps it was a question of normal gravity, or shifting plate tectonics, or even the intake of breath from the people surrounding the green, but after maybe a full second, Ricky's ball dropped into the hole and the whole place erupted.

The noise travelled down the fairway like a train. It was

such a cheer that it could only mean one thing, and after a beat, Ricky leapt into the air like a salmon on a riverbank.

Another birdie and indeed it was quickly confirmed. This was incredible; and in jubilation, he tore off his new golf cap and threw it into the crowd as hands reached up to snatch the sporting memorabilia. He hopped along the rope, high-fiving random people as only an American can get away with, his golf cap long forgotten and never to be seen again.

'...oh dear, his hat has gone. Poor old Silver Linings...'

The head of compliance at the BBC had been on high-alert all weekend. The Wayne Grady comment had been unsettling, but had been contained with Wayne issuing a complete retraction and fulsome apology, and the matter was hopefully over. But now word was getting through to him that the BBC's strict code on advertising might have been breached and it was no surprise that it was to do with the player in the bloody kilt.

A light on his phone console illuminated; a direct line from his boss holed up at the preposterously named Media City. As soon as he heard his superior's voice, he could sense something was awry. They had already discussed the new golf cap and they'd assured each other that it was nothing to concern them.

'Silver Linings is a New York hedge fund.'

Instantly, his mouth dried and he pulled his hand through what was left of his hair. A hedge fund? Only an arms manufacturer was worse - and then, only marginally.

'Jesus Christ. And they've had two mentions already...' he murmured.

'Three. They've had three mentions,' his boss corrected him. 'And there's more.'

'Oh, great. What? Don't tell me, they're long on panda pelts and short on Rhino horn?'

'Silver Linings is a Wall Street firm, owned by a Jago Silver.'

'Right - and what is he, other than rich? A paedophile?'

138

This was not a helpful or amusing suggestion, the BBC still reeling from Saville Gate.

'He's an American billionaire. And he's got interests in big pharmaceuticals.'

Hardly a day passed when potential trade deals with the United States were not mooted and the inevitable accusations of the sale of our beloved NHS to American vulture capitalists just like Mr Silver, who was now advertising his wares on the BBC.

What's next, he's married to Trump's sister?

The head of compliance pinched the top of his nose and closed his eyes. This was truly terrible news for everyone - apart from Wayne Grady, who was now well and truly off the hook.

A confidential and urgent directive was immediately fired off to all executives, and especially to the outside broadcast team. No-one at the BBC was to mention the words Silver and Linings ever again, and they would all have to hope that they'd dodged this destructive little dirty bomb.

Having retrieved his ball from the cup, Ricky continued with some high fives with people around the green, including Ben and then it just happened. Because now was the right time.

Ben felt it, and he knew exactly what to do; and Ricky knew not to argue.

Ben took off his cap and handed it to Ricky. It was a little dog eared. It was Ben's favourite cap, a present from his favourite doctor, but Ricky needed it much more than he did.

The golfer smiled and plonked it onto his head. It was a perfect fit - and the crowd cheered even louder.

Polite Notice

Please avoid slow reading. To get to this point should have taken you two hours and twenty-four minutes. Please keep in mind that other readers are behind you, as well as prospective readers waiting to know whether this book is worth reading or not. Also, keep in mind what this book is trying to achieve, so please read quickly and respectfully of fellow readers.

Thank you!

Chapter Ten

Richard Randal, ENG -5
Open Championship + 8
45th Place
Prize Money €49,318
10th Hole
472 Yards, Par 4

'... **J** ust when we all thought it was safe to go back into the commentary box, along comes a player who turns everything upside down. Out in five under... we have all sorts of statisticians exploding around us. We think this is the lowest outward nine on a Sunday in the Open Championship, but we are checking. And to return to his dress sense for a brief moment, we believe he doesn't have any waterproofs, which seems extraordinary to anyone who's ever played golf in Scotland - I mean, it's a wonder, really, that he remembered his putter. Although to be fair, he hasn't used it that often...'

John Inverdale, the on-course anchor for BBCR5 and

making his last appearance for the national broadcaster, was as animated and excited as any other journalist covering one of the more bizarre sports stories of any of their careers.

'... oh, I'm being told that an umbrella has been dispatched from the pro shop and is on its way now. And let me make at least one prediction about this most unpredictable golfer - which is simply this - if Ricky Randal has a back nine like his opening nine, then he'll be able to afford a smart set of new waterproofs for himself. Of that I am certain.'

Jago Silver was sitting on the toilet when he read Noah's text.

All done. The Silver Linings Cap is on the target head. £100k as agreed.

He smiled. He was a little irked that Noah had needed the entire budget, but never mind. He would have paid ten times that amount for this kind of exposure.

His partner for the night had tired of him not coming back to bed, and she needed to be away already for a flight to LA. She had a fashion shoot in Hawaii, and the sooner she left the better. She was beautiful and fun to sleep with - but not as much fun as watching the back nine from Muirfield with a Silver Linings cap on the golfer of the moment.

'Jago, honey, I'm outta here,' she called out, pulling on a tunic jacket over her vest.

'Er, yeah... sure,' he said, not feeling any particular need to see her off.

'So what? You wanna have lunch next week?'

'Er... yeah, sure.' Although she didn't look like she ate very much. Dining with her would be like eating alone.

'So, what - shall I call you?'

She sounded a little needy now. He sighed to himself; it was a familiar pattern.

'Er... sure... great... er...'

Jago was no actor, and didn't care if he sounded insincere, but being unable to recall her name in this instance was particularly unfortunate. Lena, maybe? No, wait, Lana...

He heard the front door of his apartment being opened.

'It's Leniah, you asshole,' she screamed - and then his front door slammed loudly. Ouch.

Jago emerged from his toilet, smiling and rubbing his hands together at the prospect of Ricky Whatsisname continuing to play well. Hell, he might even win the freaking thing. Jago imagined shots on newspapers across the world and adorning magazine covers - and all for the price of a half-decent lunch.

He rushed back into his office and leapt into his chair. A shot of Colin Montgomerie filled his screen. The classic Monty look, with the bemused Scot glaring at a ball that had dared to remain above ground.

'Come on. Who's this guy? Get to my guy. To my guy. Come on...'

A few other golfers were then featured before Ricky Randal filled the frame, and immediately Jago was confused. Randal was standing on the tenth tee, talking to no one in particular; and he was now wearing a cap... but it wasn't Jago's Silver Linings. What the fuck?

Jago stared at his screen intently, trying to make sense of what he was seeing. Perhaps this was a recording, he reasoned? Because it was definitely his guy. The giveaway being that he was wearing a kilt. Jago unmuted his set.

'...in a different golf cap now of course, after this happened on the ninth just a moment ago...'

The screen cut to a piece of recorded footage. A ball hanging on the edge of a hole, and then dropping, and an exultant Ricky Randal celebrating wildly.

As soon as Jago saw his cap being jettisoned into the crowd, his large TV screen exploded with the impact from his coffee cup, which for good measure was closely followed by a half-full bottle of Chateau Latour. The cold wine ran into the workings of the hot screen and quickly created a mass of steam with aggressive sparks firing across the room.

Jago was apoplectic. His eyes narrowed angrily as he grabbed his phone.

'Call that fuck, Noah.'

The smartphone took a brief moment to register.

'*That-fuck Noah* is not recognised. Do you wish to call...'

Sometimes smartphones can be too smart for their own good, as it proved with this particular device as it now met the same fate as the coffee cup and wine bottle, crashing into the stricken $100,000 television.

More steam billowed outwards and upwards, and the hyper-sensitive ceiling sensors now reached a critical threshold; something which Jago failed to fully register as he grappled with his laptop. But not for long, and he could not ignore the alarm and the instant downpour of water from above.

With this he was catatonic with rage. He needed to kill Noah - but more pressing was his need to get to the stop-valve in his apartment to shut down the water system. An easy thing to locate, but no small feat for a man who was temporarily blinded with fury.

Ricky was greeted with pandemonium as he arrived onto the tenth tee but he only had eyes for one person, who had magically reappeared.

Marshall was standing there to greet him, and still his carefree nonchalance remained as though he had nothing to account for.

'Fuck's sake, Marshall. Where have you been?' Ricky

seethed, although the sheer relief at seeing his caddie again was obvious. He could have hugged him, and barely managed to restrain himself from doing so.

'Sorry Ricky. Toilet break.'

Ricky glared at the man, not believing him for a second.

'Toilet break?'

'Yeah, toilet break.'

'You could have bloody well told me.'

'Yeah, well, I'm sorry. But it just comes on. As you well know, man of a certain age. You wait.'

'I had to carry my own bag.'

'Oh.' Marshall seemed to get it now and he looked a little rueful. His timing had certainly been unfortunate.

'Marshall. I'm on the bloody telly. You made me look like a right plonker. I had to carry my own bloody bag.'

'Yeah. I'm sorry. I can see that would have been awkward.' Marshall could sense that Ricky was delighted to see at him again - which was most heartening.

'You missed me, then?' he asked cheekily.

Ricky smiled a little. 'Not really. I birdied nine.'

'Yeah, I saw that. Good lad. You see, you don't even need me.'

Ricky smirked.

'From now on, you stay within sight at all times.'

'Yes, sir.'

Birdie or not at the ninth, Ricky was acutely aware of his increasing dependency on his eccentric companion, and not just for carrying his bag.

'Nice cap, by the way,' Marshall added. 'Much better than the other one. This one's perfect.'

The tee was surrounded by fans of Ricky Randal and his playing partner, Lee Pah, looked completely lost. Pah was six over par for the day, eleven shots behind his partner and he had one eye over his shoulder at his young countrymen eager to show him how it was done.

Another unhappy teenager was Ben, thanks to the swelling crowds that Ricky was attracting with every hole. If they became any larger, it would be impossible for him to follow Ricky's match shot by shot. It was already becoming something of a scrum for positioning, and Ben was never going to be able to compete.

His dad was starting to worry too. The medics had been explicit about avoiding stressful situations, particularly in standing areas, and so when Ben began to push his way through the crowd surrounding the tenth tee, his dad pulled him quickly back.

'Ben, you can't just push through like that.'

'But, Dad, I have to.'

'No, Ben. You don't. You can't. These people are ahead of you and remember what you promised your mum.'

Ben tutted angrily.

'And besides, people just won't allow it. They want to see Ricky as well.'

'But I need to watch his tee shot!'

Eric was becoming a little exasperated now. He had got away with his earlier faux pas, but he was not about to make another mistake.

'I have to watch...'

'For God's sake, Ben. What do you mean, you HAVE to? Stop being so bloody melodramatic.'

'I'm not being melodramatic. You don't understand...'

'No, I don't understand. Correct. And what I say is final, young man. You cannot see this tee shot. It's as simple as that. But if we walk down the fairway...'

Ben ignored his dad and attempted again to burrow through the static crowd surrounding the tee. It was most unlike him and Eric was growing ever more strained, clinging onto his son and pulling him back.

'Ben, please be reasonable. Let's walk on to the eleventh or twelfth tee and wait for Ricky there.'

At this Ben's eyes widened in panic. He was tearful now and thinking for a split second, he suddenly took off without warning, rushing down the fairway with his dad stumbling after him.

Eric called out after his son. He was angry now. This trip of a lifetime was getting out of control – perhaps it hadn't been such a great idea after all.

Back on the tee, despite his reunion with Marshall, Ricky too felt a little awkward. He didn't know what it was, but something was awry.

He waggled his driver, and then it occurred to him. Ben was missing. His one true and original fan, and the supplier of his golf cap.

The all-knowing Marshall seem to understand and shook his head. But there was no time, now. Ricky had to tee off.

No time like the present. Sitting in his Porsche, using his mobile phone, Noah wired the money from the Silver Linings slush fund account to the bank account of a friend who had agreed to pretend to be the agent of Ricky Randal.

This was stealing, of course. It was theft, pure and simple, but from a man who was so wealthy that he was hardly going to miss it. And if this didn't mitigate the crime sufficiently, he'd told himself, then his friend could certainly use his share of the money as a new dad and with a wife who didn't relish returning to the classroom.

He had, he reasoned, also delivered what had been asked of him and at the agreed price. So Jago had what he wanted and his subterfuge would never come to light. This was nothing more than a fair recompense then. A living bonus that the tight billionaire wouldn't ordinarily grant.

Noah breathed out heavily and congratulated himself. He checked his phone again, amazed that he'd yet to hear back from Mr Silver Linings himself. Then his phone did ring - but it wasn't Jago.

It was the bank with his verification code for the transfer. All was well. What a great day.

Ricky's tee shot at the tenth was poor. And by his recent high standards, it was very poor indeed. It lacked any real zip, and this time it kept right; heading for the rough. It was also short, and greeted by almost complete silence on the tee.

Ricky shut his eyes and hoped that Marshall had a line on it - assuming that he hadn't wondered off again, of course.

The television pictures showed Ricky's tee shot in super slow motion. The venerable, Sir Nick Faldo was now in the commentary box and he knew exactly what was wrong.

'...that, I am afraid, is just pressure. Plain and simple,' England's greatest ever golfer explained.

'He's been hitting it lovely all day and suddenly I think things have just dawned on him. Hey, this is the final round of the Open. He's at the turn in a great position and all eyes are on me. I'm heading home and this is all new. This is a place he has never been before. He doesn't have the experience to draw on. And that creates pressure, the result of which is that tee shot. No doubt about it.'

It was a fair and easy assumption to make. Peter Alliss murmured his agreement and so, probably, did the millions of people watching in homes across the world, some of whom would be hoping and waiting for Ricky's wheels to fall off completely.

But Faldo, along with everyone else, was flat wrong. It was not pressure that had caused Ricky to choke on the tenth tee, and watching at home, Maggie was quick to reassure her mother-in-law that their man was okay. Ricky's dad and Tess's husband had worshipped Faldo, and it was odd for her to hear the illustrious golfer discussing her son - and even more peculiar to hear Maggie stating that the man was plain wrong.

'Ricky's fine. I just know it.'

'Right. And how do you figure that, then?'

Maggie thought about this for a moment and shook her head. 'I don't know. But I just do.'

Tess stared at her oddly. She had been acting strangely since taking that phone call earlier, which she had yet to explain.

'You're acting very calm all of a sudden,' Tess said curiously.

Maggie just nodded. 'Yeah, well. It's what Ricky would want – for us to be calm.'

Tess was unconvinced, but said nothing and let the pictures on the television of Ricky's ball do the talking for her. His ball was buried, and would have been lost, had it not been for the ball spotters, television cameras and spectators on-hand to find it.

Ben had picked up the flight of the ball as it emerged from the tee area but then quickly lost it in flight, his eyes darting about trying to pick the ball out of the grey sky but to no avail. He stood statue-still, despite the shouts of 'fore right' and he heard a ball land quietly just ten feet to his left.

Eric ducked, and then felt embarrassed that he hadn't covered his son to protect him from the incoming ball. He hoped that this hadn't been caught on television - but he suspected that it had. It was that kind of day. He'd be a meme no doubt. Useless dad or something else disparaging. In his pocket, he fingered his phone, half expecting it to vibrate with an angry incoming call, but it didn't, and he breathed a sigh of relief.

Ben had raced up to Ricky's errant ball and was in prime position for the next shot; this was a great piece of fortune, but it would be short-lived, and his dad worried that with the ever-growing crowds that this would most likely be the last shot he would see Ricky make.

By the time Ricky arrived, marshals were needed to create his passageway through, and he was delighted to see that Ben was waiting for him. They smiled at each other affectionately as his dad looked on.

'Thanks for the cap.'

'Yeah, no problem.'

'Missed you on the tee back there.'

'Yeah, well, you're getting too popular.'

'Or infamous?'

Ricky smiled, gesturing to his kilt, and nodded at his ball position, with the gentle inference that this was in some way Ben's fault.

The rain was easing off now, but it was still a factor, and the wet grass was not going to help. Ricky discussed the shot with Marshall, and they flitted between clubs. The ball was lying poorly and advancing it any distance was going to be difficult.

'...*just get it outta there...*' Faldo said, '*This is air shot territory, which will ruin anyone's round, let alone the most important round of your life...*'

Ricky swung his club down very hard. He might as well have used a scythe for the mass of grass that he threw into the air before anything white emerged. But eventually, his ball did finally make an appearance, slowly and sleepily, like a teenager advancing towards a bath. It barely made it onto the fairway.

The crowd shuffled ahead and surrounded the ball once again, ready for the third shot from nearly three hundred yards short of where it needed to be.

Ben jockeyed with the rest of them and managed to maintain his prime position, but his dad was really panicking now; Eric knew he needed to put an end to this before his wife was on the phone again. His son was in no state to be fighting through crowds. It wasn't fair on Ben or his mum, watching remotely from Devon.

Earlier in the year, after eighteen months of waiting and the elation of finding a match, Ben's transplant had failed. His treatment had now moved to containment.

The medics had been careful not to put an exact timeframe on it, but it was unlikely to be very much longer than a year, something his mum was unwilling to countenance. Where there is hope, she would repeat over and over, and he would nod obediently and join her in prayer but only to support her - and not because he really believed in such hope.

Their son was being taken away from them, and there was nothing they or anyone else could do about it. And as inevitable as it was, should anything occur at Muirfield to hasten this tragedy....

Eric shuddered at such a prospect. Such a thing would very probably take his wife too, and he wrapped his arms protectively around his only child.

'You all right, Ben?' his dad asked a little wearily.

'I'm fine, Dad. Honestly, stop worrying about me.'

Ricky's ball was sitting up beautifully on the pristine grass. A perfect lie - and Ricky looked at the distance that he had left and began to wonder. Marshall smiled mischievously, and seemed to understand what he might be thinking.

'What do you reckon, Marshall?'

Marshall pulled at his moustache and grinned. It was an answer of sorts, and it was enough. Ricky pulled out his driver from his bag and drew gasps from everyone watching, Sir Nick Faldo included.

'*...oh, my God, spoiler alert, big mistake coming up right here. Round-wrecker coming up. Ricky Randal is about to hit driver off the deck - what is he thinking? There's been talk of his having a breakdown all morning and now we have incontrovertible proof. Back nine of the Open and he's playing an exhibition shot. Out of bounds left. Bunkers right. And into this wind, I doubt he can reach anyway... he could run up a really big number here and that will be him and his Open over...*'

Ricky, though, had other plans, and Marshall approved - which was a good thing. After all, the ball was sitting up and practically inviting him to take the shot. He just needed to be accurate. That was all.

He clipped the grass with his practice swing and then settled for a brief moment, imagined his shot, and then promptly crunched his ball away; aggressively firing it off into the drizzle.

A magnificent shot. Possibly the best shot of his career, and Sir Nick was quick to take it on the chin.

'*...okay, so what do I know? Don't listen to me, people, I know nothing. This is completely foolhardy but also top drawer stuff... what sort of bounce will it get?...oh, lovely, it bounds on beautifully - and why wouldn't it? This is Ricky Randal, and his latest shot is possibly the best golf shot we've seen here all week and I would say, by at least three hundred yards...*'

The ball settled onto the front edge of the green. A miraculous shot - and the crowds surrounding the green burst into warm applause. Ricky smiled broadly and wondered, again, if

Patrick, his absent caddie, was watching. He bloody well hoped so.

He handed Marshall his club, looking around for Ben and his approval, but the boy was gone; nowhere to be seen. He looked quizzically at Marshall who raised his hand knowingly.

'Don't worry. I'll get him.'

Ricky nodded his thanks. He was no longer spooked by the old man and how he seemed to know things instinctively, and he watched him dip under the rope and disappear into the throng.

It didn't take long for Marshall to locate Ben and his dad. They were bickering at one another a little away from the main throng of the crowd; Marshall ushered himself ever closer until he caught Ben's eye.

Their argument ceased immediately. The old man smiled. He patted Ben on his shoulder, and smiled, too, at his bewildered dad.

'This is about the crowds, I take it, and being able to watch the golf,' Marshall said kindly.

'Not just any old golf. Ricky's match is the only golf I want to see.'

Marshall chuckled at this. 'Come on, then, follow me.'

They cut a path back through the crowds easily enough, and when they got back to the rope, they dipped under and walked on to the hallowed course.

A course marshal spotted them immediately and was quickly over towards them, gesticulating wildly, which drew the attention of the nearest golfer on the course who happened to be Ricky Randal and he marched back to the scene.

'No. no. You can't be on this side of the rope. This is for...'

'It's fine,' Ricky called out loudly, 'they're with me.'

The marshal was old-school. But under the circumstances,

he was willing to stand down, although he remained less than impressed.

'But they haven't got badges or any accreditation,' he fumed.
'No, but...'

They will have soon, Ricky thought to himself, as he sought out the match referee. He was on hand immediately and it was refreshing to have an exchange with him about something other than his kilt.

'This boy is my nephew. I know it's late and there are proce-dures - but could you organise some passes for them both? Run them off and have them sent over?'

It was an instruction phrased as a question, and delivered with an air of confidence that befits a player who hits driver off the deck. It was an unusual request. Security was ever-tight-ening at such events - but the boy and his dad were hardly threatening. The referee got onto his radio, and it seemed to be a problem solved.

Ben was elated and a wave of relief washed over his dad.
'Thanks so much, Ricky.'
'Just don't say anything. And no photos or phone calls, OK?'
They both nodded vigorously.
'Good. Because I'm in enough trouble already.'

The media centre was a feeding frenzy by now and Ricky Randal was the prawn vol-au-vents of the buffet.

Anna Wade, as a freelancer, remained completely dispens-able, but she too had an air of confidence about her now as she listened to her conversation over and over - or interview, as she preferred to call it - with the man every journalist wanted to hear from. It was something of a godsend. An exclusive and a coup and way out of her experience and beyond her pay-grade.

There was a glaring issue of ethics, of course, and this troubled her. The scary words of 'entrapment' and 'clandestine' were playing on her mind.

And yet, even with a shrinking window of opportunity, she didn't feel frantic or inclined to do anything immediately. Don't be rash, she kept telling herself. Ordinarily, she would have called her dad and put her conundrum to him and his wisdom, but she hadn't done so yet - which itself was a surprise, if only for the bragging rights that it presented.

For now though, she was distracted by Ricky's new cap and its donor as she watched the curious incident on her laptop again. Even before it had occurred, she'd been researching the company Silver Linings, and decided that she rather enjoyed the ignominious spectacle of a hedge fund being tossed aside. It presented certain tasty but rather obvious possibilities as a story. *The Guardian* would clearly be interested and a good place to start. *Hats Off to Randal* sprang to mind, and she fired off a quick email to her contacts at various press agencies.

But then matters became even more exciting once Ricky Randal pulled on his latest cap, this time sporting a large yellow flower above its peak. It had yellow writing down each side which required Anna to freeze-frame her screen in order to read.

Anthony Nolan. The name rang a bell. A charity, she thought?

A simple Google search quickly joined the dots.

A charity that saves the lives of people with blood cancer.

Thoughts bombarded Anna's mind and her eyes narrowed as she studied the most enigmatic golfer on the planet. He looked utterly ridiculous in his outfit - and yet it made perfect sense also, as the whole world looked on and wondered.

Obviously, charities gave out thousands of goodies carrying their logos in the hope of generating awareness, a case in point being the pen she was twiddling with even now, marked with

Bowel Cancer UK – which she had no idea how she'd come to own. But a cap being plonked on the head of such a golfer was a remarkable piece of good fortune for any charity, and it twanged at Anna's journalistic antennae.

Her attention was drawn, too, to the cap's original owner, a young boy who'd now joined Ricky within the ropes. What a morning he was having, first with his gift of Ricky's ball and being featured all morning on television and now being invited within the ropes - but there was something else about him that piqued her interest. She froze her screen and zoomed in on his face. He was a handsome boy and appropriately wide-eyed. He was accompanied by his dad, she presumed, who had a certain defensiveness about him, standing over the young man as though protecting him from something.

Her laptop pinged. It was an email from a press agency; a standard response, thanking her for the submission but explaining that this angle was already being covered and had been placed already. Anna expected as much, but now she didn't care. This wasn't really the story, after all. Things had moved already - and had hopefully just got bigger. It was only a hunch, of course, but it felt so compelling. There was something occurring here, to do with the boy and how he might be connected to the golfer.

This was the story, and for the first time in her stuttering journalistic career, Anna felt that she was ahead of the curve and in with a shot. It was time to call her dad, for sure.

On the tenth green in three shots, having used his driver twice, Ricky now felt comfortable again and almost relaxed. Marshall was present, crouching down to get a read on his putt, and Ben was greenside as well. Everything was where it should be, apart from his ball which was thirty feet short of the hole with only one putt to make his par.

'...yep, bogey's the likely result, and how he reacts to it will be crucial. It'll be a dent in his scorecard but he must just put it behind him. Everyone will drop shots out here today. This is Muirfield. This is the Open and this is Sunday...'

Sir Nick Faldo stated all of this calmly enough. When he'd won the Open at Muirfield in 1987, he was plain Mr Nick Faldo, and he'd famously played the final round in eighteen straight pars when players all around him were dropping shots and moving backwards. Currently, his co-commentator was Sam Torrance, who knew this fact very well but chose not to mention it.

Ricky crouched on his haunches to get the best read, trying to account for every swale and borrow. It was left. Maybe as much as a couple of balls outside left? He looked over at Marshall.

'Three balls left?' Ricky suggested. The old man said nothing - which meant he agreed, presumably.

Ricky replaced his ball carefully and picked up his marker, an Isle of Man ten-pence piece that his dad had given him many years ago. Settling over his ball, he consciously eased off his grip as he relaxed and softened his hands. He exhaled slowly and then drew his club back and through, sending his ball smoothly on its way.

Too fast, was his immediate concern. Too fast, anyway, to worry about any of the most subtle borrows that his ball raced over. He walked after his ball nervously, his eye fixed on the hole ahead, which hopefully might get in the way of his ball - or else it would roll on into bogey or even double territory.

Which it duly did. It clattered into the pin and then skidded around the cup like a motorbike riding the wall of death. Around it went, and almost completed a full circle before finally gravity exerted itself and sucked the ball from view.

Ricky hung his head low, almost embarrassed at his feat; no question, the most remarkable par in his entire life. The spectators, in disbelief, were in raptures once more at the golfer who just kept on giving. Something special was afoot and they all felt part of it.

Chapter Eleven

Richard Randal, ENG -5
Open Championship + 8
45th Place
Prize Money €49,318
11th Hole
389 Yards, Par 4

Along with everyone else, John Inverdale was struggling to adequately reflect the drama and excitement that surrounded Ricky Randal. The interview that every journalist was currently after was with a sulky Michael Landale and after this, anyone at all connected with Ricky Randal. Ideally his caddie, and then his wife, his coach, his mum or dad, his agent, a friend, or indeed anyone at all who knew him - none of whom were available, so Mr Inverdale was left to chat matters through with a generic sports psychologist.

The social 'scientist' was explaining to the nation what everyone already knew; that Ricky Randal was in uncharted territory and that he would be feeling immense pressure, which might or might not have an impact on his game.

'Right, thanks for that...' Inverdale said as politely as possible. '...so, let's go now to the eleventh tee, where we'll see how this extraordinary saga continues with Iain Carter.'

'Yes, thank you, John. Well, as you say, the fireworks continue after that brave, brave par putt and so here we are on the eleventh tee. One of the shorter par fours on this famous links, and if he hits another Sunday best of a drive, it could be yet another scoring opportunity for him here...'

The tee was completely surrounded, five deep with people all around straining for a view. The rain had abated now and even the wind had dropped. It almost seemed like an invitation.

Ricky and Marshall did not consult with each other. There was no need. Ricky grabbed his driver and he winked at Ben.

Anna's instincts had been correct, and her heart fluttered with such excitement that she almost had to shut her laptop and check that she wasn't being watched by any nearby hacks. Quickly, corresponding levels of guilt and shame caught hold of her as she focused on the web page that had just opened.

The phenomenon of fundraising is becoming ever more popular amongst the family and friends of patients who are ill and most usually, when their conditions are grave - either to find a cure, or to leave a legacy for others similarly afflicted in the future, and it follows that any fundraising efforts need to be shouted about and not kept quiet. A wonderful tool, the internet, which allows us all to become such effective private detectives and including fledgling journalists like Anna Wade.

YouTube allowed her to re-watch the television interview of Ben with his golf ball in hand in order to get his surname, and then a Facebook and Google search quickly unearthed his efforts against the pernicious disease that had singled him out.

She scanned her screen quickly, discovering that Ben had been battling his illness for three years, but that his joy at finding a match had turned to sadness when his bone marrow transplant had been unsuccessful.

Anna stared at a photograph of Ben as a younger boy, standing with his mum and dad who looked more frightened than him. She noted that Ben was wearing a cap; the very same cap, in fact, that was featuring on the television today.

It was a quite a development; the kilted golfer jettisoning a US hedge fund for a cancer charity - and furthermore, taking a mortally sick child from the busy crowds and into his fold. Ricky Randal was the sports story that was fast becoming a human interest story, and more importantly, the story that keeps on giving.

She continued on with Ben's website, scrolling down various photos of people running, cycling and a roomful of grannies knitting. Only the man in a bath full of baked beans was missing, and at the end of the site was an array of methods of making donations, as well as instructions on how to make contact with Ben and his family.

Anna noted down the email address and paused over her quandary. It was possibly exploitative and definitely opportunistic - but then what if a national newspaper was interested and happy to stump up for this very worthy cause? It was a human interest story, and the Daily Mail would be all over it.

Anna opened a new Word page on her laptop. She needed to take stock. She needed to write up what she already had in the hope that some meaning might emerge. The slogan of the charity played large in her mind.

Be a match, save a life. Very noble words, and true enough, but it might even be extended to saving careers as well.

· · ·

The bad day continued for the Head of Compliance at the BBC, when security at the Open confirmed that the marshal who handed over the Silver Linings cap to the golfer of the moment had been an imposter. All kinds of alarms were sounding.

Quickly, the rogue marshal whose pass had been misused was identified. He was not trussed up around the back of the clubhouse, thank God, but rather in a champagne tent enjoying a langoustine lunch.

His days of stewarding were, of course, over, but the authorities were keen to establish that they didn't have anything else to worry about, and that the imposter did not have more sinister intentions. In these days of suicide bombs, a steward giving out free golf caps was much less troubling, but nonetheless it posed awkward questions, and so there was some relief when it turned out that he had disappeared.

'He wanted to give his company's cap to the player in the kilt. So what?' The steward stated plainly. 'No harm in that? Nike pays Rory McIlroy, I assume.'

'And why did you agree to it? Did he pay you?' the BBC man hissed.

The steward didn't respond, which was answer enough - and he looked a little worried now that this could even become a police matter. But neither the golf authorities nor the nation's broadcaster were keen to involve the law and risk any more unwelcome attention, or possibly even a full scale security alert. Sacking him and escorting him from the premises seemed to be the eminently sensible way to go.

The guilty man was led from the office, flanked by the marshal chief and his deputy. He'd been stripped of his bib and badge, but ironically, his distinctive steward's golf cap remained.

From the press centre, Anna watched curiously as this little procession made its way towards the clubhouse and exited from the complex. She shut her laptop and clutched her bag. She might be wrong, but it looked as though a marshal was being escorted from the premises - and a connection to Capgate was hardly an enormous leap.

Ricky smashed his tee shot down the eleventh fairway, enjoying the cheers of encouragement and the inevitable 'och aye, Jimmies' that were becoming ever more popular.

Ben walked the fairway alongside him in silence. As much as he wanted to chat to his hero, he knew not to. Ricky would have things on his mind, and now was not the time for small talk.

'Hey, Ben, you okay?' his dad asked. It was a silly question. This very clearly being the very best day of his life bar none. He was inside the ropes, seeing his newest favourite sportsman, and he was on the telly. *Yes, Dad, of course I'm all right.*

Seven hundred miles away, his mum was watching, swollen with pride and numb with pain.

Eric was thinking constantly of her; he decided to send her another quick text. To tell her that he loved her and that Ben was okay.

Which, of course, he wasn't – and this was exactly why Eric couldn't fully enjoy the elation of where he was and what he was doing.

Noah turned cold the moment he saw a shot of Ricky Randal on television. The player in the kilt was wearing a golf cap - but it wasn't the golf cap Noah had given to him.

His throat tightened as he imagined Jago's reaction. He

needed to think. Panicking, he grabbed for his phone and quickly turned it off. And just in time – seconds later, an incoming call was diverted to his answerphone.

'*Hey, this is Noah. Thanks for phoning...*'

Jago did not leave a message and for the second time this morning, he crunched a phone into smithereens.

This time, it was a landline handset in the hotel suite of the Soho Grande, where he had checked in while his sodden apartment was attended to by people in uniforms and names on their chests. Shards of phone flew into the air, and the glass desk cracked and chipped as the phone was repeatedly smashed onto it.

Slumping into a seat beside the ruined desk, Jago found himself idly wondering if he might jump on a jet so that he could kill Noah himself. His lawyers would get him off - and even if they didn't, it'd be worth doing time for. He popped open a bottle of Jack Daniels, emptied four tablets into his shaking palm, and quickly tipped them down his throat. He pressed his thumb and forefinger on to his eyes to gain some relief as he recognised the signs that his doctors had warned him of.

His heart continued to flutter and fluctuate and he took a long deep breath. His doctor's advice was playing heavy on his mind now. His dad had died in his fifties. Breathe, he told himself. And that this was not a big deal. This was nothing. And nothing to get upset about - not really. He breathed in again, deeply.

It had been a little opportunity that had just fallen away. No big deal. So what? And if he really wanted this kind of exposure for his fund then he could always buy it. It probably hadn't even been noticed that his cap had been tossed aside.

He squeezed his eyes shut and willed his stomach-juices to

absorb the pills into his bloodstream, as he massaged both his temples.

His aggrieved assistant, who had been dragged from her bed in the middle of the night, entered the room.

'Jago. I have a call for you from the UK.'

Good. It had to be Noah.

'That fuck Noah, right?'

'No, actually, er... Anna Wade?'

Jago looked blank. At such an early hour, it was an odd time to receive a call, and particularly from someone he'd never heard of.

'Who the fuck is Anna Wade? What does she want?'

'I don't know. Some bullshit story about a golf cap at some golf tournament...'

Jago closed his eyes. He might need to fire up the jet after all.

'*...well, if I was a betting man, I would have our Ricky sinking this for another two and his third eagle of the day - he's having that kind of magical day. Everything he tries he makes. But knowing the curse of the commentator, he'll duff this chip and three putt for bogey, so maybe I should keep quiet and just let him get on with it...*'

Ricky clipped his ball firmly off the pristine fairway, keeping it low and bumping along towards the green as links golf demanded. The ball chased onto the putting surface and made a charge for the hole.

The flag-stick clunked as the ball dropped vertically into the ground.

It was an impossible result. At that speed, it should have bounced clear from the hole - but it hadn't and everyone was agog, including Peter Alliss, who was now genuinely lost for words.

Indeed, it was Richard Randal's third eagle of the day - and another record, surely and sent commentators scrambling for the collective noun for eagles. A clutch? A flock?

Ricky held his head in disbelief as all around him went wild. He clutched Marshall's hand and shook it warmly. The roar from the green could be heard all the way back at the clubhouse.

Someone was putting a run together and by now, everyone knew who it was.

Chapter Twelve

Richard Randal, ENG -7
Open Championship + 6
40th Place
Prize Money €53,982
12th Hole
345 Yards, Par 4

'... N*oooo. That's no wa' ahm sae'in...'*

'Well, then what are you saying?' asked Fred MacAulay, the host of a special radio phone-in show on BBC Radio Scotland.

'Wa' ahm sae'in is that it's no right for an English-marn ta bee wearin the tartan. Canya nae oonderstand tha? The kilt is fa a Scots-marn and tha s'it...'

Radio phone-in shows had been particularly animated on Ricky's kilt, and particularly in the context of these times of heightened politicism, not to mention the new terror that is cultural appropriation. People's careers laid to rubble as photos from yester-years fancy dress parties emerge when an ill-judged costume had been selected. Who knew that donning a Sombrero could ever cause such offence decades ahead and presumably it rankles with the beach salesmen in Cancun, now without jobs.

The islands of Britain might be 'Great' in name, but few of its inhabitants would argue that the Kingdom is particularly united; London, after all, is an economy all on its own, and the wealth that it generates is insufficient against the resentment it creates but Fred McAuley, a proud Scot was not so offended by Ricky's kilt as some of his irate callers.

'*How can ya sae tha, Fred? Ee's no a Scot. He's a English-marn!*'

'Aye,' Fred bantered, clearly enjoying himself.

'*...but pal, lemme just sae this Fred...*'

'*Aye.* Go on, my friend.'

'*Wa we can all agree on is this – tha' this is a clear case of the wrong troosers.*'

Fred laughed heartily at this little quip, which was a welcome and neat sign-off. 'OK, very good, that was Donald in Glasgow who is not happy with Mr Randall. Let's go now to Iain in Irving. Good morning, Iain.'

'*Morning, Fred. Thanks for having me on.*'

'You're very welcome.'

'*I'm just phoning to say what fun this is.*'

'Aye, it is.' Fred agreed. 'Whoever said golf can't be fun?'

'*I'm lovin' it. I would rather it was a Scot tearin' up Muir-field, of course, but I think this Ricky character is playing so well because of his kilt.*'

'Is that right?' Fred laughed. 'You think it's the kilt that's allowing him to play so well?'

'*Aye. I do. I think it's a magic kilt. It has to be.*'

'Well, maybe you're right. We have learned that he wouldn't take it off for a pair of trousers, anyway.'

'Aye that's right. And do you know what I'd love tae see happen later today?'

'No - go on?' Fred asked a little warily now.

'I'd love to see Tiger heading out in the tartan as well.'

Fred roared at this, and so did most of the people listening.

'Because that would really put Scotland on the map, and Fred, I'll tell ya somethin' else.'

'Yes, go on, quickly, though...'

'There's been lot'sa talk aboot whether he's wearing his kilt like a true Scotsman, which is why we're all hoping that the wind gets...'

'Yes, thank you, Iain. This is a family show. Thank you.'

Michael Landale popped another couple of ibuprofen, despite the warnings on the label. He had consulted with his committee and other officials and the verdict was split. The clothing violation was a flagrant breach of their authority, but any possible sanction was complicated by the soaring popularity of the golfer and their tournament.

Michael felt physically sick. No one present had dared to mention that Ricky Randal might even be good news for the sport, but it was what everyone was thinking and along with the rest of the country, they were all rooting for him as well.

In the press tent, the editor of the Scotsman was relishing a piece on golf that he was furiously writing about a game conceived in Scotland and given as a gift by Scotland to the rest of the world. But while Scotland remained the undisputed home of golf, the power base of the sport had long been ceded to America but also to England - that irksome little country below with delusions of grandeur.

The piece he was writing was not intended for publication. Editors usually clamour for coverage and readership - but not in this case. This was a letter. A personal letter to Michael Landale; a man he now had much leverage over. A private letter, making the case why the venue for the next Walker Cup should be Castle Stuart in the Highlands, where he happened to be a member and future Captain.

Marshall and Ricky argued as they made their way down the fairway after Ricky's short drive. He had ignored Marshall's advice and hit three wood, and his caddie was not pleased.

'You're short because you didn't hit driver.'

'I've told you, I hit driver here yesterday and made seven.'

Marshall huffed a little, and that was the last they said to each other on the short walk to Ricky's ball, whereupon he conceded his error. Now he faced a long and challenging shot for the green. He consulted his stroke-saver and plucked his two iron from his bag.

He was reminded of the famous joke.

What should a golfer do if he's ever caught in a lightning storm?

Hold up a two iron - because not even God can hit a two iron.

Ricky loved this joke for two reasons. Firstly, because his dad had told it to him, and secondly, because he was able to hit a two iron - as he proved again today as his ball carried the two bunkers guarding the green and chased up onto the elusive short grass.

The relief was palpable, and Ricky allowed himself a little fist-pump as he fed his club back into his bag. *Mistake redeemed.*

'Feel free to say sorry, Marshall. Or 'good shot', even?'

But Marshall said neither, which made Ricky smile even more widely. Marshall was too old to be petulant, and Ricky was pleased to see a little crack of a smile appear on his face.

But it wasn't a smile of contrition on Marshall's face, as Ricky was about to find out.

Anna could not explain where she had summoned up the courage to place a call to Jago Silver. Totally out of character - not to mention the unearthly hour in New York.

Wikipedia was not a robust source, but Anna did not have time to go elsewhere; and the results were as interesting as they were frightening. Particularly worrying was the fact that in Jago's index was a section called 'Libel and Lawsuits'. She gulped and wondered if she should use a pseudonym.

The page on his company website, including images of his key staff around the world, joined the dots for her. A handsome chap called Noah Edwards was Silver's man in the United Kingdom, and quickly she placed him as the rogue marshal who'd handed Ricky the golf cap in the rain. It was all rather beautiful - if journalism failed, then perhaps a career as a detective beckoned.

Her mind was made up. She placed the call.

Five minutes later, Anna ended the call and glanced up from her desk at the world's best sports journalists who were all hungry but way off the scent. She allowed herself a little smile.

Surely the connection with the New York hedge fund had been made already. It had happened live on television, after all. And similarly, the human story of Ricky's youngest fan was there for the taking also - and yet, she still didn't feel any urgency or need to strike. Even her incendiary voice-recording of Michael Landale wasn't nagging at her to make her move.

She had an eerie feeling of calm, and an awareness that she would know when the time was right; that somehow, and for whatever reason, she was part of a bigger puzzle. The completed picture of which had yet to emerge.

Then her phone beeped with an incoming text. Not from her dad, as she might have expected, but from a private number and she opened it with some caution.

Her eyes widened immediately. She placed her phone face down and looked about. Nobody was looking at her. Nobody was on to her. Why would they be? In her chosen profession, she was completely anonymous.

She re-read the text. Just a name and a phone number. But not just any name.

The live television pictures showed a ball rolling across a manicured surface. It was a close shot of Ricky's ball on the twelfth green - and if the script was really being adhered to, the ball should disappear from view. Only this time, it did not hit the pin or the cup – instead, it rolled on by.

'*...steady, steady...*'

It ran on eight feet or so. An eminently missable return putt beckoned.

'*Oh, dear. Well, at least we know now that he's human after all and that there's hope for the rest of us.*' Peter Alliss mused on behalf of us all, because it seemed that Ricky's run of extraordinary putts had ended.

It had missed by only a whisker, but golf is a game of miniscule margins, and now it was Marshall looking rather pleased with himself. Ricky blew out hard as he marked his ball.

'Not a word, Marshall.'

Marshall obeyed and said nothing.

Ricky stepped back and forth; suddenly he felt vulnerable again and alone, an unwelcome return to how he had felt earlier this morning. In reality, he knew, this feeling had probably never left him but had just been masked by the spectacular nature of his game. But it caught him now and it forced him to reflect.

He certainly did not relish his putt for par. It seemed to be lengthening all the time - and he felt scared again. He looked around himself and took in his extraordinary surroundings and circumstances. The packed green, his score, Ben, his kilt, his caddie, of course, and he realised he'd normalised them all.

Was this the twelfth or the thirteenth hole? In his fluster he wasn't even sure. Certainly enough holes remained for him to unpick his magnificent score, should he lapse into another of his familiar bogey runs. Such a run from here on in and he would cede all his shots back to the famous course, and he would finish level par for the day. A fabulous score for any player today - but not now from where he currently stood. Level par would mean a spectacular collapse.

Ricky shook his head and tried to re-focus. Marshall had no advice for him, which was typical. It was unreasonable to expect anything normal from the man.

He studied his line, his mind scrambling now. He thought of Maggie and his mum and his boys glued to the telly, willing him on. He chose a line, more guesswork than engineering, and forced himself into position. He placed his hands on his grip and wondered if the people surrounding the green and watching at home could see that his club was shaking.

The moment he struck his ball, he knew he'd missed. It was going to be short, so the line was irrelevant. Ricky cursed himself.

Fuck it. Bogey.

A fucking bogey. A horrible dirty stain on his card, but far more troubling was whether it was a sign of things to come. It was something he'd become too familiar with in tournament golf; the great limp home. After tapping in, Ricky picked his ball out of the hole and skulked off the twelfth green. On to the thirteenth - and unlucky for some?

Chapter Thirteen

Richard Randal, ENG -6
Open Championship + 7
43nd Place
Prize Money €51,201
13th Hole
193 Yards, Par 3

L ee Pah had the honour now, a rare thing after his
par at twelve, and Ricky was grateful for the few
extra moments to compose himself. It had been his
third bogey of the day, but he reminded himself that he was
still six under par and set for the best round of his life.
Hopefully.

No more dropped shots, he told himself. He glanced over to
Marshall in the hope of a supportive nod or a wink, but the
caddie was lost in thoughts of his own. He looked happy
enough - and why wouldn't he be? He was having a great day
out; not only was it an adventure, it was a day out of the toilets.
Their circumstances were as extraordinary as they were ridicu-

lous, and Ricky shook his head again to try and clear his thoughts.

Then, suddenly, Marshall turned, and smiled at his charge with genuine affection. It was great timing, and very assuring; Ricky was grateful. The old boy had an imperishable inner confidence and warmth, which had been most apparent when the match referee had dismissed him so rudely, but he clearly hadn't cared a jot. He did not need to be affirmed by anyone, and his sense of poise was inspiring. Whether he knew it or not, he was born to be a wingman, and it was a tragedy if his newfound career was going to last only a single day.

Ben watched the silent exchange between the two men intently; he smiled in agreement.

The thirteenth was another par-three, but uphill all the way to a narrow green that was surrounded by sand. Ricky noted that Lee had hit four iron and had found the green. Good for him. How much would Ricky give for the same result? Anywhere on the green would be good.

He went with four iron as well, but he was unable to fully clear the recent bogey from his mind, and it was no surprise to see his ball disappear into the middle greenside bunker. He closed his eyes. His chance of making par now was remote and his anxiety grew at the prospect of another dreaded bogey run.

It was a horrible thought - maybe all of this was too much for him. He felt exhausted and spent, mindful of his lack of sleep. His legs felt heavy, and for some reason his shoulder ached; at this moment, he just wanted to head off the course and go home.

He wouldn't be the first golfer to be so overwhelmed by pressure. The Great Dane had been escorted from the course once, and even the mercurial Rory McIlroy had walked.

Perhaps Marshall's kindly smile had lost its magic? Ricky was all alone. He was terrified, and Sir Nick Faldo's sage warning was playing on the minds of everyone watching, Peter Alliss included.

'...*oh, dear. Is this the wobble Mr Faldo was warning us about? I hope not. He's played so well up until now.*'

'*Or has he, though? That's why he's so fascinating to watch. Of course, to be six under, he must have played some spectacular golf, and he has. But he's had some preposterous good fortune as well, rattling in putts that really could have scooted by. And he's played some very ordinary shots as well. His chip at the first and his fairway wood... on eight, was it?*'

'*But he's still six under par, which makes this a round of golf that only the late great Seve could really understand, God love him. Much missed and always will be. Never to be replaced. But this is how he played the game. The great Ballesteros. This is his golf. And if he's up there looking down, he might have a few words of advice for our Ricky –*'

'*– and now would be a good time, because he's looking worried as he trundles along. Another bogey here and I fear for him, I really do...*'

In Skibo Castle, to the west of Dornoch in the Scottish Highlands, a highly groomed man sat in his large suite transfixed with the golf on television.

His wife had already disappeared for her range of beauty treatments and would not reappear until lunchtime - looking exactly the same, but feeling better, which was the main thing. He had an exciting day planned: taking delivery of his new powerboat at Lake Windermere in Cumbria with a quick jaunt south in his helicopter. The boat had been made to his exact specifications, and with nearly twenty months under construction, he'd needed to be patient.

But as excited as he was about his new 150mph toy, he

hadn't planned on Ricky Randal tossing a spanner into his carefully made plans. Half an hour ago, he'd even considered breaking his flight for a pit-stop in Edinburgh to see the man for himself, but had since reconsidered.

Like everyone else watching the television, the recent bogey had come as a setback. And like most people, he hoped that Sir Nick Faldo was wrong and that Randal would recover. It was all most peculiar, and his interest took him by surprise because golf was certainly not his sport - not dangerous enough, not to mention, too damn difficult. He had played in the odd charity game, and he did own a couple of golf courses - but only by default. They'd come with properties he owned and an island.

He called his PA and explained that he would not now be heading down to Windermere until later. He couldn't say when, exactly. However long it took for Randal to finish his round.

He'd waited almost two years for his new boat, so another hour or two wouldn't do any harm; and besides, he was more than just a run-of-the-mill billionaire. He was that rare breed of businessman, the universally-recognised household name. Regularly invited on to a raft of television shows for his celebrity status which he rarely agreed to but he appreciated being asked all the same.

His knighthood, on the other hand, had been a blessing like no other. It had been coming for years, of course – appropriate recognition for his philanthropic work, not to mention all the bloody tax he'd coughed up. He enjoyed the title, though, and the doors that it opened.

In short, he enjoyed being a celebrity - and aren't celebrities supposed to be late?

. . .

Maggie studied her husband's face as he considered his ball in the bunker. It was clear to everyone watching that he was under considerable strain. Her mother-in-law could barely watch, and she was happy to have her grandson, Paddy, to distract her with his ongoing explanations of the *Itsy Bitsys*: how they attack but, most importantly, how to kill them.

'And who do you fight them with?' Tess asked the little boy.

'With my dad,' Paddy blurted happily. 'Only my dad knows how to fight them properly, but he taught me, so I can help him.'

Tess grabbed at the child, pulling him into her ample bosom and cuddling him as she stole a quick glance up at the television, where Paddy's dad was now in the fight of his life. She'd never played golf, but she understood enough to know that the impending shot was pivotal, and she found it easier to listen for Maggie's reaction rather than to watch for herself.

There were no groans anyway, so he must have exited the trap at least. Maggie glared at the screen and waved both her hands at the television, urging his ball on towards the pin.

Tess buried her head into Paddy's neck, thinking of her husband and how he was missing out on this special day. It was the day he'd dreamed of ever since Ricky first picked up a club. A day that, in the end, had come too late for him. Tess squeezed little Paddy tight, and his squeal and wriggle made her cry.

'...*well, not bad. Not bad from there. Fifteen, eighteen feet left for his par and a chance, I guess. He needed to get it out and he couldn't have put anything less on it for fear of leaving it in the sand. But he hasn't done that. So well done. He's on the green and he has a putt for par. An outside chance, but a chance all the same...*'

· · ·

For Scotland's First Minister, the day just continued to get better; Scotland and Scottishness was featuring heavily on news bulletins across the globe and naturally her opinions were in high demand.

Politicians are no different from actors, sports stars or any other form of celebrity. They bask in any limelight they can find - and this was very welcome light indeed. This was attention on a global scale, and it gave her a glimpse of what life might be like if her nation decided to allow her another referendum and make her a world Statesperson. Intoxicating stuff.

The Ricky Randal story was an unexpected bonus to today's various shots of the beautiful Muirfield - along with the talk of Scotland, its outstanding beauty, traditions and the cultural heritage of this fiercely proud nation.

She received a jubilant phone call from Angus McLeish of the Scotsman who explained his unlikely leverage over Michael Landale and what he planned to extract for Scotland in return. She had met Michael Landale of course and instantly disliked him. A patrician Englishman with the temerity to preside over a Scottish game.

'Great stuff, Angus.' She cooed into her phone. 'Do remind him of our friendship in case he needs any more persuading.'

On the thirteenth green, Ricky was taking his time, studying his putt from every possible angle, determined to keep a successive bogey off his card.

Phil Parkin was commentating greenside, and speaking quietly into his lip-mic.

'It's pretty straight. Perhaps a smidgen right to left, but this will depend on how hard he wants to hit it - and I would strongly suggest not as hard as the other putts he's rattled in. Twenty feet, maybe, to get his round back on track...'

Under the circumstances, Ricky was delighted with his bunker shot, because at the very least it'd given him a chance. He prowled the green back and forth, trying to get a feel for the shot but more importantly, trying to calm himself down and get his rhythm back. Marshall was less aloof now, as though he sensed the panic within his man, and he was gently smiling and offering his assurances.

He didn't say much, though, which Ricky now understood. It was straight.

Ricky brushed the surface of the green with his hand just ahead of his ball, more out of nerves than a real attempt to remove anything from the surface.

Finally, he sent his ball on its way, and the distance was immediately in doubt as the ball began to slow and hold up with only half the distance travelled. The nervous golfer is always short, and Ricky Randal had never been as nervous as he felt now.

The ball continued to lose energy as it neared the hole, but it still had a chance. The line was good but would count for nothing if it couldn't reach the hole. Within inches now and moving so slowly, the branding and markings on the ball were almost legible as it advanced achingly slowly and finally running out of energy and stopping on the very edge of the cup. Agonisingly close. But from here, gravity took over and after a short beat, it pulled Ricky's ball down below the ground.

Instantly, a roar reverberated around the thirteenth green. Unlucky for some - but not Ricky Randal. A par. A sandy par. A sand save, and the most sensational par since the last sensational save on this most extraordinary round. And judging by Ricky's euphoric reaction, perhaps the most important par of his entire life, and television editors were already beginning to think of a possible par montage sequence for him. Ideally they would need one more, but Ricky still had five holes to play - so who knew?

Ben screamed his approval and slapped Ricky's outstretched hand. Even his dad lost control now and grabbed at the golfer who was having such an effect on his son. Marshall, too, was clearly aware of the moment's significance, but he was not a man given to wild celebrations and his warm hand-slap communicated all that was needed.

Seeing his ball disappear meant more to Ricky than anything that had gone before; even his ace at the fourth, both because of its significance for his round, and because he had made this putt even while he'd been terrified all over again - just as he had been at the start of his round.

A good sign, surely for the remainder of his round?

Chapter Fourteen

Richard Randal, ENG -6
Open Championship + 7
43th Place
Prize Money €51,201
14th Hole
478 Yards, Par 4

The fourteenth hole was a very long par four, which Ricky was happy about; with adrenaline coursing through his body, it rather suited him to thrash at a ball with everything he had. He was forced to wait, however, until Lee had fired off first, retaining the honour after his own par at thirteen.

He drummed at the shaft of his club impatiently until Marshall reached over, gripped his arm gently, and gave it a little squeeze. *Calm down*, the gesture said, which Ricky understood and he nodded.

'Remember you're still wearing a skirt,' the old man said cheekily.

Ricky smiled. He hadn't needed to pinch himself all morning, because his exposed knees had been reminder enough, but he didn't care anymore. Keeping the kilt had been the right thing to do. If nothing else, it was his connection to Marshall - and he understood now that Marshall was a large part of his success.

The referee had been clear that there could be repercussions of the stance he'd taken. He'd even warned Ricky that shots could be docked, but it no longer mattered. Maggie, his mum, his boys, and everyone else watching would know what he had shot here today. Everyone could count and everyone would know.

With a sense of newfound defiance, he sought out the lens of Daniel's television camera that had followed him all day and looked straight into it, the way that tennis players do with usually a pen in hand. It felt liberating. Like he was looking directly into his lounge at home where he knew his family would be. He smiled, and thought about giving a wave, but decided against it. Too cheesy!

Lee hit off, and now it was his turn. He set his tee peg into the ground and after a quick practice swing he crunched his ball away. *Bogey run, my arse.*

Tess hugged Maggie, who had been correct after all because Ricky was fine. Sure, his wobble had been a worry, but her belief in him had remained. She understood all too well the hurt that her son had endured for decades as a professional golfer; his unfulfilled potential and his hopes continually dashed no matter how hard he worked. It is this backdrop that made this day so far so overwhelming, and Ricky's look down the television lens spoke volumes. It made her weep. Maggie, too, was relieved to see his ball bounding safely down the fairway - and then her phone rang.

Tess sighed. She wished people would leave them alone. Maggie, however, was happy to take the call. She cleared her throat and took a quick beat before answering.

'Hello.'

'Ah, hello - Mrs Randal? Is that Mrs Randal?'

It was a woman, and Maggie could hear that she was anxious.

'Yes. Speaking.'

'Oh, hello, great - I'm sorry for calling now. At such an awkward time for you, what with the golf on, but I just felt that I should call...'

'No, no, that's OK, pet,' Maggie said calmly. 'How can I help?'

'WHO IS IT?' Tess mouthed, but Maggie gestured that everything was okay.

'My name is Anna Wade. I'm, er...'

'Are you that journalist lady?' Maggie asked. On hearing the profession, Tess began muttering angrily to herself.

'Er... yes... I suppose, I am.'

'No, that's okay,' Maggie said. 'And you're in Muirfield, are you?'

'Er, yes, I am. I'm... er, covering the golf... '

Anna petered out, recalling how Mrs Randal had referred to her. 'Sorry, Mrs Randal, you said *that* journalist? Were you expecting my call?'

'Well, I'm not entirely sure. Not really. But I was expecting a call, I suppose. How did you get my number?' Maggie asked, but not in an accusatory manner. It was a kindly enquiry, and in contrast to Tess, who was frantic now - and understandably so, given what they had agreed.

They had been fielding such calls all morning. At first, Tess had been keen, particularly when money was offered, but Maggie had disagreed and they'd argued about it, especially when Sky News offered them £10,000 for an exclusive interview.

But Maggie had refused point blank and Tess had been aghast. She'd asserted that her son would be furious with her for turning down such money, but Maggie was adamant. Just a feeling she had. She would not speak to any journalist, not for ten grand and not even for the generous and exciting offer to be flown to Muirfield in a celebrity's helicopter.

Tess thought her daughter-in-law had lost her mind.

'And you're calling about Ricky, I presume?' Maggie asked.

'I am, yes.' Anna felt embarrassed now. 'And I'm sorry for intruding. I expect you've had other calls like this one...'

'And how did you get my number again?' Maggie repeated.

'Er...' Anna dithered, contemplating whether or not to lie. 'Actually, someone texted it to me. But I'm afraid I don't know who or why.'

'Oh, only 'cos I got a text as well,' Maggie said.

'Oh, really.' Anna replied, unable to disguise her surprise.

'Yes. It was just your name, Anna Wade, and it said that you'd be calling.'

The line went quiet as Anna dwelt on this and tried to process and search for an explanation.

'And now, here we are.' Maggie continued.

'Yes. But, er...' Anna continued to scramble. 'Do you know who you got the text from?' she asked hopefully.

'No, not a clue.'

Anna didn't know what else to say now - which did not bode well for a career in journalism.

'It's a mystery, then,' Maggie laughed. 'Like the whole day, really.'

'Who is it?' Tess barked, angry now because Ricky had just

played his second shot on fourteen and Maggie had missed it completely. Maggie glanced at the telly, and was relieved to see a shot of a green. The fourteenth, hopefully?

'So can we speak later on, then?' Maggie said into her handset. 'It's just that I'm a bit busy at present.'

Anna was watching the same pictures on her monitor and understood.

'Yes, of course. Of course.'

'Okay, then, so if we talk once his round is over then - and I can get Ricky to talk to you as well if you like? Is that okay?'

Anna's eyes widened. She could hardly breathe. It sounded as though she was being offered an exclusive; and if not, then at least the chance to speak to the man making all the headlines.

'All right, then; we'll speak later, okay?'

Maggie ended the call.

Anna was completely overwhelmed. Mrs Randal hadn't hung up on her like she had feared - but then again, given the mysterious text messages, why would she?

They were meant to speak with each other, although neither of them understood why.

On the fourteenth green in regulation, par was almost a certainty. It was Muirfield's hardest hole, and it would be Ricky's first par in four attempts if he managed it. Marshall seemed happy enough and skipped alongside him as they headed for the green.

'I took triple here yesterday,' Ricky said, but the old man did not seem unduly concerned.

'Yeah, well, everything for a reason, eh. Including what happened yesterday.'

Ricky shot his caddie a quick glance and then chewed on

this cliché for a moment. He gestured to Marshall for an explanation.

'What?' Marshall shrugged.

'That?' Ricky stated. 'That little pearl of wisdom? You're just putting it out there but you aren't going to explain it.'

Marshall chuckled. 'Me?' He pointed to himself for extra effect. 'I can't explain any of it I'm afraid. But I expect it will become clear. I bloody hope so, anyway. Otherwise I've put my back out for nothing.'

Ricky looked at him oddly, but Marshall rebuffed him. He had nothing more to say.

'And it's no good looking like that, either. You found me, remember?'

Ricky didn't reply. By now they were on the green, which was surrounded by people applauding him warmly; and naturally he doffed his cap, which made Ben swell with pride even more.

A flurry of calls to and fro, and there was much excitement amongst the employees and management of Anthony Nolan. The chairman of the charity was nursing a sore head and had to wait for his vision to clear to see if it was indeed true.

He had planned to watch the golf anyway, but this was a remarkable bonus for him. An Anthony Nolan cap, live on television and furthermore on the head of the world's most featured sportsman. It was an old cap of theirs, but no matter; he agreed with his fundraising director that it was an impossible stroke of good fortune and immediately they set to the task of making sure it counted.

Who should he call first: the BBC, the newspapers? His wife wasn't sure either. And with time pressing on and their window of opportunity diminishing, they needed to act now.

He brought himself up to speed with events as best he could, and the rest was filled in for him on a Skype call with the charity's head of marketing. Most importantly, she explained all he needed to know about Ben and his condition. The young lad's consultant had been tracked down; he was in South Africa with his family but like so many others, he was watching the golf. Even the lions and rhinos were having to make way for the Ricky Randal Show.

Ben's mum remained rooted to her sofa; her phone had not stopped ringing all morning. She had ignored most of them, but decided to take a call from the chairman of Anthony Nolan. She was delighted that her son had managed to bring the charity into the spotlight, but inevitably this made her tearful as well.

The chairman had a difficult balance to strike. As thrilled as he was, he was sensitive to her circumstances and acutely aware of the agony and strain in her voice.

Before making the call, he'd read Ben's file and adequately prepped himself. He showered, had a shave and got dressed, as though he would be meeting the mother in person. He was calling a mum who was preparing to bury her son, and he wanted to thank her for what the young man had done for the charity.

She was grateful for his call, during which she kept an eye on the television, where Ben was beaming from ear to ear and, it seemed, without a care in the world. He was a picture of perfect happiness as he bounded down a fairway with his dad next him. It was the happiest she had seen him since his diagnosis.

She ended the phone call and stared at her beautiful son. Ben had been right all along. Going to the golf had been a wonderful idea.

The chairman, too, watched his television and tried to

imagine a mother's pain - but now was not a time to dwell. He dragged his laptop across the table and wrote out a five-hundred-word press release. He had complete clarity now and knew exactly what to write.

His wife put a cup of tea down in front of him, but he didn't touch it. He wrote continually, and he didn't check it over once he had finished. He fired it off to his head of marketing, with instructions for all key personnel to be copied in. By the time his email was on its way, Ricky was putting for his par on the fourteenth green - and the chairman of the charity with its name on the golfer's head would have staked his house on Ricky making the putt.

For such a short putt, Marshall was particularly involved - almost animated. He wasn't taking anything for granted, and if anything, the uncustomary caution on his part was a little unnerving. Was there something in the shot that Ricky hadn't seen? There'd been less pressure on his first putt, because it was never likely to drop. But the five-footer left for par was loaded with expectation.

'It's not as fast as it looks.' Marshall mused, taking Ricky by surprise.

'Really, you think so?'

'Yeah, it just looks a little more sticky, that's all. So get the line and give it a bang, I would.'

Ricky wished that he could. He recomputed his calculations and what he had to do. Speed hadn't really been a factor in his mind until now, and Marshall was even crouching on his haunches now to make sure of the line. He had never taken so much time.

'Quarter ball, outside left and firm.' Marshall said definitively, and he even stayed in position behind him while Ricky lined up. Ricky moved his club face a fraction to his left.

'That's it. Perfect. Hit that firmly and it'll drop.'

Marshall, the expert caddie from nowhere, scampered out of the way, and a moment later Ricky did what he was told to do - and so did his ball. Another surge of relief, but only a small fist punch this time for his par, and not the celebrations that the TV people were hoping for.

Ricky smiled broadly at his caddie and nodded knowingly. He hadn't seen the speed of the putt and he might well have been short. But Marshall had, thank God.

'Jees, mate. That was a Grisham. Thanks.'

Marshall looked bemused.

'A great read,' Ricky repeated. 'A John Grisham?'

Marshall shook his head uncomprehendingly.

'Forget it. You live under a bridge, I forgot.'

Chapter Fifteen

Richard Randal, ENG -6
Open Championship +7
43rd Place
Prize Money €51,201
15th Hole
447 Yards, Par 4

John Inverdale had time to fill, and he was happy to do so musing on one, Richard Randal.

'...but what this really demonstrates is real courage on his part, isn't it? Because we've had umpteen pundits and golf experts on - people who we mortal amateur golfers defer to, all predicting this great wobble over the back nine where the Randal wheels would fall off, and now here we are, two incredibly brave pars later, and that's looking much less likely now.'

'After that bogey, he's righted the ship and he's still hogging all the limelight - and deservedly so. How his wife and family must be coping, goodness only knows. Mrs Randal, if you'd like to text in or tweet, we'd love to hear from you. The whole coun-

try, I'm sure, would love to get your thoughts on just what is happening to your husband today. Because everyone here is talking about only one player and let me tell you, everyone here at Muirfield wants Ricky Randal to continue what he is doing - with the understandable exception of his fellow players who he's leaping over, because he is really charging up the leaderboard.

'And if the wind picks up or, dare I say it, we get some more rain... well, he can't win this Championship, Ricky Randal, but who knows how high up the leaderboard he might yet finish? And here to discuss this very point now, I am delighted to say, is none other than Justin Rose - a man who knows a thing or two about pressure on the back nine on a Sunday.

'Justin was in the Walker Cup team with Ricky Randal many moons ago, so he knows the player better than most. Justin is not out on the course for another few hours yet but he is on the range - where else? - and Andrew Cotter is down there for us. He caught up with Justin a moment ago, and this is what he had to say...'

Anna Wade had a wry smile on her face as she listened to Mr Inverdale on her radio, confident that Mrs Randal would not be getting in touch with the nation any time soon. She'd played their recent conversation over in her mind, and had given up trying to make any sense of it. She had also tried to trace the mystery text, but a nice lady in Mumbai working for her network could not help her and suggested that she might need to go to the police if any messages were troubling her.

Another press agency mailed her with the news that her angles for stories were already being covered - only this wasn't bad news anymore. Anna brought up her inbox and re-read the e-mail she had written to Mrs Jean Costello but had yet to press send.

It had not been an easy letter to write, and it'd taken her much more time than a hack could afford, but it made perfect sense to take such care because, under the circumstances, she needed it to be perfect.

She adjusted the final paragraph and checked it briefly once again, and then typed out the email address and hovered her cursor over the Send/Receive button. She checked it one final time and was pleased to change a comma for a semi-colon and insert a missing 'the'.

It needed to be perfect. Anything less would feel like an insult.

She clicked Send and watched her screen as her words travelled through the ether, and then she called her dad again who she had yet to speak to. He would be watching the golf, no doubt fretting and wondering why she hadn't rung him yet. Not even he would be able to offer any explanation for her morning so far; her fear being that his strong faith would have him plumping for a celestial explanation which would be no use to anyone, and especially not hard-bitten editors.

'Your mum keeps praying for you, you know.' She could hear him saying already - although this phrase had been previously referring to the Almighty providing her with a handsome husband, and not for gifting her with a scoop.

Something was now afoot in Skibo Castle and the timing of the whole thing was almost digital. His service director in London had called to explain that the jet he had ordered nearly an hour ago out of a Newcastle airfield was in the air and P.O.B (Passenger on Board) bound for Edinburgh. Now he just needed to flag up his intentions with his PR people. They would bleat and moan of course, but so what?

He congratulated himself warmly on hearing Mr Inverdale reference an event which was going to be a great publicity coup for him. The commentator had unwittingly teed it up, so to speak, and he remained glued to his television where Ricky had arrived on the fifteenth tee.

On the tee, Ricky caught Marshall looking a little reflective - almost fretful. He was standing with Ben, who oddly, looked a little sombre also.

What now? He glanced over at the match referee, but fortunately, he seemed happy enough and even gave Ricky his thumbs up.

Ricky raised his eyes at Marshall enquiringly, but the old man just shrugged and gestured towards the tee. Ricky had the honour back now, and things to attend to. He went for his driver, but quickly Marshall shook his head.

'No, not here, not now,' he said, almost flustered.

'Really? What do you mean? I'm hitting it great.'

Marshall just screwed up his face.

'Bloody hell. What is up with you? Has anything happened?'

'No, nothing, but driver is wrong. This is a short par four. So hit three.'

Ricky bit at his lip and mulled on this for moment. Well over four hundred yards. It wasn't *that* short, and earlier today, Marshall had barely even known what a par four was. And now Ricky was relying on him.

He continued to ponder. His dad had always encouraged him to push harder when he had any momentum. 'Foot down, son,' he used to say.

Ricky smiled as he thought of him, and then in this moment everything froze once again - just as it had done on the fourth hole. Just how it happened before, sounds became muted, everything slowed, and he was able to take stock and view the scene before him.

But this time there was something else even stranger and even more wonderful.

Ricky's attention was held by a man who he had not seen for years. It was his dad. He was grinning, and looked much younger than he was when Ricky had last seen him. He was strongly-built and lean, just like he was when he used to caddie for his only son. And in this vision before him, it was a cold day - late autumn perhaps, and his dad was wearing insufficient clothes – just like he always did.

'What do you mean it's cold?' he used to say. It had driven his mum mad.

And next to his dad, Ricky now glimpsed himself, bending and swinging, as a young amateur, and suddenly it all made sense and he understood. This was not just a random day from the past and a chance apparition on some golf course of his beloved dad. This was a special day, the day at Muirfield over twenty-three years ago, when Ricky had played in the hallowed Walker Cup with his dad on his bag. It had been a biting cold day, and it had caught many of the Americans out, he remembered. But Ricky had still lost his singles match.

And then as quickly as he'd appeared, his dad was gone. Vanished. The bubble popped, and he was back in real time. He looked around for Marshall – who, thankfully, was real enough, still present and ever-smiling. A little dazed, Ricky cleared his mind and needed to re-focus yet again on his task in-hand. Momentum being with him or not, *sorry, Dad, but I'm going with Marshal.*

Ricky pulled out his three wood.

'Let's hope you're right, Marsh,' he said to himself as he waggled his club. A wind had picked up now, and blowing straight off the sea and down the hole, it helped Ricky's ball as it climbed skyward from the tee box, with Ben leading the calls of 'shot'.

His ball bounded on and settled a short distance shy of a fairway bunker which he would have reached with driver. Ricky nodded his thanks at Marshall. Another great call.

But Marshall looked reflective again, and even a little sad - and now Ricky suspected he knew why.

Patrick was a little nervous as he walked the high street of Gullane, a few miles south of the famous links. He didn't know how long this was going to take, so he'd let his taxi go and would need to book another one.

He didn't care to be recognised, and so he pulled his golf cap down low. His photograph had been all over the television all morning. He saw the shop ahead and quickly ducked inside, welcomed by a loud bell and an old fashioned clattering wood-and-glass door that sprang shut behind him.

After such a leisurely morning, he was now in a hurry and could not wait to get onto the course, if only to see the action – and besides which, he hated not knowing how Ricky was faring. He had watched his tee shot on fifteen, but then his cab had arrived and he'd needed to leave if he was going to make it. He was as excited now as he was nervous.

The shop was immaculate; a throwback to yesteryear, and no doubt enjoying its best trading week of the year and possibly the decade. Not a hair out of place.

There was only one person serving, which came as a surprise, and she did not appear to be rushing either. She was old. In her sixties and well preserved, wearing a red cardigan and heavy blouse with white hair pulled into a neat bun. She was completing a huge order for a Japanese couple; an American lady waiting next, followed by a Swedish family.

Patrick shifted from foot to foot. He wouldn't have time at

this rate - but he didn't have any choice. The old lady appeared to have only one gear and it was first.

But then she looked at the wall clock, and peered at the queue ahead of her, and then finally she looked directly at Patrick and tutted her disapproval.

'I'm sorry, everyone, but this young man is in a dreadful hurry. Would anyone mind if I just served him ever so quickly?'

Jago Silver was a results man and the player in the kilt was not wearing a Silver Linings cap. Totally unacceptable. Noah had failed, and no excuse could ever make it right and as such, he needed to be punished.

Noah was in a full-blown panic at this point. Jago Silver was a man without the words 'forgiveness' or 'mitigating' in his vocabulary. He was going to be fired just as soon as he decided to turn his phone back on. Going incommunicado had been a mistake as well, because it implied that he had something to hide. By now Jago would have noted that one hundred grand had been debited from the Silver Linings UK hospitality account - and for what?

A shaft of ice-cold fear gripped Noah and he shuddered. Getting fired was the least of his worries. Even if he returned the money, his fate was already sealed. It would leave a trail which Jago would definitely sniff out. *Jago doesn't do forgiveness, ever.*

His ploy would come to light; he would be ruined. Jago would set his attack-dog lawyers loose, and once they connected the dots between the two university buddies, then Jago would set about ruining his life. It was the only sport he actually played. Noah was frantic now.

He fingered his phone and took a moment as something occurred to him.

His access to the Silver Linings hospitality account had already been cancelled. A very bad sign. Sitting in his hotel room at the Balmoral, he half-expected a knock at the door. This could even mean jail-time.

It was theft. And apparently there was no way out.

'Fuck. Why couldn't that arsehole just have kept his fucking cap on?'

He turned on his phone; and he did not need to wait long.

A few moments later, Jago's name appeared on his screen, accompanied by an insistent vibration, and he deliberated. But then he answered.

'Jago, hi. I can explain.'

'Where's my money and why is it...'

'It's been given to a charity.' Noah blurted desperately.

Silence.

'A kid's cancer charity,' he added quickly, 'and that's the cap Randal's wearing. So the money...'

'*...fuck you, Noah.*'

'But this could be good for you,' Noah pleaded.

'I don't give a shit. I don't give a rat's ass. I haven't got kids, so why would I give a fuck about kids with cancer? Fuck 'em. I'm sick of seeing their bald heads and their clawing eyes...'

Noah almost dropped the phone as Jago continued to rage. The man was simply revolting and terrifying; he hung up and ran to the toilet because he needed to throw up.

Michael Landale's day continued to worsen. The people gathered in the member's lounge of the clubhouse were quietly applauding Ricky's approach to the fifteenth green. Having all played the famous course themselves, they appreciated just how brilliant his golf was.

The camera followed his ball on to the green and then

quickly cut back to a close shot of the player himself. He touched the peak of his Anthony Nolan cap as his kilt billowed in the Scottish breeze - managing to look both magnificent and ridiculous at the same time.

Landale ordered himself another large scotch.

The fairway was lined with people - three deep, all the way from the apron to the green, and the crowds cheered him on.

'Go on Ricky,' rang out from all around, along with the very common wolf whistle and 'give us a twirl' - which he had yet to agree to. On the eighteenth, maybe?

He had fifteen feet to go, and it was pretty straight. Given his form today, it was almost a gimme.

He marked his ball and noticed that Marshall was chatting to Ben again. Perhaps, he thought, the old boy was explaining how to become a caddie to the wide-eyed youngster. But Ben looked pensive; the old man brushed his head affectionately and then turned his attention back to the green and the putt in hand. They had time to spare, because Lee was in yet another bunker and had still to play.

Marshall wandered back over, a little sheepishly.

'Good of you to join us,' Ricky said, sounding a little jealous.

'Yeah, well, it's nice to be needed. He's a lovely lad, that Ben.'

'Yeah. He's got vision, anyway, because he's stuck with me all this time.'

Ricky gestured to the putt he was facing, but Marshall's thoughts were apparently elsewhere. Leaning on his putter, Ricky took his weight off one foot. Perhaps it was the pressure of the day, but suddenly he felt exhausted. Finally Lee Pah landed his ball onto the flat surface. Poor lad - Ricky understood very well the youngster's torment – the young Korean had picked the worst day to have such a calamitous round.

Ricky had a decent read, but he deferred to Marshall, who reluctantly got to work.

'My worry here, Ricky lad, is that you're becoming a little too reliant on me.'

'Yeah, well, not long now and we're through,' Ricky chipped back at him and his caddie chuckled.

'But I'm only good for the next hole though and then that's me. I'm outta here.'

'Yeah, fine,' Ricky answered, playing along.

'Dead straight,' Marshall said.

'Yeah, I figure that.'

'No, I meant I'm only good for the next hole,' Marshall said, but Ricky didn't laugh.

'Dead straight?' he murmured.

'Yep, like a spirit level. So just aim at it and hit it. Simple physics.'

Just as Ricky had seen it - and he reminded himself that he had two putts for it to disappear.

'*...he'll be wanting birdie here. It looks dead straight to me. About the only straight putt on this green, so very makeable, especially with the way he's been putting. To get him to seven under. Extraordinary stuff.*' Peter Alliss mused.

'*Remember, he was two over after two holes today. A birdie here and perhaps one more on the par five sixteenth will give him a sixty-three - and that will be the lowest round of the entire Championship, let alone today's final round. And on that I will stake my entire reputation... What do you think, young Wayne?*'

Wayne was still a little shaken by the reaction to his earlier attempt at levity, and now he was taking no chances at all.

'*With this chap Randal, I'm not making any predictions at all.*'

202

'No, very wise. I suppose it's a good job Sir Nicholas isn't here. He's still waiting for the wheels to fall off and might be predicting three doubles to finish.'

'A la Van De Velde?' Grady added.

'Now, Wayne, steady... this is the BBC and there will no swearing on live television. That name's a little bit like the Scottish play that nobody dares mention, especially up here...'

More hoots of laughter emanated from the commentary booth.

By contrast, a very serious-looking Ricky Randal was now ready. He softened his hands once more, before passing his blade through. His ball did not deviate a fraction, and Peter Alliss called it immediately.

Ricky held his putter aloft as he stared after his ball. A cheer of encouragement began to gather volume as the ball got closer, and then it became an enormous roar as it dropped; Ricky punched his fist and then pointed at Marshall, who was impassive as ever, standing next to Ben, who was screaming wildly.

Chapter Sixteen

Richard Randal, ENG -7
Open Championship + 6
32nd Place
Prize Money €75,484
16th Hole
188 Yards, Par 3

He was still in his suite at Skibo Castle but now fully dressed. Time was running out if he was going to make it himself, and on seeing Ricky's latest birdie, his mind was made up. He should have left earlier, of course, but now he was certain.

It would be a spectacular reunion - and naturally, he should be a part of it. It would cause painful disruption to his PR team, but so what? Billionaires are allowed to change their minds.

But this was a very late curveball, though, and it would smash the very best and carefully laid plans of his staff. Tantrums and vernacular behind his back, no doubt - and so he decided to lob in this particular grenade by text. Less bother-some and quieter. For a few moments, anyway.

Having pushed 'Send', he enjoyed the peaceful silence for a couple of minutes before his door exploded open - and in swept his staggeringly angry personal assistant. It was a look he was familiar with.

'What?' he began, with a shrug and his trademark grin.

'WHAT?' his PA spat. 'Jesus, Richard. Everything's been arranged for months. This has taken me months. No! Years of planning. Years.'

'Oh.'

'Is that it?' She spat. 'Everything's ready and everyone is waiting for you at Windermere - and you just say 'oh'?'

He stayed silent. He didn't know what to say, and so he tried another one of his shrugs. Softer and more apologetic this time, but it made little impact. Detouring to Edinburgh might even mean delaying the launch of the boat until tomorrow. The boat master would freak out - and understandably so. He'd flown in from Queensland especially and all of his people had travelled up from Dorset for the unveiling; they would all need to be accommodated. The flights? The press? The pilot's hours? Landing permissions?

'Bloody hell, Richard, this is a fucking nightmare. And just because you want to watch a bit of golf?'

Another shrug. It was the best he could do.

'But you don't even like golf.'

Another shrug.

'Can you at least explain why?' she asked, anticipating the fury of the people stranded by a lake with a fifty million-quid boat itching to get wet.

'I don't know. It's just one of these feelings I get...'

She threw her hands in the air. He was famous for his

'hunches', but only his inner circle were aware of his paltry hit rate.

'Fine... we'll go to Edinburgh.'

'Good. Thank you - and I'm sorry.'

She wasn't interested in his apology and waved her hand in the air. 'To leave, when?'

He glanced back at her from his television. 'Now. We need to leave now.'

Her eyes widened and her aggressive demeanour shifted to somewhat defensive. She was imagining his helicopter pilot, who, when she'd left her room this morning, had still been comatose in her bed.

She fingered her phone. She had calls to make.

'And your wife?' she asked. But he shook his head without looking at her.

'She's in the spa, right?' he asked hopefully.

His PA consulted her clipboard and looked at her watch.

'Yes, currently, she's having her colon slooshed.'

'Oh, right, well no need to disturb that,' he said, grinning. 'We can always pop back for her if she really wants us to.'

'Fine.'

She slammed the door as she left; his phone rang. It was the call he'd been waiting for.

'*Richard. It's Peter. Okay, it's all set up. I've got a call in to a journalist who's coordinating at the course and I'll come back to you. But assume that it's on as we discussed - and if it's going to work, then you need to be wheels-up minutes ago.*'

The sixteenth hole was something of a special hole for Ricky. It'd been here yesterday where everything in his professional world had gone completely haywire. On the tee box, he and Marshall were deep in conversation.

Ben looked on with great interest. His dad was tutting loudly, tired of feeling excluded from whatever the hell was going on.

'What the hell is he doing now?' he asked Ben, but he was shushed rudely by his son. Eric looked to the skies, less than impressed and more than a little put out, which Ben obviously registered, because now he answered,

'They're talking. I think it's about his caddie.'

Eric sighed and shook his head. Completely bemused, he too, was having an extraordinary day. Seeing such drama and at such close quarters was exciting, but more noteworthy even was the odd behaviour of his son.

And he felt ashamed too since he was feeling sorry for himself. This was supposed to be a day out for them both, a father and son bonding day, but he could sense that he had become completely expendable. If any bonding was taking place it was between his son and a bizarre golfer, neither of them had ever heard of until today.

It was all completely mystifying, and any attempts to discuss it had been stonewalled. It was though Ben had something to hide. And so it had gone on; the eye contact, the little nods and gestures, and Ben's apparent and complete understanding of a situation that was mystifying to everyone else.

Even worse, he felt jealous - an ugly emotion anyway, but jealousy of his own son was particularly unpleasant. And his sense of isolation was compounded because he couldn't discuss it with anyone. Not with Ben, and certainly not with his wife who wouldn't understand such feelings at all.

He coped by settling on the idea that his jealousy was towards Ricky and this made good sense. Contesting the Open as he was. Playing like a God and captivating everyone he encountered. And, no doubt, a fat cheque and media interviews would follow his round, so why wouldn't an insurance broker from Torquay be a little green?

Ben was clearly besotted with him, just like he worshipped Lionel Messi - but there was something else here as well – somehow a connection between the two of them.

Suddenly he felt a movement in his hand. It was Ben grabbing for it, and his spirits soared. It was something that his son would not normally do in public, especially since there was a good chance of it appearing on television. Ben glanced up at him and gave his hand a little squeeze. It was timely and heartening - as though his boy understood his anguish and knew what he needed to do.

Guilt set in fast that he should ever have been so needy and putting himself first. But then Ben smiled at him. A smile of confidence and complete and utter happiness.

Eric smiled back and did everything he could do to quell his tears.

'Dad, everything is brilliant. Really, it is. Everything is fine.'

Eric's throat continued to swell and ache; he managed a brief nod to his son, and then he looked over to the remarkable golfer who was at the centre of it all. And now he too, smiled.

'It's time, son.' Marshall had said with his hands gently holding Ricky's elbows, and he half-smiled and nodded back at the tiny man before him.

It was not exactly an epiphany for Ricky, but he finally understood what was happening to him, if not the methods behind it. It was a lot to take in - overwhelming, in fact, which Marshall understood and seemed to acknowledge.

Ricky was a different golfer now. A completely changed man. He stared affectionately at the old man who had appeared from nowhere, and he thanked him silently.

Marshall had a mischievous glint about him. All around them was searing energy, with people calling Ricky's name and encouraging him onwards, but Ricky and Marshall were able to shut it all out for their special moment together. Perhaps even their final moment.

'Marshall, I... don't know what to say.'

Marshall just grinned. A smile that Ricky had grown very fond of over the last few hours.

'I've played Muirfield before, you know...,' Ricky began but then stopped himself, realising that Marshall already knew all about his last tournament here.

His throat tightened at the memory of his dad on the eighteenth green that Sunday all those years ago. He'd been struggling not to cry - and not because Ricky had lost his singles match in such cruel circumstances. And he could feel his dad's consoling bear hug, now, as he'd lifted his son off the ground, and he could hear the words he'd whispered into his dad's ear on that cold day and the promise that he had made him.

Ricky was crying now as he bent down to speak with Marshall.

'I do the Itsy Bitsys, you know?' he whispered. It was ridiculous thing to say, but he didn't care. 'With my youngest, just like Dad did with me.'

Marshall nodded knowingly, but he had a sense of urgency about him now.

Ricky wiped his face and he understood. What would he tell his wife and everyone else watching? Where would he even begin?

'Your dad is so proud of you,' Marshall said. 'So proud of you. And I've got to go now. But you know that, right?'

Ricky nodded as Marshall continued to hold him. 'So, son, you get on with what you've started here... and me and your dad, we'll be watching.'

And then Marshall released him. He let him go.

And the little old man was gone and this time, Ricky knew not to look around for him.

Most striking now was the silence as people looked on at the stricken golfer who was weeping openly and live on television for the billions watching. Fittingly for a man of seniority and wisdom, it fell to Peter Alliss to articulate what he saw.

'...well, now, this is all terribly sad, and something that many people have been predicting all morning. Ever since he arrived on the first tee in his kilt and without a caddie, we've been asking ourselves just what the dickens is going on and I think we can now see for ourselves.

'We've had doctors and psychiatrists speculating on whether Ricky Randal is having some sort of breakdown, and the R & A have been deliberating on whether he should even be allowed to continue with his round on medical grounds. Never mind any rules that he might have broken. But they allowed him to play on, no doubt affected by his splendid scoring, and it now seems that this might have been a mistake because the occasion and emotion has rather overcome the man, I'm afraid.'

'And what a sad end it would be if he is unable to continue. We've seen it at other tournaments, of course, but never at our Open Championship and never with so few holes to play and with such a prodigious score. It is really quite a unique set of circumstances we've seen here today. He's carried his own bag for the whole round, wearing a kilt, and he just happens to be seven under par. Remarkable, extraordinary. Utterly unique, I could go on. Where's a medic when we need one? Surely there's someone who can help him. Or a kindly steward to go and put an arm around him...'

St. John's Ambulance had been duly summoned and were charging to the scene, but nobody around the tee had the confidence to approach Ricky.

At the fifth hole, a local golf professional had offered to caddie for him, but he'd been told brusquely by Ricky that he already had a caddie, thank you very much. A line that had been quoted on many of the news bulletins and did much to feed the story of his mental incapacity and imminent breakdown.

Ben, though, understood what was happening - and he understood also exactly what he needed to do. Leaving his dad behind, he came forward and caught Ricky's eye; they smiled at one another.

Ricky was still processing his revelation, but he could see now that it was something that Ben had in shared also, to some extent, at least.

Ben smiled again, just as Marshall would have done. Ricky wiped his face and chuckled.

And then Ben took a club from his bag and handed it to Ricky - they both laughed. It was all the crowd needed. The relief was palpable.

Ricky looked up and nodded his assurances that he was all right, offering his thanks to the people who had followed him all morning and helped him so much without even realising it. Someone began clapping; the noise grew, and in a few seconds it became an almighty roar of encouragement.

Their man was not bowing out. Far from it. Their man was back.

Ricky smiled broadly, but pulled at his left shoulder again which suddenly ached and throbbed – no surprise, given he had hauled his own bag across the links. How odd it must have looked; a golfer carrying his own bag and chatting with someone that only he could see.

He looked to Ben for some assurance, which he duly received; it came as a relief. At least he hadn't imagined the whole thing.

He thought of Maggie again. He couldn't wait to see her. The ambulance screamed into view, but he quickly waved at the referee that it would not be needed. There was no break-down. Nothing to see here. Just a bizarre series of incidents which he would never be able to explain.

The cheering and clapping were now a continual roar, and even his playing partner and caddie were clapping as well.

A further quick glance at the on-course scoreboard, just to make sure that everything was in order, and now Ricky Randal was back and fully in the zone.

He stared at the hole ahead like a man possessed. Marshall had chosen this hole for a reason - because this was where the whole bizarre chain of events had started. He knew that now. A par-three that had cost him seven shots yesterday, and where he and Patrick had parted company.

Marshall had gone, but Ricky knew that he wasn't alone.

Noah was now having a similar moment or movement to the one that had overcome Ricky Randal outside the pro shop at the very beginning of the day. He was completely frantic, and without any idea what he could do to save himself - especially when the bloody golfer concerned was going to be interviewed on every media outlet once his round was finished. Urgently, he called his friend who had received the money, and who was most likely enjoying the golf along with everyone else.

'Tom. That money? You need to return it.'

'What? Why - what's happening?'

Noah shuddered at the horrible realisation that his old pal was complicit also in this theft; Jago would have him too, new dad or not. Noah couldn't think straight. His vision narrowed.

'Tom, you need to send it back. Just send it all back to the account where it came from. Do it now.'

'*Why, though? You said...*'

'I know what I said, Tom. *Fuck*. But it's all gone to shit.'

Noah's phone bleeped. The +001 was all he needed to see. A call from America - and a call he could not take. He had no answers for anyone. He rejected the call. It felt almost liberating, in the circumstances.

He stared at his TV screen. A woman was being interviewed, and under her face was a caption - **Chief Executive of Anthony Nolan.** And then in that instant, something occurred to him.

Maggie had torn around her house, grabbing whatever she might need, as the sleek black Audi purred outside and had curtains twitching all along the street.

Paddy had screamed that he needed to go with her - which probably had more to do with the mode of transport than the destination - and it was his granny's suggestion that she allow him to accompany her. There wasn't any time to deliberate. Paddy was helicopter-bound and he was beyond excited.

Maggie grabbed her keys, which she wouldn't need, and Paddy grabbed his plastic golf club.

'Tess, I'll call you.'

'Yeah, you'd better.'

'I will, I promise. Keep watching.'

Tess tutted and waved them off.

On the sixteenth tee, it seemed that Ricky, without Marshall now, was going to be tested immediately, as he watched his ball find the same greenside bunker that had been his undoing yesterday at this fiendish par-three.

It was a poor shot, and not what Ricky had expected.

He waited for Lee to fire his tee shot and was happy to accept the kind offer from Eric to carry his bag. Most likely, it had been Ben's idea and very welcome, too, because his shoulder continued to ache. Eric was delighted also, finally able to play a role he had craved all day, and he got a particularly big cheer the moment he got under the bag.

Peter Alliss was the first correspondent to notice that the cavernous bunker was not the only thing waiting for Ricky.

'...stone the crows and hold the front page but do you know what - if my eyes don't deceive me, isn't that Patrick Walsh standing greenside? The absent caddie of one Richard Randal. I think it is, you know...'

Daniel, the fledging television cameraman, was now urgently scanning the crowds surrounding the green as his director barked directions into his ear.

'...the caddie. His caddie. The mad fucking caddie is back'. Daniel, get a single on his bloody caddie, damn it, this could be awesome. They might even kick off...'

The television pictures jarred and shuddered for a moment, but nobody would complain once Patrick Walsh came into view. He looked resplendent in his kilt, complete with woollen socks and his black leather golf shoes.

Standing next to the bunker, he was staring towards the tee as Ricky approached with his bag finally being carried for him. Patrick was aware that he had now been identified and that it was highly probable that he was featuring on the telly at this very instant. And if onlookers were hoping for a contrite man with his tail between his legs, then they were disappointed. If anything, Patrick looked defiant and proud. He was certainly proud of what his man had achieved so far today - and he was excited to see him again.

Eric, too, was basking in the spotlight - and what an honour it was, he thought, that had been bestowed upon him. It was something he would dine out on for years and it was all because of Ben. He was pleased, though, that he only had two more holes to complete because the bag was mighty heavy - and he marvelled even more now at Ricky's remarkable achievement so far.

Ricky walked alongside him and continued to pinch at his throbbing left shoulder. It really hurt now. It might even have been the reason why he pulled his tee shot so badly. It was no bad thing that his round was nearly complete; level par from here would be a magnificent way to finish.

'...well, he certainly doesn't look like a man who's worried about being late for work. What the devil is he going to say? 'Sorry, boss, my alarm didn't go off.' It wouldn't surprise me if he's given short shrift here and told to clear off - with some vernacular, I shouldn't imagine, which I'm sure the BBC editors will be mindful of with the on-course microphones all over the place...'*

Ricky spotted Patrick from mid-fairway, and the precise moment was caught on camera by the steady and trusted camerawork of Daniel Colindale. But it was not the reaction that onlookers expected or even wanted to see. Everyone watching was perhaps a little disappointed to see Ricky smile broadly, and then break into laughter when he clocked Patrick's kilt.

Sure, the man had a lot of explaining to do; but Ricky suspected that, like him, Patrick wouldn't really know where to begin.

The crowd looking on all held their breath as Ricky got to the green, and the two men embraced each other like long-lost brothers. Ricky hadn't even yet looked at his ball and how it was lying.

'...well, well, well. Who'd have believed this? I really don't know what to say,' Peter Alliss mused on behalf of the nation.

'...*quite emotional, if you ask me, Peter.*' Wayne Grady chipped in. '*Two men who obviously love each other, hugging on live television...*'

Immediately the antennae of the BBC producers pricked up. Where was Wayne going this time? Not the gay lobby, surely, but their concerns, however, quickly passed.

'....*quite beautiful, if I'm honest with you. These two men have obviously been through something together, something only they can explain...*'

Anna Wade was now the busiest and most in-demand sports journalist on the planet. Her phone was bleeping constantly, and she fielded her calls judiciously.

'Dad. Hi. Can't talk now. No, I'm fine. Really. Everything is brilliant. I'll call later.'

Helicopters were airborne and all coordinated by her. She'd just got off the phone with the Chief Executive of Anthony Nolan, a bright and accommodating lady who was happy to be interviewed to discuss her charity's unlikely coup and explain the impact it might have on people afflicted with blood cancer and other blood disorders. Anna hadn't asked for exclusivity, but the chief executive suggested it herself.

'*I'm getting lots of calls, but I won't speak to anyone else, then - and I'll wait to hear from you, Anna?*'

This was unusual, given that Ricky's round was coming to a close, but it suited Anna and she had learned by now to trust events as they occurred. Her in-tray continued to fill up with gold. The charity, too, was having a bonanza of a day. Their media mentions and internet traffic were off the charts, which would inevitably lead to increased revenue and no doubt, people registering to donate their stem cells. Unbeknownst to him, but Ricky Randal was saving lives.

But what was really needed was a big signature donation to really kick things off.

Anna's phone bleeped. She answered it immediately.

'Anna Wade?' a man asked.

'Yes, speaking.'

'Ah, hello. You don't know me. My name is Noah Edwards...'

Anna smiled and grabbed a pen.

Ricky shifted in the sand, hovering his club just above and behind the ball. Eric had been immediately relieved of his duties, and he was quietly delighted. As excited as he was to have his role, he was also terrified of saying the wrong thing or - God forbid - suggesting the wrong club. Still, he'd been a caddie in the Open Championship. On the final day, no less, even if only for half a hole.

Patrick had grabbed the golf bag without even any discussion with the golfer himself. It was as if nothing had happened between them, and they both knew the roles they had to play. Just as though he was a little late for work and nothing more. *Bloody traffic.* He pulled out the 58-degree wedge, towelling the blade and the grip before handing it to his boss.

Yesterday, it had taken Ricky three attempts to extricate his ball from the very same bunker, and even when he'd finally managed to do so, it had been a poor shot and he'd needed three putts to get down. And then their confrontation had occurred - and the beginning of a chain of events that none of them could have ever predicted.

But with the pin placement for the final round, his final 'poor' bunker shot yesterday would be the perfect shot today, and this was something that Patrick had quickly seized on. It was a shot that had been played yesterday in anger. A petulant shot, borne out of frustration, and now Team Randal needed precisely the same result.

Patrick and Ricky eyed each other briefly but neither man said anything. They didn't need to.

'*...nothing at all would surprise me here. Apart from Ricky Randal getting out of the trap and then taking two putts for bogey, because that's what is supposed to happen...*'

Patrick picked up his bag and cleared out of his boss's eye-line - and moments later, Ricky splashed his wedge in to the crisp sand and his ball duly took flight.

Ricky replicated yesterday's swing precisely – albeit in such different circumstances - and his ball responded dutifully. It barely arced over the lip of the bunker and landed softly

eight or ten feet above the hole but with enough energy to roll out - and as soon as it started to advance, everyone watching willed it on in disbelief. Quickly, Ricky clambered back and out of the trap to get a view. Just in time to see arms all about the green thrown into the air, accompanied by yet another almighty roar.

Ricky rocked back and tossed his club high in the air. It twisted like the baton of a band leader and was ably caught by his trusted caddie.

Peter Alliss, John Inverdale, Phil Parkin and correspondents from all over the world floundered for superlatives at what they were seeing. Randal was eight under par with two holes to play - and now he had a caddie again, anything could happen.

Chapter Seventeen

Richard Randal, ENG -8
Open Championship + 5
26th Place
Prize Money € 109,037
17th Hole
578 Yards, Par 5

Patrick had a driver ready for his man on the penultimate tee; with nothing ahead, and the honour on their side, he was keen for Ricky to crack it away. It was such a contrast, he thought, to how they had behaved on this same small rectangle of grass just yesterday, when they hadn't been speaking and could barely look at one another.

Ricky swung the club a few times. He was thinking about Marshall and what he'd said about his father watching him. Recalling that length had been his dad's golf obsession provided him with a little more speed and zip to his drive, as he crushed his ball and watched it climb high and off into the distance.

Good enough for you, Dad?

It was a massive drive; his best of the day and put him in range for his second shot. His dad would be cheering.

Patrick murmured something positive, hitched the bag up onto his back, and the two men got on their way in a contemplative silence. They had much to catch up on - but where to start?

'And the kilt?' Ricky asked suddenly.

Patrick chuckled. 'Dunno. Solidarity, I guess? I didn't want you looking like this on your own.'

'No, good plan,' Ricky answered.

'And yours?' Patrick continued.

'Don't ask. Long story... but an explosion was involved.'

'OK... say no more. They're quite comfortable, though, right?'

'Oh, really? I haven't really thought about it. Been a bit busy, if I'm honest.'

'Crazy what's happened, though, huh?' Patrick offered almost glibly.

Ricky nodded, wondering what Patrick already knew or understood.

'You didn't see Marshall, then?'

Patrick shook his head. 'Marshall?'

'I've been carrying my own bag, right?' Ricky asked, a little tentatively.

'Yep. How's your shoulder?'

Ricky didn't answer as he pinched the aching muscle once more. His mind a flurry again; he imagined how odd this must have looked to everyone watching and the fuss it must have caused. He thought about the offer on the fifth hole from the assistant pro to caddie for him, and how he had sent him packing. And how the match referee had reacted on the first tee - particularly so when he'd introduced him to Marshall.

He recalled the referee's face at this specific moment, and

he laughed to himself. He looked over at the poor man who was still on his blinking radio and offered him a thumbs-up of his own as a kind of thank you for the support that he had shown.

'Patrick... this feeling you had?'

'Yeah. It wasn't explicit.'

'No.'

'I didn't hear voices or anything, although I did get a phone call. It was more just a feeling of... you know, just knowing what I had to do.'

Ricky nodded. It was all he needed to hear for now and they could catch up later. He was nearing his ball, and had a decision to make.

He glanced down at the loyal and ever-present Ben and leant down so that they could have a quiet word together.

'Hey, Ben. You saw Marshall, right?'

Ben smiled. 'Yeah, of course.'

'Good, that's good.' Ricky nodded. 'Just making sure I'm not as mad as everyone must think.'

Ben and Ricky chuckled together. When his round was over, they would need to sit down together, just the two of them.

And on reaching his ball, he realised that the fear was gone. He was living entirely in the present now, but he was a different man. He'd changed, and nothing would ever be the same again. Whatever other people couldn't see; Marshall had been real alright and so was his score.

And all he could think about now was Maggie, Tess and his boys.

The idea had come to Noah in a flash; it was an inspired move. Since he couldn't risk venturing on to the course again, Anna had agreed to meet him in the pub a little way along from the links. She had hardly any time and he needed to be quick and to the point - which was a shame, because he was easy company and she would have liked to stay. He looked lost and vulnerable and she liked the idea that she might be able to help him.

Anna had already pieced together what might really have happened to Noah, and that the £100,000 donation to Anthony Nolan from Silver Linings was, in fact, his GET OUT OF JAIL card. Whatever the motive, the money generously donated by the New York hedge fund would be gratefully received by a charity for its vital work.

She thanked him and explained that a press release would go out immediately. Then she smiled at him, shook his hand and handed him her card. He looked relieved and promised her that he would call her and she believed him.

And then she was gone; in her waiting taxi, and heading back to Muirfield, where she had much to attend to.

Noah breathed heavily.

Jago would still be after his scalp, but the donation would hopefully reduce his options - because he'd be unable to assassinate his ex-employee without undermining the sincerity of his generosity.

Noah thumbed her business card; thinking and pondering, and then grabbed for his phone to type out a text.

Thank you Anna. Enjoyed meeting you. I'll be in Edinburgh this evening. Perhaps we could hook up later and I could explain more fully what really happened? With you being a journalist, it might make an interesting story. Best, Noah.

He read the text again before sending it. Then he went back in and added a 'V' before 'Best'. More personal and heartfelt. He liked her. But anxious now, he read it yet again. The line about her being a journalist had been added so that he wouldn't come over as too forward, and so he wondered if he should delete it. He wanted her to register his interest but the Me-Too minefield nagged at him. How do people meet these days and stay within the law?

He added an 'x' after his name, and studied it again. Too pushy? Too girly, for sure, which is yet another can of worms to avoid. And so, he deliberated back and forth and fretted before concluding, so what. He no longer had a job he could be sacked from, plus he meant it, so the 'x' should stay. He wanted to be forward and his advances could always be spurned. Old school.

Thank you Anna. Lovely meeting you. I'll be in Edinburgh this evening. Perhaps we could hook up later and I could explain more fully what really happened? Might be fun and will certainly make for an interesting story. V best, Noah, X

He hit 'Send' and stared at his screen with an intoxicating sense of hope. Now the call from Jago was no longer the most important thing occupying his mind. His phone bleeped almost immediately, and his heart leapt.

Lovely. I'd like that. A X

Ricky and Patrick both stared at the golf ball, computing the distance that remained. Ricky had never attempted this green in two shots but he was going to now. The pin-prick green ahead was surrounded by a crowd eight deep, as was the fairway, lined with people on either side, and expectation hung heavy all around. If such scrutiny was making Ricky nervous, then he didn't show it. He had Patrick and Ben in place - and all-seeing-eyes above, as well.

'...he's going for it, as we all expected, and I would venture that this shot coming up, is perhaps the shot of his life, Wayne?'

'I guess so, Peter, but there's been so many already. Saved putts. His driver off the deck.'

'Very true. A round like no other, and I expect we'll never see it's like again. I hope not, anyway, because at my age I'm not too sure if it's been good for me. I have him making this shot, though. The shape is right and he has the power. We've seen that already. And he has the temperament as well, which we know for certain now because he hasn't killed his caddie...'

As yet, all broadcast journalists had managed to avoid mention of a certain number – specifically, fifty-nine. Every sport has its hallowed number. The 147 in snooker. The 9-dart check-out. The hat-trick in football. All very creditable, but they pale against the mark of fifty-nine in golf, a feat that does occur, but only rarely on the tour, never in a major championship, and certainly never on a Sunday.

Ricky clipped his ball off the surface with his two iron, flying it low and straight to keep below any breezes that the hole might have defending its honour ahead. Standing rock-solid with all his weight through and onto his left foot, he glared after his ball. He could not have hit it any harder - and it appeared that this was a good thing as it zoned in on its target, flirting with the traps but clearing them and bounding on.

Peter Alliss was quick to herald Ricky's efforts as the ball caught a kindly down slope, bounded on towards the green and finally crept tentatively onto the very front edge, like it was entering a party and didn't know anyone present.

'Clever shot. Using the terrain and accounting for the elements. A links master like the great Tom Watson would have been proud of a shot like that.'

Ricky slapped the outstretched hand of his caddie and breathed out hard. Risk and reward; and now yet another eagle putt beckoned and he had form at this mark.

Peter Alliss, meanwhile, had a note shoved under his nose

which made happy reading and was further good news for team Randal.

'*...and news just in, related to our man in the kilt and wearing the Anthony Nolan golf cap. I am delighted to be able to inform our viewers that in the last few minutes, the Anthony Nolan charity has received a donation of one hundred thousand pounds, which is very welcome news indeed, and I'm sure the good people there are overjoyed. Our source is that the donor is a chap called Jago Silver, so thank you, Jago, whoever you are... Strange things, these 'sources'. A source says? All very mysterious to me...*'

But not so mysterious to Anna Wade, who'd just got off the phone with a very excited marketing manager at Anthony Nolan; immediately afterwards, she took a call from ITV, keen to organise their exclusive interview but it wasn't the right time. She thanked them, but didn't commit, hung up, and looked at her watch and then to the skies.

Not long now. Her phone rang again but she didn't answer it. Her man, Ricky Randal, was on the green and she wanted to watch him putt. Everything else could wait.

In the media room, all eyes were on the big screen for his latest eagle attempt and people now expected him to hold it - but no one was more captivated by the action than Anna.

Somehow, she knew by now, that she'd become embroiled in the unfolding events for a reason. It was as though she'd been singled out by the remarkable story and appointed by it. Although, she didn't know why or how. So much was unexplained - and she reminded herself that she must warn her dad before she appeared on any television interviews as the official spokeswoman of Ricky Randal.

She checked her phone, just in case. Noah had texted her again.

· · ·

Jago sat with his lawyer and nursed his metaphorical bloody nose as they took stock of the situation; the damage and the potential upside. He'd been excited at the prospect of destroying Noah Edwards, but his ex-employee's latest move had both surprised and upset him.

It certainly had been devilishly smart. A move that showed cunning and an ability to think under pressure, which were precisely the qualities he needed from his people - and a possible reason to rehire the thieving son-of-a-bitch.

The coverage of his gift was also good, both live and online. His company, Silver Linings, had not been mentioned but his name had been, and in a positive light, so hurling the book at Noah made little sense. One of three PAs explained that his apartment had been signed off as safe by the authorities, but that Jago needn't bother getting back there just yet.

Then his phone beeped. A text from Noah.

JAGO. WHAT CAN I SAY? BBC JUST MENTIONED YOU. LATER PM I'M MEETING WITH MEDIA HANDLER. WILL MAKE SURE THE GLORY IS YOURS AND IT WILL BE BARGAIN PR FOR 100K. NOAH.

Jago bristled. The absence of an apology was glaring, but another of his own mantras occurred to him; *never explain and never apologise*. It rankled being outmanoeuvred by the little shit – but still, he did have a point. And he could use some good press for a change.

He decided not to reply, which was as much as letting Noah know he'd got away with it.

Morag McKinnie practically spat her false teeth out across her lounge in Dundee when she heard the name on the BBC - and by the venerable Peter Alliss, no less. Jago Silver. It had to be the same Jago Silver. How many Jago Silvers could there be?

'The freakin cheet-en bass-tard.'

Morag was barely able to breathe; she had a long memory and had been waiting for her chance since 2007 to avenge any of the protagonists involved with the collapse of Scotland's Royal Bank and particularly the twelve thousand shares she had accumulated and still owned over a career spanning thirty years working for the bank, and on which she had planned out a comfortable retirement. But along with the highly qualified 'expert' economists, Morag had not foreseen the financial melt-down of 2008, which put paid to her plans as her lifesavings practically vanished. From almost £70 per share to less than a £1 at their lowest before her tearful eyes and although some careers had been extinguished, no one was deemed guilty of any crime. Billions of pounds simply evaporated. Salted away from ordinary people and yet not a single days jail-time for any of those responsible.

Morag had been left bereft - but at least then she had a new purpose to her life. She became an expert online campaigner, representing people less able than her and vowing to expose those responsible for decimating their savings.

She twiddled her fingers impatiently as her computer laboured into life. Although now, it felt less computer and more like a machine-gun loading; the crosshairs came sharply into focus now, and so did her target.

Jago Silver had long been on her radar, but he'd proved to be one of the many untouchables. Using her knowledge and some judicious google searches, she quickly pieced things together and then a further internet search provided the name Anna Wade. Fully zoned in now, Morag, she fired off a pithy email.

We need to talk about Jago Silver. I can help you take this thief down. Call me...

Ricky and Patrick had the line of the putt now. A foot outside the left, and firm to account for the break, which was more shallow than it looked. The birdie was assured, but Ricky had become much greedier now - and why not? It was that kind of a day.

Patrick surveyed the line again, looking for any imperfections, but there were none. The green staff had been busy and his man was good to go.

'Firm, Rick. Just roll it clean and firm.'

Patrick waited until Ricky replaced his ball exactly on their agreed line, and he had picked up his dad's marker before clearing out of the way.

There was absolute silence surrounding the green. Ricky set up square, placing his club behind the ball. He glanced at the target, took a beat to settle himself, and then stroked his ball on its way.

The crowd cheered immediately, roaring his ball on, as Ricky and Patrick stood motionless. The line was good as the ball began to take the camber and track towards the hole. A little pacey, though. It certainly wasn't going to be short.

The ball hit the edge of the cup at speed and was flung off its course, finishing eight feet to the right, and the crowd groaned their disappointment as Ricky held his head and Patrick pulled his hand through his hair. Close then, but no eagle - and the birdie was no certainty either.

Ricky quickly marked his ball and lined up his birdie putt. Eight feet.

He marched back and forth to get a good view but with some haste now but he didn't know why. Just felt right. He bunched down on to his haunches to peer over his ball one more time.

'Half a ball off the right?'

Patrick nodded but said nothing.

Two quick practise shots and then he sent his ball on its way. He heard it drop before he saw it fall. The crowd roared once again. Yet another shot gained and his extraordinary ascent up the leaderboard continued.

Ricky had just one hole to go - and he couldn't wait.

Chapter Eighteen

Richard Randal, ENG -9
Open Championship + 4
19th Place
Prize Money €141,339
18th Hole
473 Yards, Par 4

The headphones practically subsumed little Paddy's entire head, but he insisted on wearing them as soon as he clambered on board. He'd seen helicopters on television, and the passengers always wore headphones.

Maggie was much less happy about the thought of anything touching her head. During the short car journey she'd done her best with her hair, and now she wanted it left alone. She sat at the back of the private craft and worried about the next hour and what it might hold.

Anna had arranged it all, explaining that she would be there to meet them at Muirfield. This was strangely reassuring, given that she'd never met this woman before, and had only spoken to her a couple of times. But she'd sounded confident. The sort of person who was always in complete control, and so now here was Maggie, thousands of feet in the air, looking down - which felt appropriate because someone was certainly smiling down on her Ricky today.

And long may it continue, she thought.

She glanced down at the green patchwork quilt below and thought of Ricky. He'd been on the fifteenth when they'd taken off, and she prayed that she might be there to see him finish. His face would be a picture, she thought wistfully.

She snapped photographs with her phone, mostly of Paddy with his thumbs up and smiling like a maniac, and everything else from the ground upwards. *What a bloody day.* Ricky had said as much. As soon as he'd qualified for the Open, he'd promised her that it would be special, and that he would make her and his dad proud. But she hadn't really believed him at the time, and felt a little ashamed now.

The excitement of making the cut had been terrific, but it had soon faded once his third round started to disintegrate - and now here she was, in a private helicopter chartered especially for her by one of the world's most famous entrepreneurs. *What a bloody day!*

Instinctively, she pushed her hair up again. She didn't know what was more exciting; seeing her husband finish his round or meeting the man himself, who apparently was on his way in his own helicopter, travelling from a castle retreat in Scotland.

Maggie pulled strands of hair over her fringe and used the window as a mirror as best she could. With no time to spare, she'd grabbed whatever make-up she had to hand. It had all been pretty garbled, but Anna had explained that because this was Sir Richard's idea, not to mention that he was paying for it, then it could be that their meeting would be filmed. Maggie gulped and pushed at her hair again.

Anna went on to say that because publicity was his oxygen, the press would most likely be there in force - but not to worry, because Anna would be there also. And as assured as she sounded, no doubt, handling the press was her thing.

Michael Landale had been canvassing opinion from close sentries, and the consensus was that he should concede defeat, although none of them put it quite like this. Strictly speaking, it was agreed that Randal could be docked shots - for disobeying orders of the referee, if for nothing else. But under the circumstances nobody thought this would reflect well on the fuddy-duddy R&A.

For Landale, this was a particularly bitter pill to swallow. The public were certainly on Ricky Randal's side and there was no disputing the magnificence of his round. Worse yet, it had been confirmed now that the man's wife was indeed pregnant and was en-route to the bloody course. The whole thing was surreal. Like a freaking Disney film. He groaned.

'Michael, I think it's the best play. Really, I do,' a colleague wittered on. 'Not that we are condoning his behaviour. His dress code violations. But certainly, we should embrace the man and the golfer. The man and his journey.'

'The man and his journey,' Landale spat. 'His fucking journey?' He loathed clichés. 'What are we, writing a fucking novel here?'

'No, but it's a round of golf that's going to go down into legend. The caddie-less golfer shooting the lights out. The ultimate underdog coming good - and I just think that the R & A is better served if we are a part of it. But woe betide the next golfer who ever tries such a thing.'

Bitter though it was, it made sense. Landale rubbed his eyes.

'We'd explain to the press that that you never approved, but that you were always supportive and privately, that you wished him well-'

Another of his aides stepped in now with a more measured, and altogether more English, approach.

'Michael. It's the sensible and pragmatic line. But by all means, tear a strip off the little bastard when you get him alone.'

The aide gently nodded to the clock and eased open the door of the office.

Another thing that they'd agreed on was that Michael and his officials should be on the eighteenth green to see the man home. It was just a lob wedge away - and given the interest in his concluding round, they had better hurry.

Ricky stood on the eighteenth tee in something of a daze. His entire career came down to this day and the final hole ahead. He knew this now. He understood.

How many golf shots had he played to get here? Millions. Too many to ever quantify - but they all counted. Every shot had contributed to where he now stood, on the final tee box at the Open Championship with the chance to shoot a score that would go into the record books.

His head had cleared now, and the haze had shifted. He still had more questions than answers, but at least now he knew why it was all happening.

He watched yet another helicopter coming in to land. A familiar sight at The Open, with a constant stream of dignitary's toing and froing; he lingered on this particular bird however, with more interest and wondered idly who it might be conveying.

The long narrow patch of raised turf at the eighteenth tee was cordoned off on three sides with banked seating, and not a spare seat, such was the fevered interest surrounding Ricky and his caddie. Not a vantage point was left empty anywhere. Similarly, the fairways were lined with people eager to get a view of the world's most infamous golfer and so too on the green ahead, where anticipation and hope hung equally heavy.

Ricky graciously accepted the applause, doffing his golf cap, and when he pulled out his driver, this received another, by now, familiar cheer. All eyes were fixed on him; the tee box felt like a pressure cooker, and a decent drive was the valve that was needed.

Patrick, being a latecomer to the Ricky Randal Show, was rather overwhelmed by it all, and grateful that he was a caddie and not the player who needed to hit the shot. In his youth, he'd played off scratch and better, and had even flirted with turning pro himself, but now he realised that he'd been wise not to bother. He could hardly imagine how Ricky was coping.

'Hey, Ricky - you good?'

Ricky didn't reply, his chest pounding.

'This is all a bit different, huh?'

Patrick chuckled. 'Yeah, tell me about it. Some contrast to yesterday, eh?'

Ricky smiled.

'You're good, though, right?' Patrick asked, unable to mask his anxiety.

'When I get this one away, I will be. So, what do you think? Right side?'

Patrick nodded. 'Yep, that's it. Anywhere right. Two eighty. Two ninety. I tell you what, two seventy will be fine. No need to smash this one any further. An easy swing. Just like you've been doing all day.'

Ricky recalled his first tee shot and smiled to himself.

Ricky looked ahead over the channel of land, lined on both sides with his ardent fans. It would be a spectacular walk. But as much as he wanted to savour these moments, the highlight of his professional life, he couldn't wait to get it over with either.

Anna Wade was standing by the VIP tent, a little away from the landing site. Sir Richard had arrived already; she'd greeted him graciously and with great poise and purpose.

As he'd come in to land, his spirits had soared. He'd eyed the hordes of people and press that were waiting for him. This was going to be a triumph - he could feel it in his bones.

He'd shaken Anna's hand and was immediately taken by her. She was clearly efficient. But she was confident, too, and self-assured. When people first encountered him, they were often nervous and anxious to please - but not her, which was refreshing and even something of a challenge. It was no surprise to him that she'd collared the big sports story of the day, and would be handling all things Ricky Randal post-round as well.

Her phone rang as she was updating him, and he was happy to be interrupted. Clearly she was a busy lady with much to do.

'Hi, Morag... yes, I have this covered. I have a meeting scheduled with the chairman, and I'll put that to him. And I've drafted an email to Mr Silver, which I'm running by a lawyer now. But it'll have to wait until later, because I have matters here to attend to, I'm afraid...'

Anna watched the second helicopter hover a foot or two

before finally reconnecting with earth. Mrs Randal had arrived, and Anna knew precisely what to do.

Ricky's drive on eighteen was short of his best, but it drew rapturous applause nonetheless.

He put his driver away for the last time today. It felt like a tremendous relief. The club had been formidable and it deserved a rest as much as he did. Adrenaline coursed through his system. His lack of sleep and weary shoulder were both forgotten now – he'd never felt quite so alive.

'Well, remarkable scenes here on the eighteenth at Muir-field. Scenes we expect to see for the final pair and the year's Champion Golfer elect... but what we have here is the people's champion in Ricky Randal. Whatever he makes from here - whether he makes a birdie or even has a double - nothing would surprise me now. Not after what I've witnessed today.'

The crowds were enormous and loud, without a space to be had on either side of the fairway. It had been a good idea to invite Ben and his dad inside the ropes, otherwise they would certainly have been lost.

Ricky doffed his Anthony Nolan cap and smiled; people were shouting his name and calling for his attention, and he was happy to oblige.

'...well, wonderful stuff. Really wonderful and thoroughly deserved. Do you know, it reminds me of that time at Royal Birk-dale and the finish of a certain young Justin Rose. Just an amateur, then, of course. When was it? 1998? I can't recall. Someone will tweet in, I'm sure. Anyway, golf fans will all recall young Justin, a slip of a lad who happened to finish fourth that year.'

'And when the young lad marched up the eighteenth, he

looked almost overwhelmed by the reception he was getting. He practically smiled at each spectator individually, and I tell you what? The way that Justin finished that day, in with his third for a birdie? What our Ricky wouldn't give for that now. He'd be signing his card for a sixty one - which would be, without a doubt, the most remarkable round of golf in Open Championship history...'

The news of the special passenger on the inbound helicopter had been first picked up by BBC Radio 5 Live, and John Inverdale was charged with sharing such exciting news with the nation.

'...thank you. That was Anna Wade, spokeswoman for Sir Richard, who has himself just arrived here at Muirfield. Goodness me, it's all happening today. And as we heard there from his spokeswoman, that he's also arranged for Ricky's wife, Maggie to be flown here for what I am sure, will be a very emotional reunion here on the 18th green of this famous links.

Anna got back to Sir Richard quickly and efficiently.

His personal assistant was clearly deeply aggrieved at being usurped - and was keen to reassert herself.

'All press requests from now on,' she snapped, 'like that radio grab, will need to come through...'

Anna raised her hand to stop her and she kept her gaze on her new boss.

'There will be no more press for now.'

Richard grinned easily.

'With time as it is,' Anna continued, authoritatively, 'I suggest for now just a photo with Maggie but no questions.'

'Yes, thank you,' this angry PA snarled. 'But I think you'll find that I'll decide...'

Anna shook her head and raised her finger also for good

measure. She was a completely different woman now and didn't have time for a hurt ego.

'I expect Maggie will be quite anxious about speaking to the press,' Anna explained, 'and she'll want to watch Ricky finish, of course - which is the money shot, after all.'

Richard readily agreed. *Whatever you decide, Anna.*

'So we need to get going. The eighteenth is just this way.'

Maggie needn't have worried about any headphones messing with her hair - because the overhead rotors took care of this completely, forcing her coiffure as flat as a mortarboard.

Instinctively, she crouched down low and clutched at an exhilarated Paddy as Anna greeted them, ushering them both to a private area - which turned out not to be so private after all, because the world's press were waiting for them, along with a beaming billionaire.

She thanked him immediately, accepting his warm embrace as though they were old friends, and the photographers clicked into action, calling out for another kiss and a wave from the pair of them.

And then it was time to get going. Ricky was about to play his approach to the final green.

Sir Nick Faldo had joined Peter Alliss in the commentary box now, and was happy conceding that he'd called it wrong.

'... *it just goes to show why golf is such a wonderful game. Every golf pro - or every tour pro, at least - is capable of extraordinary shots and can knock it round in a very low number when it doesn't count...*'

'*But what if the stars align and these wonder shots all pile up, one after another? I'm talking Oosthuizen's albatross at Augusta. Rocca's putt at St. Andrews. Casey's tee shot at the Ryder Cup, or*

Clarke's for that matter. That they come all at once, and then what you have is alchemy. It's pure gold. Which is precisely what has happened today to Ricky Randal. It began with everything going wrong. His trousers. His caddie. His bogey-bogey start - and yet everything since then has gone so, so right...'

Peter Alliss murmured his agreement, but he had some concerns as well, and he was quick to interject his timely wisdom.

'Well I wouldn't say that just yet, because he's not quite finished. He's still got hopefully just one more iron shot to play, and then we can genuinely start to celebrate. Assuming he doesn't five putt, of course. I saw a player from Japan yesterday - can't remember his name, which is probably a relief for the poor fellow, because he took an eight here and should a similar fate befall our Ricky now...'

The cheering finally abated once Ricky reached his ball; by the time he was ready to play, there was complete silence.

He waggled his four iron gently, feeling the breeze and imagining the shape of the shot that was called for. The flag was cut on the left of the green, and Ricky's tee shot gave him a good angle of attack. Anywhere on the green would do.

Patrick checked his yardage book again and affirmed the club selection. He had it right on the limit of Ricky's range and this was a good thing.

'You can give this a real whack, Rick. Full swing and right through it.'

Ricky understood. He nodded and brushed the grass with his practice swing. He clipped the turf perfectly as thoughts of Marshall and his dad continued to drift through his mind.

Just one more shot, Dad.

Ricky softened his arms, loosening his hands and edged his club to nestle behind his ball. He breathed in softly, before drawing his club away, before beginning his downswing and firing his ball off into the distance.

Immediately, Patrick shouted, 'Go', which might have indicated that it was short - but soon the cheers from ahead began and washed down the channel towards them both. They came as a wonderful relief.

His ball bounced a little short, but it had enough energy to continue its path onto the green. Not the shot that Justin Rose, the amateur, had managed but it was good enough. He and Justin had always been on different golfing trajectories; it was something he'd long accepted. But he was on the green, and this suited him perfectly.

Two putts for the best round of his life and the lowest round in Open history? He'd need to check that latter assertion, but the former was not in any doubt at all.

'...well done. That'll do. Club short, perhaps, but on the green, with thirty, thirty-five feet to complete what will be a sensational and, I suggest, a truly unique round of golf...'

The walk ahead to the green was euphoric; the greatest walk of Ricky's life. The people were cheering him all the way. He raised his cap and smiled broadly at both sides of the fairway.

It was overwhelming anyway, but particularly so given who he now understood was responsible for his day. He thought of his dad, and even scanned the crowds in the hope of seeing him. A single tear dropped down Ricky's beaming face.

'Bloody hell, Ricky,' Patrick said amidst the mayhem. 'Soak this up, mate. Soak this up.'

'Mad, eh?'

'Bonkers.'

'What must we look like?' Ricky said, looking down at their kilts. They both laughed.

'It's your day, as well, you know?' he added, glancing at his trusted caddie. 'But you know that already, right?'

Patrick nodded; he gripped Ricky's hand and thrust it aloft. A little premature, perhaps, but the onlookers didn't seem to mind, given the further roar that it inspired.

'So... when you say you weren't alone?' Patrick said, a little seriously. 'You know, back on seventeen?'

Ricky stared at his caddie intently now.

'Yeah, I did say that - but I didn't say I could explain it.'

'No... but you don't need to. I get it. I think.'

Ricky thanked him quietly.

'Strangest and best day of my life,' Patrick said.

'And it isn't over yet. Who knows what's next?'

'You in front of Michael Landale, I should imagine.'

Ricky continued to wave and smile for the crowds. 'And you just had this feeling, right? This peculiar feeling?'

'Yep. Soon as I woke up. Weird. Like nothing I'd ever experienced before. And somehow I just knew what I needed to do.'

Patrick laughed and Ricky joined him as they continued towards the green. The cheering continued, and even swelled.

'I could get used to this,' Patrick mused but Ricky looked a little doubtful.

'Then you might need another bag,' Ricky said, 'because I've a feeling that this could be my lot. And I can't see you getting on Adam Scott's bag after today's no-show.'

Patrick roared at this – and Ricky did, too.

The green, when they reached it, was surrounded by brand new Ricky Randal fans - along with a few special people to whom he owed everything.

He stepped on to the shorn grass to rapturous applause; taking off his cap, he turned full circle, waving warmly at everyone.

Marking his ball with his dad's coin, he then looked back up to take it all in - and in particular, those people within the ropes. Daniel was in precisely the right place, as he had been all day, to capture the moment when Ricky set eyes on his wife, Maggie.

He smiled broadly, and gave her and little Paddy his thumbs-up as the cameras whirred all around him. He should have been astonished to see his wife and child - but he wasn't, of course. Nothing could surprise Ricky now.

Maggie looked lovely, but completely overwhelmed, which was understandable. She was standing with a woman who Ricky assumed was Anna Wade. A woman he'd never met - and yet he knew her name, and what she looked like, and that she was in charge from here on in.

He bid Anna a polite hello, which she returned. They'd have much to organise between them later, not to mention trying to make sense of their respective days. But for now, Ricky continued his search for the other people he needed to acknowledge.

Marshall was leaning against a golf cart - perhaps tired after the exertions of his day - and standing next to him was his dad. Only now, his dad looked as he should. He was old – just how he'd looked when Ricky had last seen him.

He smiled, and his dad beamed back at him. Here he was at the Open Championship after all, his lifelong ambition, just as they'd promised each other all those years ago. His father had a mischievous glint in his eye; he looked happy and proud of his only boy. He held his thumb up and Ricky waved back at him.

The driver of this particular golf cart who was sitting alone, was naturally bemused that he should hold the attention of the golfer on the eighteenth green - especially when his wife and child were greenside. He waved back tentatively and Peter Alliss, too, was rattling around for answers.

'I don't know who that is in the golf cart. Must be someone

Ricky knows, I guess, and a very nice touch too. But he has matters to attend to now. Plenty of time to catch up and glory in what has just happened. But the round is not yet over - and a couple more blows will be very good indeed...'

Just off the green, Ben and Ricky were having a hushed conversation. Ben explained his idea, and Ricky nodded without any hesitation. It was an excellent plan.

Quickly, Ben made his way over to Maggie, with his ever-clueless and bemused dad in tow. He introduced himself to her; she hugged him warmly as though they'd known each other for years. Eric got a formal handshake and no more - and crucially, nothing approaching an explanation either.

Anna grabbed Ben's hand and squeezed it tightly.

'Ben, this day isn't over, you know,' Anna whispered.

'I know. Marshall explained it to me.'

Anna nodded gently. Who was Marshall, she wondered?

'I can't wait to tell my mum.'

Ben responded, and then he moved on to the next grinning spectator.

'Hi. I'm Richard...'

Ricky pulled his cap down hard. It was a way of putting everything and everyone out of his mind so that he could concentrate on his final two shots.

He cupped the peak of his cap with his hands, focusing only on his ball and the flag. Nothing else.

Patrick paced the putt again. Two balls outside right, he was thinking, but neither man had said anything to each other just yet. A hush fell on the green. All eyes were on Ricky – if occasionally darting back and forth to his wife and to the driver of an empty golf buggy, who had some explaining to do.

Ricky continued to stare at his ball. He was standing on the biggest stage in the world of golf. A stage which, in all likelihood, he would never grace again.

'...well, dare I say it, but if this were to go in... it'd get him to three over for the Championship. A share of fourteenth place and a place at next year's Open...'

'What are you thinking, Pat?' Ricky finally asked.

'Two balls outside right. You?'

Ricky grimaced a little, unsure himself.

He looked over to the golf buggy again. His dad and Marshall were laughing raucously – and, it seemed, without a care in this world. He wondered if he could appeal for some guidance from either man, but it appeared not.

'Why?' Patrick asked, as he started to look again. 'You think less?'

But Ricky was not sure at all. 'I don't know. Maybe more. Depends on speed, right?'

Patrick looked anxious now. The speed was crucial, of course, but he didn't want to put any doubts in his man's mind. At such a juncture, it was better to let the golfer follow his own instincts - and so he surprised himself by piping up again.

'No, Ricky, two balls right. No more. Two balls and firm. That's it.'

Ricky processed this information, considering the logic. It was good that Patrick was being emphatic. His dad and Marshall remained deep in their banter by the golf cart and were no use to him whatsoever - and so he needed someone to take responsibility.

'OK then. Line me up.'

Ricky set up with Patrick crouched behind him. He waved his club backwards and forwards to get a feel for the weight, and then he nudged his blade in to position so Patrick could get the line. He squeezed his left eye shut to get a better focus.

'Fraction left...'

Obediently, Ricky adjusted his club.

'...smidge more. That's it. Right there. Hit that.'

Ricky breathed in slowly. He imagined the roll, and as he exhaled he passed his club across his body and felt his ball moving away, his head remaining still. He closed his eyes.

His entire day was racing through his mind. The most incredible day, which he'd started on his own, and would finish with his wife and dad looking on, and his mum back home watching on the telly.

By the time he opened his eyes, the roar from the crowd had already started. Everyone watching knew from six feet out where the ball was heading.

It was as though it was on rails, and Patrick was the first person to leap into the air. It was his read, after all, and it was the perfect end to his perfect round.

As the ball disappeared, hands were thrust into the air. The roar was deafening, like an aircraft blasting off. Ricky held his face and made no gestures of euphoria at all. His shoulders slumped at the relief of it all. He looked to the golf buggy again but already knew that it would only be the bemused driver there now.

Patrick grabbed him by the waist with both arms and lifted him high into the air, and when he landed, he turned to see his wife and little boy rushing towards him. Ricky hurried to meet them, conscious that Lee had yet to play - plus there was the little matter of the entire field behind him also.

Paddy was beaming at his dad and suddenly began his Itsy Bitsy dance, punching his little arms out to each side and thrusting his hips back and forth. Ricky laughed at the little man as he scooped him up into his arms; and he kissed Maggie as she arrived.

Anna held back to allow the family a little time to themselves, as freelance photographers tried to get the shot that would be appearing on websites across the world within seconds.

'*...ten under and sixty-one. Oh my Lord. And other than that, I really don't know what else to say - which is a problem for a chap like me, I suppose. But what does one say about this young man, Richard Ricky Randal...*'

Ricky waited for his playing partner to putt out for yet another bogey, and then he took off his cap and shook his hand warmly and embraced him. The young golfer looked shocked at his own collapse - but even more so at what he'd seen at such close quarters.

'Wow, man, what just happened out there?' he asked.

Ricky just shrugged. It was a perfectly reasonable question, one which the whole world would require him to answer. But this was something that Anna would have to figure out for him - and until then, everyone would just have to wait.

Ricky shook Anna's hand and they formally introduced themselves to each other.

'If you sign your card,' Anna said, '...and then we can make some plans.'

Ricky nodded. Neither of them felt any need to explain themselves.

'*...we're going to try and get a word with Ricky Randal just as soon as we can and when we do, we will bring it to you immediately...*'

As he walked to the scorer's tent, Ricky shook hands with Sir Richard; they had a brief and incoherent conversation that didn't make much sense to either man.

Ricky was being pushed from all sides now. He needed to get to the scorer's hut but before that, he still had one matter to attend to. He smiled at young Ben, reached for his cap and handed it to him.

'I take it, that this was only a loan?'

Ben laughed. 'Actually, yes. It's my lucky cap.'

Now Ricky laughed too. 'Your lucky cap?'

'I can get you a new one,' Ben beamed. They give them to me for nothing and they have a new design now, anyway.'

Ricky smiled. 'But maybe I should have that one back just for a little while longer... in case I get to do any interviews.'

Anna's phone continued to beep and hum for her attention but she felt no need to answer anyone's calls just yet. For now, everyone could wait - even Noah.

Rather fittingly, Justin Rose was present as well, adding to the sense of excitement. Justin had already explained on-air about their unusual exchange earlier in the day, but now he wanted to congratulate his old friend personally and was not giving any further interviews with his tee time fast approaching.

Ricky emerged from the scorer's tent and spotted Justin immediately. They smiled at each other and warmly embraced.

'You know that feeling I was talking about?' Justin began, steering his friend away from any journalists and their prying microphones.

'You called it right, then,' Ricky chuckled, suddenly exhausted now.

'Er, yeah, I'd say so. Sixty-one! Dude, what the hell just happened, man?'

'Jeez, man, who knows? I can't explain it. I wish I could.'

'Well, it was unbelievable. No one can quite believe it. Carrying your own bag. The get-up. Jesus, hitting driver off the deck? Seriously, man, what the fuck?'

'I know. I wish I knew, honestly.'

Ricky left it at that, happy to leave it all oblique.

'And hey - go well today, Justin. You shoot par and I figure it might be enough.'

'Yeah, so ten shots worse than you and I get to win?'

Justin Rose, the world-famous golfer, raised his open hand above his head and the two pro golfers high-fived for a photo that would go around the world - and become even more valuable after Rose duly delivered a round of level par and was announced as the year's Champion Golfer, one shot better than Ricky Fowler and the new golfing star, Tommy Fleetwood.

Epilogue

Ricky finished the Open Championship having accumulated all sorts of records - as well as a cheque for €207,663, his highest purse ever and more money than he had won over the previous three years.

His twelfth place finish was enough to get him into the next year's championship, which Ricky accepted would be his last. He just wasn't a good enough player to play with the elite golfers - not without his dad's help, anyway, and this was not something that he could count on.

But his story and the impact of his round continued to reverberate long after the Open had finished.

The interview Ricky gave to the BBC shortly afterwards with John Inverdale wasn't terribly enlightening, but it was the best he could do. It was much simpler than telling the truth, anyway. That he did have a caddie. That he was called Marshall, but that only two people could see him, and that his deceased father had been present as well.

His round was confirmed as the lowest ever in Open history. The lowest ever in any major championship. The greatest climb up a leaderboard. The most eagles in any one round at a major championship. The lowest round ever with three bogeys on the card. And so it went on – and, of course, the only golfer to carry his own bag on any PGA tour event, and the only golfer to ever wear a kilt. The round immediately went into legend; it was quickly coined The Miracle at Muirfield, and Ricky's bounty continued to grow under the careful and skilful stewardship of his public relations manager, Anna Wade.

Anna offered a little more explanation during her live interview for Sky News later the same day. She talked about Ricky's family and their importance to him, and how elated they all were, of course. And she alluded to Ricky's father, and how the memories of his dad and the promise that they had made to each other had been playing large in his mind all day. It was an evocative image, and the man's mystique only grew.

Michael Landale had to lick his wounds. He gave an interview through gritted teeth and gave up any ideas he had of tearing a strip off Randal when Anna introduced herself to him. She looked somewhat familiar, and he was aghast when she reminded him of their buggy ride earlier in the day. She certainly didn't look sick anymore - and he eyed her narrowly, recalling his rather crude pass at her. Anna smiled at him coolly - she did not need to suggest that he leave her man alone.

Over the next week, Ricky was interviewed in twenty-three magazines worldwide, featuring on twelve covers sporting a brand new Anthony Nolan golf cap - and with such coverage, the sponsorship deals cascaded his way. Everyone, and every company, it seemed, could not get enough of Ricky Randal. Banks, cars, insurance companies, airlines, pharmaceutical giants and retail Goliath's; they all wanted in and Anna made hay on his behalf.

But Anna and Ricky both understood that the story was

ever-evolving, and was about to dwarf anything that he had achieved with his clubs - and it was fitting that Anthony Nolan should become Ricky's banner sponsor, which shed further light on their lifesaving work.

As much as Ricky's life had changed that day, it paled by comparison to the life-changing event that Sunday 16th July had been for Ben Costello. After the Open, Ben, too, was in great demand from the media and he featured prominently, speaking confidently and bravely about his condition and his need for another bone marrow transplant as his only chance of survival.

Anthony Nolan matches people on their donor register with patients in need of a transplant - and it follows that the bigger their register, the more lives they can save. Tom Holland, a young actor and famous for his role depicting Spider-Man, was already something of a figurehead for the charity in their hope to encourage young men to join the register, and now he and Ben made a further recruitment video which reached over twenty million people within its first month alone. Donors and funds poured in, including a registration from one Daniel Colindale, a young man who had graduated from trainee cameraman to seasoned operative in a single day at Muirfield.

This was all very heartening and exciting, but the euphoria surrounding Ben's newfound celebrity was quickly overshadowed once his disease reasserted itself, just as his doctors had warned it would. He was forced to curtail his fundraising activities, and within a month he was back in his familiar hospital ward. His team now explained that his condition was going to worsen over the next few months – and the unspoken implication was that his next destination would be a hospice, rather than coming home. His mum wept with anger and hurt. Eric felt impotent and helpless, quite in spite of Ben's chirpy demeanour and insistence that everything was going to be well.

Daniel Colindale was not surprised to receive a call from Anthony Nolan just a few months after he had submitted his sample of saliva and given how gravely ill the young patient was who he was a match for, he agreed to fly home from Seattle where he was covering an extreme sports event for Sky Sports.

Daniel's genetic match was as close as it could be, and Ben's doctors were excited to share the remarkable news with Ben and his family. But even though it was a closer match than the donation Ben had previously received, the medics still advised caution.

By now, Ben's mum was a wreck with the anxiety and hope that came with the news, and Eric did his best to support her - while Ben continued to smile brightly and assure everyone that he was going to be fine. It was all just as Marshall had explained.

Ricky was in constant touch, and on the day of the transplant, he charged down the M5 with Anna to be with his most important fan.

The doctors ran some immediate tests and explained that they wouldn't have any news for two to three weeks. His mum could not stem her tears and continued to call upon whichever deity would listen. Ricky sat with Ben by his bedside, and they chatted about things that only they could share with each other.

Twelve months later and following more positive tests, the doctors finally gave the Costello family the news that they had all been waiting for - apart from their son, who knew everything already. The reality was that the young man was still dying, but only as the rest of us are with each passing day. Ben was in remission.

Two weeks after the Open Championship, Ricky was contacted by a certain Barry Singleton. Anna had fielded thousands of calls and requests for Ricky's time, but they both agreed that Barry was someone Ricky should see.

They met for a coffee in a local hotel, along from the Belfry where Ricky had just finished playing an exhibition match, and he listened to Barry's story. How he'd woken up that morning with a strange feeling which led to him winning enough money to change his life.

His wife was present at the meeting as well, a formidable looking woman - and Ricky realised that the compulsion that had overcome Barry must have been strong indeed. Barry and his wife were now relatively wealthy, and his desire to write out a hefty cheque was understood by all present, including Mrs Singleton - and the coffers of Anthony Nolan continued to swell.

Noah proposed to Anna within a month of the Championships, taking everyone by surprise. Her parents were thrilled on every level. Her dad, particularly so. After a career in a classroom, he hadn't wanted his daughter to jump into the perils of teaching, a job full of ironies - as the exams become easier, the work becomes harder. But he could never have imagined that her career as a journalist was going to bear such fruit. And now here she was, presiding over the story that kept on giving and managing a sports star the whole world had warmed to. Not to mention meeting a husband.

Others, though, fared less well from the exploits of Ricky's final round at Muirfield Golf Club - chief among them, Jago Silver. Morag McKinnie had indeed been thorough and Anna helped her with compiling and collating her evidence of negligence into a report. Noah read it, and agreed it made a compelling case - but knowing the man as he did, he worried that it would not be enough. He would just lawyer-up and they would need something more tangible. He smiled mischievously at the thought.

Noah flew to New York with one of London's top lawyers, working on a pro bono basis, to put the charges to Silver and suggest a way forward and possible solution. As expected, it was an ugly meeting - it was no surprise to anyone that Noah and his team were searched before entering the office and very quickly, fruity vernacular and ugly threats coloured the air.

But Team UK held firm - and particularly forthright was Morag McKinnie. Originally it had been her intention that Silver should spend the rest of his life in jail. But this was folly, she soon realised, and never going to happen.

What she really wanted, most of all was a victory; and this could only come in the form of regaining her retirement funds and recouping all of the money she and her colleagues had lost. Money that had not evaporated or been burnt - but happened to be in Jago's coffers and not hers nor the sixty-seven other co-employees she represented. All of whom wanted what was rightfully theirs, and not a penny more.

Silver sneered at such a risible notion.

'You people need to get the fuck out of my office,' he spat dismissively.

Noah had expected this, of course, and quickly he went online with a laptop as the lawyers continued to exchange blows. After a few seconds, when he had what he needed, Noah asked for silence. Then he hit the return key - and quickly, Jago's eyes widened.

'...*fuck you, Noah. Do you think I give a shit about charity? I don't give a rat's ass. I haven't got kids, so why would I give a fuck about kids with cancer? Fuck 'em. I'm sick of seeing their bald heads and those clawing eyes...*'

Noah hit another key and the recording stopped.

Jago glared at the bastard he had once employed. Hearing his words fired back at him was doubly difficult, not least because this was all just bravado on his part. He was just playing a role - and it was now playing him into a hole.

The demeanour of his lawyers, changed instantly. It was

inadmissible, of course, but a courtroom hearing was not what anyone was worried about here. Morag had a blog, and the incendiary recording had a whiff of viral about it; it could cost much more than any potential settlement. All of a sudden, 'just what we are owed and not a penny more' seemed very attractive.

The legal team were in agreement, and Jago realised his stance was crumbling.

'You wouldn't put that online,' he began, sourly.

'No, he mightn't,' Morag sneered back at him. 'But I will.'

'Yeah, and I'll sue the shit out of you.'

'Oh, really? Then go ahead - because I haven't got anything left, you stupid numpty. You have all my shit already, remember.'

It was a beautiful retort, which Morag enjoyed tremendously.

'Fuck you, lady...'

But Jago was silenced by his chief counsel, who placed his hand firmly on his boss's arm. This battle was over and Jago had lost. The mighty Wall Street titan humbled by a spinster from Dundee.

'You fuc...'

'Jago. Not a word. Not another word.'

Jago Silver picked himself up and rushed to his private bathroom.

He closed the door quietly and then began to smash the tiling to pieces, adding to the already gargantuan bill that the Muirfield Open had cost him.

In the end, his lawyers would sell the settlement to him as a small price to pay for his glorious contribution to humanity and the plaudits that would continue to shine on him.

'Jago, you'll be saving lives!'

Jago bit his lip and said nothing.

Just to be certain, the legal team drafted an airtight agreement that the settlement today was final and that it could never come to light; that the tapes would be deleted, and no other claims could ever be laid at his door.

Noah agreed, as did his new negotiating partner. Morag and her colleagues got their lives back, and Anthony Nolan took in its biggest ever single donation. All in all, it cost Jago Silver a cool $9 million. A snip to him - and yet the biggest and most bitter pill he had ever had to swallow.

Six months after that Sunday in July, things had settled down; a pattern had re-established itself. Ricky was playing on the tour again, but in trousers now, and always with Patrick, his trusted caddie. He was making the cut regularly but never really troubling the leaderboards - and Maggie and his kids were able to accompany him as well when it wasn't so far away.

Anna and Noah, the perfectly matched couple, were about to set a date, and her new PR agency had already attracted two new sports clients. Ben was the face of a new television advertising campaign for Anthony Nolan and their register of donors was swelling daily.

A remarkable outcome from a single round of golf.

As to the truth of the matter, Ricky had confided in only Maggie. It was a story which she accepted completely, and she didn't seek any further explanations. And why would she, given what had happened?

Ricky sat at home, on his sofa, in their unfamiliar, gleaming conservatory which had been hastily planned and executed just in time for the new arrival. An army of workmen had worked all hours to get the place finished.

He watched Paddy in the garden, gallivanting about on his adventure playground, with his new son bouncing on his knee.

The boy had been born bang on his due-date, and a third son was no surprise to either of them. They had deliberately not discussed names in the hope that they might be blessed with a girl - and Ricky had guffawed when he saw the bright red male bits of his new baby.

'What about names, then?' Maggie had asked, nestling her little boy on her chest.

Ricky smiled.

'What?' she said.

'What do you think of the name, Marshall?'

It wasn't to Maggie's tastes at all. She was a traditionalist. Peter. Richard. James. John. Luke. Daniel. Jack. And never a modern name, and certainly never a bloody surname, which is now all the rage.

But something glinted in her eye as she mulled it over.

'Yeah. Do you know what? I like that. I don't know why... but I do.'

Ricky smiled again.

'Yeah, so do I.'

THE END

Afterword

Open Links is, of course, a fairy-tale. If there really is a Marshall out there somewhere, emerging from a locker room to revitalise the flagging careers of plucky underdog golfers, mankind has yet to meet him.

But there's one miracle at the very end of this delightful novel that, to me, rings very true indeed – the extraordinary moment when Ben Costello and his parents find a selfless donor willing to undergo a stem cell transplant and give the young man a chance of life. Thanks to the work of Anthony Nolan over the past 50 years, scenes just like this one now occur four times every single day in the UK.

It's a strange thought - perhaps just as strange and wondrous as any of the events of *Open Links* - that a random stranger somewhere in the world can provide a patient with the lifesaving transplant they need. And as an organisation we find ourselves continually humbled, too, by the humanity and generosity shown by the 900,000 people who've signed up to our donor register in the hope of saving a life.

But they aren't our only supporters. Anthony Nolan owes

its thanks not only to our donors, but also to the kind people who raise funds for us in so many ways: running marathons, cycling in the pouring rain, volunteering, and even, like my good friend Dom Holland, writing novels on our behalf. And since all authorial profits of *Open Links* is going towards our lifesaving work, we also have to thank you for buying this book.

If you've enjoyed reading it (and we hope you have), then we'd like to ask you to go one step further. Please, tell your friends about this novel. Share it with others on social media. Write a review on Amazon.com or your blog. Every single person who reads *Open Links* is supporting what we do, day after day.

The odds are often against us. In the UK, around 41,000 people are diagnosed with blood cancer every year. This equates to one person every fourteen minutes. For many people with blood cancer or a blood disorder, a bone marrow or stem cell transplant is their best chance of life. But the stark truth is, for every life saved by a transplant, another life is lost.

We're determined, however, to face up to this momentous challenge. Our work will continue until we accomplish the vision of our founder, Shirley Nolan; one brave mother who was so determined to save her son's life that she set up the world's first stem cell register 50 years ago.

This created a lifeline for patients in need of a transplant to find a matching donor and since then, the extraordinary Anthony Nolan community has been saving lives - many thousands of them, across the globe.

Half a century later, stem cell registers bring hope to patients. Every match gives a second chance of life, transforming the simple act of joining the register into an extraordinary lifesaving gift. And the next 50 years offer a fantastic opportunity to transform many, many more lives through new cures and therapies.

Afterword

Ours, then, is the ultimate underdog story – and like Ricky Randal, we'll strike hard, strike true, and aim for that perfect shot and match.

Simon Dyson MBE

Chairman of the Trustees of Anthony Nolan

Anthony Nolan

For many people with blood cancer or a blood disorder, a bone marrow or stem cell transplant is their last chance of life.

Only a third of UK patients who need a transplant will find a match within their own family.

Anthony Nolan uses its register of more than 900,000 people nationwide to match donors with patients in desperate need.

We helped find a match for over 1,400 people with blood cancer and other blood disorders last year (2022/3).

That's three transplants every day.

Since 1974, we've given over 25,000 people the chance of life.

But it still isn't enough. We need more donors to come forward.

To find out more about blood cancer and stem cell transplantation, if you're interested in joining our register of life-saving donors, or if you'd like to support our work by volunteering or raising valuable funds, please visit anthonynolan.org.

Anthony Nolan

Thank you.

Also by Dominic Holland

Fiction

Only in America

The Ripple Effect

The Fruit Bowl

I,Gabriel

Made in England

Non-Fiction

Eclipsed

Takes on Life, Vol. 1

Takes on Life, Vol.2

Short Stories

Hobbs' Journey

The Surgeon

Lucky No. 7